D0002162

Bad Day
at Willow Creek

Ralph Cotton

WHEELER PUBLISHING
A part of Gale, Cengage Learning

GALE
CENGAGE Learning·

Detroit • New York • San Francisco • New Haven, Conn • Waterville, Maine • London

GALE
CENGAGE Learning·

Copyright © Ralph Cotton, 2006.
Wheeler Publishing, a part of Gale, Cengage Learning.

ALL RIGHTS RESERVED
This is a work of fiction. Names, characters, places, and incidents either
are the product of the author's imagination or are used fictitiously, and
any resemblance to actual persons, living or dead, business
establishments, events, or locales is entirely coincidental. The publisher
does not have any control over and does not assume any responsibility
for author or third-party websites or their content.

Wheeler Publishing Large Print Western.
The text of this Large Print edition is unabridged.
Other aspects of the book may vary from the original edition.
Set in 16 pt. Plantin.

LIBRARY OF CONGRESS CATALOGING-IN-PUBLICATION DATA

Cotton, Ralph W.
  Bad Day at Willow Creek / by Ralph Cotton.
    pages cm. — (Wheeler Publishing Large Print Western)
  ISBN 978-1-4104-6363-0 (softcover) — ISBN 1-4104-6363-X (softcover)
  1. Western stories. 2. Large type books. I. Title.
PS3553.O766B33 2013
813'.54—dc23   2013026564

Published in 2013 by arrangement with NAL Signet, a division of
Penguin Group (USA)

LT-W

Seneca Falls Library
47 Cayuga Street
Seneca Falls, N.Y. 13148

Printed in the United States of America
1 2 3 4 5   17 16 15 14 13

For Mary Lynn . . . *of course.*

PART 1

CHAPTER 1

Lawrence Shaw had heard the thunder of horses' hooves from the north trail long before the five riders slid the animals to a halt out front of the plank shack. He'd heard them stop suddenly, fifty yards away, and he'd pictured the riders sitting there discussing him in the pale purple darkness, deciding the best way to kill him. After a moment he'd heard the horses come forward again, this time slower, with stealth and deliberation.

Oh, yes, they mean to kill me, Shaw told himself. He could somehow hear their intent in the sound of their horses' hooves. They had ridden away two days ago, did their robbing and killing and gotten full of themselves. Now nothing would do but for them to ride back to the shack on the west fork of Willow Creek and kill Fast Larry on their way south. Shaw sighed quietly, yet he made no attempt to save himself.

9

He did none of the things a man might do under such dire circumstances. Shaw had lost interest in such matters of life and death. They would arrive to kill him; but he would kill them instead. It was that simple. The matter deserved no deeper thought. If he was wrong, so what? Living wasn't all it was cracked up to be, he reminded himself.

He remained lying on the rough plank floor, wrapped in a ragged blanket in front of the waning fire, a man marked for death, yet so undisturbed by the prospect of dying that death would have to do better than this just to roust him to his feet. When he heard his name called aloud amid a scuffling of boots on the front porch, he did not stir, not even when he heard a gasp from Rita Vargas, who sat in a wooden chair in a dark corner.

"Mr. Shaw, get up quickly!" she whispered urgently, her voice trembling in fear. "They have come back here for you!"

"I'm asleep," Shaw whispered.

Rita sat taken aback for a moment, hearing rough voices talk boldly back and forth on the porch. "You are *asleep*?" She stared as if in disbelief at the ragged bundle stretched out in front of the dimly lit hearth. She heard the sound of a gun hammer cock. But she wasn't sure from which direction

10

the sound came: the front porch or the ragged blanket. *"Asleep?"* she whispered in an even lower, more confused tone.

But when Shaw offered no other reply, Rita understood; and she tried settling herself in her chair, her hands cradling her rounded stomach as if to protect her unborn child from the harsh ugliness of this world soon to receive it. *"Madre santa del Dios!"* — holy Mother of God — she whispered to herself and to the unborn child beneath her fingertips.

Lying stone-still in his blanket, Shaw repeated to himself the next words he knew would come from Rita's soft trembling lips. *Madre bendecida del Dios,* she would say next, the way he had heard her whisper the two lines in unison these past weeks she had traveled with him.

Holy Mother of God . . . Blessed Mother of God. Always the same short, efficient prayer, Shaw reminded himself, giving no more thought to the men's boots stamping through the door until he heard the man standing above him say, "Wake up, *Fast Larry!* I came back to see just how gawdamn *fast* you are!"

"This ain't a good idea, Brady," a voice behind the man said. "We need to cover some ground if we're supposed to meet

11

them come daylight." Only three of the five riders had stepped down from their saddles and walked into the shack. Two sat waiting restlessly, keeping a wary eye on the dark trail to the north as they watched through the open door, seeing everything in the dim glow of firelight.

"Shut up, Bratcher!" said a young gunman named Tommy Childers who stood beside the bearded old gunman. "Brady knows what he's doing."

Brady Katlin reached out and poked Shaw with his boot toe. "Hey, *'Fastest Gun Alive'!*" he said mockingly, a sneer coming to his hard face. "Wake the hell up, you old scarecrow! Are you dead, or just acting like it?" As he asked the bundle of rags on the floor, his eyes slid over to Rita as if questioning her.

Rita shrugged. "He sleeps," she said, her hands spread protectively on her tight, round belly.

"Oh, he sleeps." Tommy Childers laughed, elbowing Bratcher, who let out a guarded chuckle himself.

"Well, I'll be gawdamned!" said Brady Katlin in disgust. His hand fell from the handle of the big Colt holstered on his hip. "We've got a whore who can't do nothing below her waist, and a gunman you can't keep awake long enough to *kill*!" He shook his head and half turned from the hearth toward the pregnant woman. "Is this what the Wild, Woolly West has come to?"

"To hell with the *Woolly West,*" said Childers. "Let that turd sleep." He turned toward Rita's dark corner as he loosened his gun belt. "I know you're bellied out, little darling," he said. "But doing nothing from the waist down don't keep you from doing something from the neck up."

"That's it for me, boys," said Bratcher McBain, seeing what was about to happen and wanting no part of it. He took a step through the open door onto the front porch. "I'll be out here smelling air with the Russians."

"You care, Brady?" Childers asked. He slung his gun belt over his shoulder and unbuttoned the fly on his denim trousers.

"I don't care what you do," said Brady Katlin, turning back to Shaw and his ragged blanket. "If I can't wake this fool, I'm going to shoot him full of holes whilst he sleeps. You're my witness, Childers . . . I'm the man who killed the fastest gun alive."

"You go right ahead and kill him," said Childers. "I'll watch over my shoulder." He stepped closer to Rita, exposing himself, saying, "It's time you and ol' Wooden Head shook hands and got acquainted."

"No, no, señor, por favor, mi bebé!" Rita pleaded in her native tongue, her hands drawing more protectively to her belly.

"Your little *bastardo bebé* will never know," Childers said, mocking her. "I know you're dumb, but damn, surely you're smart enough to su—"

A shot exploded in the room, cutting Childers's words short as the bullet bored through the back of his head and sent a spray of blood and brain matter all over Rita and the wall behind her. Standing above Shaw with his feet spread, Brady Katlin looked down wide-eyed at the blue-red streak of fire that had erupted from Shaw's Colt.

"Jesus Chr—" Brady shouted, reaching for his gun, feeling the heat of the explosion lick at his trouser legs. But his words were also cut short. Shaw jerked his smoking Colt up and fired again. His second shot slammed Brady's head back as the bullet ripped upward from beneath the doomed outlaw's chin and mushroomed in a sharp spout of blood all over the low rafters.

Shaw sprang catlike to his feet, his gun, his eyes, and every fiber of his being poised toward the open door. He stood braced, prepared for Bratcher and the two Russians

14

to come charging in, guns blazing. This was not the same Lawrence Shaw who had lain there only moments ago awash in self-pity, fostering some dark, secret wish that these men might rush in and put an end to his misery. This was Fast Larry on his feet now, acting with the tightly coiled instincts of a rattlesnake.

He waited, watching the open door and the blackness beyond. But beneath the sound of Rita screaming while she rubbed Childers's warm blood and gore from her face with both hands, he heard the sound of horses racing away into the darkness and realized the fight was over. He'd lived through yet another attempt on his life. "Lucky you," he murmured dryly, uncocking the Colt.

He opened the cylinder, dropped out the spent brass shells, and replaced them with cartridges from his gun belt. He turned to Rita and said between the rise and fall of her endless screaming, "It's over." But Rita continued screaming until she ran out of breath.

Shaw shook his head and looked away, out through the front door and across the dark, rolling hillside along the creek. When Rita's screams finally subsided and she began sobbing under her breath, she felt all around on her swollen belly as if checking on her unborn child.

"Are you all right?" Shaw asked flatly.

Without reply, Rita stared into his eyes for a silent moment, then raised her bloody hands, looked at them, and began screaming anew.

"Sorry I asked," Shaw said under his breath. Stepping over to Childers's body, he stooped down, gripped the back of his bloody shirt collar, and dragged him outside, the dead outlaw's exposed genitals flopping and bouncing across the rough pine floor.

He dragged Brady Katlin outside and dropped him facedown beside Childers in the strip of wet ground along the hitch rail where steam still wafted above fresh horse urine. The dead outlaws' horses shied to one side of the rail and stared at Shaw from caged eyes.

Shaw picked up a pouch of chopped tobacco fixings that had fallen from Brady's shirt pocket on his way across the low boardwalk. While Rita continued to scream and sob, he rolled a smoke, lit it, and stared off at the pale glow on the eastern horizon. "They shoulda had me, Rosa," he murmured to the misty, dark heavens, his eyes moving upward into the deep, endless void

16

with longing, as if he wanted to step into its welcoming arms.

He visualized himself lying dead and at peace, his gun cocked and ready, yet forever silent in his hand. What was that about . . . ? he asked himself, feeling a slight chill dance across his shoulders, then vanish.

Morbid curiousity, he told himself, shrugging it off through a gray stream of cigarette smoke. But he knew there was more to it. Shaw realized what a miserable, tortured piece of work he'd become since the death of his wife, Rosa, at the hands of violent men, gunmen who were in many ways no different from him.

I almost did it this time, Rosa, he said inside his mind, seeing her face as clearly in death as he had ever seen it in life. *A minute longer and we would have been together . . . the two of us, joined again for all etern—*

Stop it . . . Shaw warned himself, feeling the familiar cold, aching pain of her death draw around him so tightly as to shut out the rest of the world and carve away whole spaces of time from his consciousness. He felt the cigarette stub burn his fingers. He shook it away and heard its death sizzle as its light turned black on the wet strip of ground near the dead outlaws. He looked all around as if questioning how long he'd

17

been standing there.

You're alive, make what you will of it, he reminded himself, his inner voice sounding harsh, worn out, disgusted with him. Behind him, Rita had stopped screaming and sobbing. Shaw took a deep breath of chilled air and enjoyed the silence for a moment longer. "Someday . . ." he whispered. Then he turned and walked back inside the plank shack.

Rita had pushed herself up from the chair and stood supporting herself on the edge of a battered wooden table. "I . . . I think I am having my baby now!" She quickly crossed herself. "All of this excitement . . ."

Shaw just looked at her, uncertain what he should say or do. Finally he said, "Let's get you over to the bed. I'll spread my blanket on it."

Rita stopped him from ushering her toward the bed. She remained leaning on the table. "No, wait . . . the pain has passed. I will wait a moment and see if I have another pain."

Shaw said, "Let me know," and turned to walk to the fire.

"Take out your pocket watch and time the pains for me. When they grow closer together, we will know the baby is coming."

Shaw stopped at the blackened hearth and

reached for his watch fob before realizing he no longer owned a timepiece. When the realization came upon him, he looked all around, dreamlike, and said, "I . . . I lost my timepiece, Rita. I lost it a good while back. . . ." His words trailed off; he looked a bit bewildered.

Rita sighed, one hand clasped to her belly, the other supporting her against the table. "I must get all of this blood off of me," she said, gesturing toward herself and nodding at puddles of blood on the floor, the wall, and still dripping from the ceiling. "I am afraid that seeing all this will mark my baby!"

"Don't look at it, Rita. Don't think about what happened here," Shaw offered, knowing nothing else to say on the matter. "You sit still and take it easy. . . . I'll get our things together."

Rita looked astonished. "We cannot leave, Mr. Shaw. Do you hear what I say to you? I am going to have my baby this morning."

"Begging your pardon, Rita," said Shaw, keeping his voice even and his tone kind, "but you have been about to have your baby four times this past week. I figure the best thing is to get you up creek into town before you have it sure enough."

Rita took on a pouting expression. "The

19

first time I only told those pigs that so that they would all leave me alone." She paused, then added, "So they would not force me to lie down with them."

"Yes," said Shaw. "I understand . . . and it worked. But still, we need to get to Willow Creek. There's a young doctor there — a good one, as I recall."

"And then you will leave me?" Rita asked, giving him a searching stare.

"I have to go on, Rita," Shaw said quietly. "I can't stay in Willow Creek."

"Oh? Go where?" she asked.

"I don't know where," Shaw replied, at a loss. "But I've got to go."

"It is because you cannot stand the sight of me, isn't it?" she continued. "It is because you do not want to be the father of my baby."

"Rita, let's not start thinking I'm the father of your baby," Shaw said gently but firmly.

"You might be," said Rita. "I told you that you might be the father."

"Yes, you did tell me that," said Shaw, being patient with her. "But you also said you had narrowed it down to either me or Henry McCarty or Jimmy Blaine or —"

"Enough, stop it," said Rita, cutting him off. "I gave it some more thought and it is

20

not Jimmy Tutt's or Macon Bill Thompson's."

"Oh," said Shaw, "then it's down to just me, McCarty, and Jimmy Blaine?"

"*Sí,* I mean yes, it is one of you three," Rita said with resolve. "I am now certain." As she spoke she supported her belly with a bloodstained hand.

"Well, of the three, I would hope it's Jimmy Blaine's if I was you," Shaw said. "He's an honest man, as much as I know of him. He tends to his spread and minds his own business."

"We must wait until my baby is born and see who he looks like. It is the only true way to know who his father is."

Anytime Rita had talked about her unborn baby she referred to it as *he.* Shaw wasn't about to tell her that she could be wrong. Instead he said, "You don't want me or McCarty either one to be its father. McCarty's never going to settle down and be anybody's father. He's changed his name to William Bonney, has everybody calling him *Kid.* He's on a wild, dangerous trail, doing business with the Katlins."

"What about you, Mr. Shaw?" Rita asked. "I think you would make a good father."

"No, Rita, I wouldn't," said Shaw. "I'm honored that you would want me, a beautiful young woman like yourself. But I'm no good for you." He shook his head. "I'm no good for anybody. I paid to go to bed with you. . . . I would pay to do it again some-day." He shook his head. "But it would be a mistake for you to pin any faith on me be-ing a good father to your child. I don't have it in me."

Rita stood in silence for a moment, letting his words sink in. Finally she cradled her belly in both hands, walked to the smolder-ing fire, and picked up a poker to stoke up some flames from the dying embers. "I will cook some coffee; then I will wash this blood off of me and prepare for the ride to Willow Creek," she said quietly. "I feel pity for you, Mr. Shaw, that you think so little of yourself."

Shaw turned, facing the endless darkness through a dusty windowpane. "Don't pity what you don't understand," he said almost to himself, wishing he'd given Brady Katlin just a moment longer. Turning away, he walked to the open door and looked out at the silver sunlight wreathing the horizon. "I expect we'd best get a move on, if you're able. Katlin's whole family will be down my shirt when they hear about this."

CHAPTER 2

William "the Kid" Bonney sat atop his big paint horse, a few feet apart from the other waiting horsemen. He watched Uncle Linton and Hyde Rudabaugh finish off a bottle of whiskey and saw Rudabaugh toss the empty bottle away alongside the trail. "Don't fire that smoker, Hyde," the Kid warned, seeing Rudabaugh lay a hand on the battered handle of the Dance Brothers revolver holstered on his hip. "What's wrong with you anyway?" the Kid chastised the older outlaw. "We got law on our tails, you know."

"I wasn't going to shoot at it," said Rudabaugh, letting his hand slip down from the holster with a half laugh. "I was just *scaring* it some." He raked his fingertips back and forth through his wiry gray beard, a bit embarrassed.

Beside him, Uncle Linton said just between the two of them, "Looks like you've been properly reprimanded. I expect you're lucky he didn't come over here and slap your hands."

Hyde Rudabaugh gave him a hard look. "I'm not a man who would take a hand slapping — haven't been since I was a young boy killing cats." He spit a stream of tobacco juice close to Uncle Linton's boot. "Don't make the foolish mistake of trying to instigate trouble between me and the Kid. He or I will more'n likely kill you for it."

Uncle Linton, seeing that his nephews, T. J. and Lane Katlin weren't paying much attention to him and Rudabaugh, decided to let the matter drop. Besides, he hadn't purposely meant to stir up trouble. Uncle Linton had a sour disposition that managed to seep into anything he had to say.

On his horse near the Kid, T. J. Katlin shook tobacco into a poised strip of cigarette paper and said as he rolled himself a smoke, "If you don't mind me saying so, Henry —"

The Kid cut him off by saying sharply, "It's not Henry, it's *William.* William Bonney, remember?" He sat staring coldly at T. J.

"No offense, *William,*" said T. J., he himself not looking too pleasant. "Some of us are going to take longer than others to get used to your new name." He returned the cold stare, licked the edge of the rolled cigarette, and ran it in and out of his mouth.

"Yeah?" said the Kid. "I reckon there's some who never will. Are you going to be one of them?" He made no gesture toward the Colt Thunderer lying loose in his lap; but he didn't have to in order for T. J. to catch the veiled threat he'd just made.

"No need to get your bark on, Kid," Lane Katlin cut in, hoping to avoid trouble. "We're all a little testy, waiting for our brother this way." He looked off along the trail. "Damn Brady anyway, wanting to kill that damn gunman."

"What gunman?" the Kid asked, knowing they were waiting for Brady Katlin, but not knowing or even caring why. The Kid and Hyde Rudabaugh had agreed to meet the Katlins here and provide them with a string of fresh horses. They had done their part. The Kid was ready to go.

"Lawrence Shaw," said T. J. He offered a slight grin. "I expect you've heard of Fast Larry Shaw . . . the fastest gun alive?"

"Yep," said the Kid. "And your brother Brady has gone to kill him?"

"That's right," said Lane Katlin. "Shaw showed up at the shack on the west fork with some border whore. Brady got it stuck in his craw that he wanted to kill him. But

25

that's over by now. Him and Bratcher and the Russians are on their way . . . you'll get their swap horses anytime now."

"Shit," said the Kid. He turned in his saddle and said to Hyde Rudabaugh, "Hyde, get a horse between your knees. This deal is as done as it's ever going to be."

"Whoa, Kid," said Lane. "Not so fast. I don't want to send you away five horses short."

"You're not," said the Kid. "I'm taking back five of the fresh horses we brought you . . . unless you want to pay me an extra fifty dollars a head for them."

"You can't leave Brady and the others riding worn-out horses, Kid," said Lane.

"If they went to kill Lawrence Shaw," said the Kid with finality, "they won't be needing horses, fresh or otherwise."

"That's a hell of an attitude, Henr— I mean, Kid," said T. J., catching and correcting himself. "Brady is as good as any man I ever saw with a gun."

"Suit yourself," said the Kid, dismissing the matter with a slight nod. "Hyde, let's get gathered and gone," he said to Rudabaugh. Then to T. J. and Lane, he said, "Let's see now . . . you're five horses short, at fifty dollars a head. That comes to . . . ." He stalled and tapped his thumb to the tip

26

of three fingers, adding to himself. "Fifty and fifty is a hundred, another fifty is . . ." He stopped as if having to think about it for a moment.

Atop their horses alongside the Katlins sat a burly gunman named Harvey Sturgis and a frail-looking young outlaw named Sal "Free Drink" Stemlet. The two looked at each other; then Free Drink said in a soft, clear voice, "It's two hundred and fifty dollars, Kid."

"Obliged, Free Drink," said the Kid. Like the Kid, Free Drink had also undergone a recent name change. Having hidden from the law in San Francisco dressed as a woman, Free Drink Stemlet had been known as Wild Rose before coming back to the Western Territories.

"You're welcome, Billy," Free Drink said.

Turning back to the Katlins, the Kid said, "That'll be two hundred and fifty dollars. Else we're taking back five of the fresh horses."

"Hold everything," Harvey Sturgis cut in, gazing out along the trail in the morning sunlight. "We've got riders coming."

Rising in their stirrups along with the others, the Katlins saw Bratcher McBain riding at the head of a cloud of dust. "Looks like you were wrong, *William,*" said T. J. with a smug grin.

The Kid didn't bother looking to see whether Brady Katlin was among the riders. He shrugged and sat comfortably in his saddle until Lane Katlin, staring anxiously along the trail, said, "Damn, I see Bratcher, the Russians . . ." He paused, then said, "I don't see Brady or Tommy Childers."

Free Drink gave the Kid a knowing look and rolled his eyes slightly upward.

Under his breath, the Kid sighed and said, "So long, Tommy."

Without saying anything to Rudabaugh, the Kid motioned him toward the five fresh horses standing beside the string of tired horses they had collected from the outlaws.

Still staring intently toward the riders as they drew nearer, T. J. said to his brother, "Brady and Childers are all right. Shaw couldn't have killed them unless he killed everybody. Bratcher and the Russians wouldn't have stood still for it!"

Listening, the Kid only chuckled grimly to himself and stepped his horse over closer to Hyde Rudabaugh and the horses. "Gather up, Hyde; it's time to go," he said quietly.

"Can you wait just five gawdamned minutes longer, Mr. William Bonney?" T. J. said, giving his words a sarcastic twist. "This *is* our brother Brady we're talking about here!"

"If you're saying wait for Brady, five minutes won't get it," said the Kid. But he and Rudabaugh gathered the horses and moved over closer to Free Drink and Sturgis. "Boys," he whispered to the two, "I'm about half sorry I put you with these blockheads."

"Don't worry about it, Billy," said Sturgis. "A job's a job. I'm still beholden." He patted his shirt where he'd stuffed his share of the mine-payroll robbery. "We made out real good."

While the riders drew closer, the Kid asked Sal Stemlet in a guarded tone, "Are you good, Free Drink?"

"I'm fine, Kid," said Stemlet, batting his eyelashes a bit girlishly. "I only wish you'd rode with us."

"Naw, I didn't want it," said the Kid. "Me and Hyde made good with the horses."

"I don't know why you ride with that trash," Free Drink whispered.

"Ol' Hyde?" The Kid grinned. "Because he's Arkansas Dave Rudabaugh's cousin. That's good enough for me."

"Arkansas Dave is exactly the kind of trash I'm talking about," said Free Drink, again rolling his eyes upward.

"I thought he might be." The Kid chuckled.

They sat watching the three riders climb the last thirty yards up the trail to them. When Bratcher McBain swung his horse sidelong T. J. and Lane Katlin, fear showed in his eyes. The Russian brothers slowed their horses and stopped a few feet farther away. McBain called out, "Lane, T. J. I've got bad news!"

"Um-hmm." The Kid nodded expectantly and lowered his hat brim.

"Brady's dead," said McBain. "So's Tommy! Shaw killed them both! Me and the Russian brothers barely got away with our lives!"

The Katlins looked at one another, stunned. The Kid shook his lowered head slowly. Free Drink and Sturgis stared blankly. "Gawdamn it!" T. J. Katlin finally shouted. Jumping his horse forward, he drew his Colt, cocked it, and pointed it back and forth between McBain and the Russian brothers. "I better see some wounds! Something to show me you backed my brother's play!"

"Don't shoot, T. J.!" Sturgis pleaded. "This was Fast Larry Shaw we're talking about! How the hell could we back Brady against the likes of this kind of gun handling? I told him we ought not go there! Shaw's a stone-cold killer! What else could I do?"

While T. J.'s Colt stayed fixed for the moment on McBain, in unison the Russian brothers raised their rifles from their laps and held them with their hands around the stocks, thumbs across the hammers, ready for use if needed. Raising his lowered head, the Kid said to T. J., "Brady had to show the world what a fool he was, T. J. Are you going to do the same?"

T. J. turned from McBain and replied in gruff tone, "Don't crowd me on this. Brady's my younger brother! This can't go unfinished. Shaw has got to die for it!"

"Yeah, but Shaw ain't the one you're flashing your gun at," said the Kid. He'd taken on a bearing, his hand near his Colt. Free Drink and Sturgis stepped their horses sideways, making room. "You lost your younger brother . . . Do you want Lane here to do the same?"

Lane cut in, saying again, "There's no need to make threats here, Kid."

"Then tell your brother to holster his smoker," said the Kid. "I'm getting tired of looking at it." His eyes fixed on T. J.'s. "One Katlin in hell is all the devil can stand."

"Why you . . ." T. J. clenched his teeth; his

31

reddened face trembled. But he made no effort to turn the gun toward the Kid. Instead he jammed the gun roughly back into his holster.

Bratcher McBain gave the Kid a grateful look. The Russians lowered their rifles a little, but kept them handy. "T. J. and I are going after Shaw," Lane said to the Kid as he stripped stolen dollars from a thick wad he jerked from his shirt pocket. "Here's your horse money. Are you riding with us? Tommy Childers *was* a friend of yours."

"There's friends, and there's good friends," said the Kid. "Tommy Childers is not one I'd pull iron over. We knew one another. I won't be taking flowers to his grave."

"Still," said Katlin, "you owe him a share of vengeance."

"What? Against the fastest gun alive?" the Kid asked, feigning a look of fear. "No, sirree! Not me! I know Shaw. I have no fight with him." He watched Uncle Linton step up into his saddle and join his nephews.

Lane glared at the Kid, then turned to Free Drink and Sturgis and said, "You two can ride with us or go your own way."

"Lawrence Shaw never done nothing to me," said Harvey Sturgis. He patted his stomach where his money lay inside his shirt. "Besides, I got some spending to do."

"So do I," said Free Drink, smiling, his wrists crossed a bit daintily on his saddle horn. "But don't think this job hasn't been a hoot." He backed his horse up a step with a touch of his knees. "If you need any more help robbing, I am your huckleberry." He gave them a limp wave of his hand.

T. J. growled under his breath, "That *she-male*-looking sonsabitch." Then he said to his brother Lane in a louder voice, "Forget these three! We don't need their gawdamn help anyways." He jerked his horse roughly toward the trail. "There's still six of us."

The Kid chuckled and said, "That's the spirit, T. J. Six to one. Any more than that, it might start looking cowardly."

T. J. flared again, this time starting to jerk his horse around toward the Kid. But Lane pushed his horse into T. J.'s and said, "Pay him no mind, T. J.! Let's get going before Shaw's trail gets too cold to follow."

The Katlins, the Russian brothers, McBain, and Uncle Linton rode away in a flurry of dust. Once they were well on their way along the trail, the Kid fanned his hat back and forth and placed it back atop his head. "Now, there go some unhappy fellows," he said.

"What say you, Kid?" Sturgis asked after

spitting a stream of tobacco juice. "Will Lawrence Shaw kill all six of them?"

"Who can say?" The Kid stared after the riders as if contemplating what the outcome would be once they caught up to Shaw.

"It certainly wouldn't surprise me. He is the fastest gun alive," Free Drink interjected.

"There's no such thing as the fastest gun alive," the Kid replied. "If there was, I would be *it*." He took the lead rope to the string of tired horses from Hyde Rudabaugh and nudged his big paint onto the trail.

"Are you saying you're not as fast as Shaw?" Sturgis asked.

"Here now, watch your mouth, Harvey!" Free Drink chastised him. "Nobody is faster than our Billy. Right, Kid?"

"Fast? Hell, I don't know," said the Kid. He frowned at the perplexity of having to give thought to the matter, then said, "Anybody fast enough to be alive is fast enough, I reckon."

"But Shaw's faster than just staying-alive fast," said Sturgis, "and he's killed many a noted gunman who was more than just staying-alive fast."

"That didn't make him the fastest gun alive. That just made him the fastest gun that day," said the Kid. He led the string of horses along at an easy walk. "A man might be the fastest today because he's in a killing mood, or because somebody's wronged him." He shrugged. "Maybe he wakes up tomorrow and killing is the last thing on his mind. He's thinking different, acting different. It's got to affect him . . . slow his hand, keep his aim from being as sharp."

"Has that ever happened to you, Billy?" Free Drink asked in a guarded tone, in case the Kid took offense at such a question.

But the Kid smiled a crooked smile and said, "No, but I can't say it won't happen someday. Life can always catch a man off guard and drop him dead." He paused and thought about it for a second. "I expect it will catch me someday . . . unless I die in bed with my boots off."

"Maybe that's the thing I'm saying about Shaw," said Sturgis. "He's never off guard. He's always on a sharp edge. That's what makes him the fastest gun alive."

"Whatever suits you, Harvey," said the Kid, staring straight ahead. "Let's get these horses into Willow Creek and get them sold. I'm growing homesick for Lincoln County."

CHAPTER 3

For over thirty-two hours Lawrence Shaw had sat sweating alongside Rita's bed, in a small, hot room in the Kratz Hotel, the only place of lodging in the town of Willow Creek. Rita lay resting quietly now, a folded wet cloth lying across her forehead. Shaw watched Dr. Adrian Hauler check Rita's pulse before stepping back from the bed and shaking his head slowly, as if in exasperation.

"You were correct, Mr. Shaw: She is a screamer indeed," the doctor said in a tired voice.

"Yep, she's a screamer," Shaw confirmed, staring up at the doctor from his chair. "How much longer, do you suppose?"

The doctor paused for a second, considering the question as he rolled down his shirtsleeves and buttoned them. "To be perfectly honest, I expected her to have had the child hours ago." He sighed and continued patiently, "Although I have seen women take longer than this. The first child often takes longer."

Shaw nodded. He noted to himself how much Dr. Hauler had aged since the last time he'd seen him. This was the young doctor he'd told Rita about three days ago. Yet the man standing beside Rita's bed was no longer the clear-browed young physician Shaw remembered who had once taken a bullet from his shoulder, but rather a seasoned, slightly stooped middle-aged man whose sandy hair had begun turning gray at the temples.

Watching the doctor turn to adjust the pillow beneath Rita's head, Shaw let his hand go idly to the empty watch fob on his vest and toy with it for a moment. How long ago had that been? Shaw asked himself, picturing this same room overlooking the dirt street. His eyes moved across the faded flowered wallpaper, and he remembered, picturing a pile of bloody bandages lying beside a pan of pinkish water on the oak nightstand.

"Why don't you go have yourself some breakfast, Mr. Shaw?" he heard the doctor ask. "I sent the desk clerk for my wife. She'll attend to Rita and let us know of any change."

"Your wife?" said Shaw. "You weren't married the last time I was through here."

"That's right, I wasn't," the doctor replied, a tired smile on his lips. "But I've been married for quite some time now. I married my assistant, Hilda. Perhaps you remember Hilda?"

Hilda. Hilda . . . Shaw searched his memory for a moment before coming to a sharp recognition of the young woman who had watched over him those first few days while his wound began to heal. Oh, yes, he remembered now. In his mind he saw the two of them locked in a lover's embrace on the very bed where Rita now lay sleeping. Damn, how had he forgotten Hilda? Lovely, gentle, hot-blooded Hilda . . . Hilda . . . What was her last name? he asked himself. Then, remembering instantly as he stood up, hat in hand, he said with a poker face, "Yes, of course, Hilda Stevens?"

"Hilda Stevens *Hauler,*" the doctor replied with his same tired smile, picking up his black leather medical bag from the edge of the bed. Glancing toward the door as it opened with a creak, he said, "Here comes Mrs. Hauler now."

Shaw wasn't prepared to meet a woman he had once known so intimately yet long since forgotten. But there was no escaping an encounter with Hilda Hauler. Before he could even forge another poker face with which to present both her and her husband, she stepped into the room, caught sight of him with a jolt that caused her to halt in her steps, and stared at him blankly for what Shaw considered an awkward moment.

"Hilda, dear," said Dr. Hauler, "I'm sure you remember Mr. Shaw."

"I . . . I . . ." Hilda blinked hard as if to make sure this was real and not some sort of bad dream. But then she recovered quickly and said with an expression no more revealing than Shaw's, "Of course! Mr. Shaw! What a surprise."

"Ma'am," said Shaw flatly.

Hilda gestured toward her husband. "Dr. Hauler said he had a gentleman who'd brought a young woman to town about to give birth. But he failed to mention that you're the gentleman he referred to." She looked at Rita, who lay sleeping on the bed. Then she gave the doctor a somewhat less than pleasant look. Dr. Hauler seemed not to notice his wife's expression. He busied himself slipping into his suit coat and straightening the lapels.

"So, Mr. Shaw," said Hilda, "I trust your shoulder healed adequately."

"Yes, ma'am," Shaw said, rounding his

shoulder a bit as if to prove its capability. "You and the doctor took good care of me."

He hadn't meant for his words to carry any sort of ulterior suggestion, yet he noted a blush on Hilda's cheeks as she looked away from him and stepped over beside the bed. She looked down at Rita for a moment, then said in a quiet tone without looking at Shaw, "Your wife is very beautiful. Very *young* and beautiful," she emphasized.

"She's, uh, not my wife, ma'am," said Shaw, somehow feeling he needed to explain. "She's a young woman I'm helping find her child's father." He looked from the woman to the doctor and added, "I'll be riding on once I get her and her baby settled in here."

"And who is the child's father?" Hilda asked, trying to be delicate about the matter.

"Jimmy Blaine," said Shaw without hesitation. "A young fellow who runs a spread near here." He looked at the doctor. "I hoped you might know him."

"Yes, we know him," said the doctor, taking off his wire-rimmed spectacles, folding them, and sticking them into his coat pocket. "He's a good man, Jimmy Blaine." He looked at his wife as if for support on the matter. She nodded in agreement.

"Yes, I know," said Shaw.

"Oh, good." The doctor looked relieved. He said solemnly, "For a moment I thought perhaps you were looking for him to settle some sort of score on the young lady's behalf. . . ." His words trailed off as he looked at the big Colt holstered on Shaw's hip.

"No," said Shaw. "I am helping to unite her and Jimmy Blaine . . . nothing else. You have my word on that."

The doctor studied his eyes, remembering Shaw to be an honorable man in spite of the kind of life he lived and the trouble that seemed to seek him out. "Jimmy Blaine's spread is thirty miles out, across the grass range just west of the Little Blackfoot. I expect you remember that area."

"Yes, I remember," said Shaw. He recalled the range war that had brought him to Willow Creek and cost him the bullet wound in his left shoulder.

"Ride carefully out there, Mr. Shaw," the doctor warned him. "I'm afraid the small cattlemen and the settlers alike are expecting trouble most any day." He gave his wife an expectant glance, as if Shaw's arrival served as some dark omen.

"Trouble?" Shaw asked firmly, drawing their eyes back to him. "What kind of

41

trouble?"

"Range trouble. The same kind of trouble that drew you here before." He shook his head with a dark chuckle. "Then it was settlers against cattlemen. This time the settlers *and* small cattlemen are banded together against a large European spread that's on its way, moving a large herd up into the grasslands."

"That must have been the big cloud of dust I spotted on my way up yesterday," said Shaw.

"Ironic, isn't it?" said the doctor. "It's as if these terrible range disputes run in some sort of cycle."

"Let's get the record straight," said Shaw. "I wasn't drawn here because of that last blasted range war, and I'm not drawn here to fight anybody's battle now. Last time I came here to help old man Frock Elders. He once saved my life, and I meant to repay that debt to him. It was unfortunate I arrived the day of his funeral. Everything that happened after that was pushed upon me."

"Yes, yes, of course, Mr. Shaw," the doctor said quickly. "I'm sorry to have implied anything to the contrary. We both know the circumstances you found yourself in! You had every right to defend yourself. I simply refer to the irony of it."

Shaw looked from one to the other for a moment, then said, "Excuse me if I seemed upset. It's just that I recall how quickly things got out of control back then. I don't want my purpose for being here mistaken. Rumors spread like wildfire."

"Indeed, you are correct," said the doctor. "I will not mention your being here to anyone, if that is what you prefer. I certainly don't want to cause you or any of us any trouble."

"Obliged, Doctor," said Shaw. "I have enough people wanting to kill me as it is —"

"In order to make a name for themselves," Hilda Hauler cut in, finishing his words for him. She shook her head and commented, "I find that so ugly and wretched, to think that one man must kill another in order to prove he is faster with a gun."

Shaw and her husband looked at her. "Hilda, please," said the doctor. Then to Shaw he said, "Excuse my wife, Mr. Shaw. I'm afraid she and I have seen too much bloodshed between men with guns."

"She's right, Doctor," said Shaw, looking at Hilda as he spoke. "Killing is ugly and wretched."

A silent pause settled in for a moment, until Hilda Hauler said, "I came to sit with

43

your patient while you make your rounds, Doctor. So please excuse yourself and get under way."

"Yes, of course," said the doctor. "Mr. Shaw, please excuse me." As he stepped over to the door and opened it, he said to Shaw, "If you'll follow my advice, you'll go get yourself some food and rest while Hilda is available to sit with the young lady. We have three other women about to deliver their children at any time." He smiled in parting. "These settlers are doing their part to fill this vast frontier."

Shaw and Hilda watched the door close behind him. As soon as the doctor had left, Hilda let out a sigh of relief, as if weary from supporting a strained pretense for her husband's sake.

"I'm sorry, Hilda," said Shaw in a lowered voice. "Had I known you and the doctor were man and wife I would have never —"

"Yes, I realize that," Hilda said in a clipped tone, cutting him off. "The fact is, you had forgotten I even existed until I walked through that door."

"That's not true, Hilda," Shaw lied. He remained in the same spot, but Hilda took a step toward him, almost instinctively. "I've thought of you many times over these years. I've always hoped the very best for you."

"Please." She stopped only inches from his face and said wryly, "You no more remembered me than you would some dance-hall girl you had." Her expression softened a bit as she gazed into his eyes. "I didn't expect you to," she said, her voice also softening. "At least, not the same way I would remember you." She lifted a hand as if to touch his cheek; but then she caught herself, stopped, and sighed. "You were my first. Did you know that?"

Shaw said quietly, "Yes, I knew. I felt special knowing it." Not wanting to rekindle anything between them, he said, "I want you to know, a lot has happened since you and I last saw one another. I . . . I married for a while."

"Oh?" Hilda glanced at Rita, asleep, a wisp of her long dark hair lying across her cheek.

"No, Hilda, it's not her . . . and it's not what it looks like," Shaw said. "My wife is dead. Her name was Rosa, and she's been dead now for . . ." His words trailed off. The distance between the present and his wife's tragic death seemed cloudy and uncertain. Hilda saw his hand almost reach for his watch fob before he seemed to snap out of some confused state of mind. "For a long time," he said finally.

45

"I'm sorry, Lawrence," Hilda said, taking a half step back from him.

"I don't know why I told you," Shaw said quietly. "It's not something I talk about." He lowered his head for a moment, then looked back into her clear blue eyes. "I felt like I should."

"I'm glad you told me," Hilda replied in almost a whisper. She had no idea what she'd expected to happen, stepping so close to him. Had she wanted him to touch her? She wasn't sure, she told herself. Had he attempted to kiss her, would she have allowed him to? Or had she made herself available only for the purpose of stopping him had he tried? She didn't know; but now that the moment had passed, she felt relieved. What had she been thinking? she asked herself.

Shaw saw a difference come over her, and he too knew that something had passed. "I'll just go get some breakfast now," he said, passing his hat brim back and forth between his fingertips. "It's good seeing you, knowing everything has worked out for you here."

"I'm not young and pretty anymore, Lawrence," she said in a rush of emotion, like water suddenly spilling over a dam.

"Hilda, that's not so," said Shaw, a bit taken aback by how she had blurted out her feelings, as if she'd waited forever to confide in someone. "You are a beautiful woman. Just as beautiful as I remembered you to be." He only partly lied, Shaw told himself. She *was* a beautiful woman. But his memory of her had been lost, never to have returned had he not traveled to Willow Creek and seen her in person.

But she didn't know he was lying; she didn't seem to even hear him. She clasped her hands together against her bosom. "I . . . I waited for you," she said, struggling to hold back tears. "You never came back."

"Oh, Hilda," Shaw said as gently as he could, "don't do this. I never said I was coming back. I made it a point to tell you as clearly as I could that I was *never* coming back. You had to know that."

"I know, I know," said Hilda. "I'm not blaming you. You said you wouldn't be back." She paused to keep herself from crying. "But you were my *first,* Lawrence," she said. "It didn't matter what you told me. A girl always believes her first love will come back for her someday."

"Hilda, I'm sorry," said Shaw, not knowing what else to offer her. "Every day I've spent on this terrible trail I've chosen, I wished I was off of it. If coming back to you and settling in Willow Creek would have

47

kept me from being what I am, I wish to God I would have done it."

She stepped forward. Yes, she wanted him to hold her. She needed to be held, she told herself. Yet, as she drew nearer to him and Shaw started to reach his arms out in an embrace, the sound of a footstep creaking outside the closed door caught their attention. Hilda froze, not so much from hearing the footstep as from seeing the big Colt streak up from Shaw's holster with such vicious intent. He'd spun suddenly toward the door, the gun cocked and pointed.

"Oh, God!" Hilda gasped, seeing a dark transformation come over him, as if she'd witnessed a man overtaken by the devil.

But Shaw raised his free hand toward her, gently coaxing her away from him for her own safety. "Shhh," he whispered, without taking his eyes or gun from the door.

She backed away three feet, then stopped, unable to force herself away any farther. Shaw stepped silently to the door. As he did so he heard another creaking step, then another, moving away down the hall. Opening the door a crack, Shaw peered out in time to see Dr. Hauler disappear down the stairs.

"Jesus," Shaw whispered. He closed the door, then lowered his Colt as he uncocked it and slid it into his holster. "It was your husband. He must have been listening through the door."

"Then let him listen." Hilda looked relieved once again. "I could tell he always wondered about you and me, but he never asked. Now he knows. . . ." She paused, as if giving the matter more consideration, then added with finality, "I'm *glad* he knows." She stepped closer, her gaze intent upon him. "I never loved him, Lawrence. I've always loved you. . . ."

CHAPTER 4

In spite of his hunger and weariness, Shaw walked toward a restaurant at the far end of the dirt street with more on his mind now than simply food and rest. Finding a forgotten lover had left him unsettled. How could he have ridden into Willow Creek without the slightest memory of a woman he'd made love to? He shook his head as he pondered the situation with shame and regret. What the hell had he been thinking?

There had been a time in his life when he might have taken some strange sort of pleasure in having another man's wife ready to forsake her husband for him. In fact, he had to admit, searching in his mind, back to that time and circumstance, part of his attraction to young Hilda Stevens had something to do with her and the doctor and the respectable lives they led. He hadn't loved her, yet he had to have her.

Hilda had been a beautiful young woman

back then, he reminded himself, but that wasn't it. At that time Fast Larry had his pick of beautiful women. All he had to do was ride into a town and be recognized. Women flocked like mares in season around him — around him and his big Colt, he reminded himself. And they were the kind of women a man like him wanted back then, the fast ones, the ones who had made it their life's calling to please a man.

Why Hilda . . . ? he asked himself. But then he saw her as he'd seen her then, her firm, naked skin warm against him, the velvet feel of her, the depth of her eyes, the fine beads of sweat on her brow as she moaned and closed her eyes and drew him deeper into her. *Stop it. . . .*

He didn't want to look back upon the memory of Hilda Stevens Hauler with anything other than shame, he thought, realizing that even as the young doctor and his innocent young assistant had attended to him day after day in order to save his worthless life, he, like some low, petty thief, had worked his way into her life for the sole purpose of taking, stealing something of a most personal nature from both her and the young man who loved her.

Jesus, what a no-good son of a bitch . . .

But that was Fast Larry, not him, Shaw

51

told himself, stopping in front of the restaurant. He was a different man now. He wouldn't allow anything to happen between himself and Hilda Stevens Hauler. She was unhappy. He had once taken advantage of her innocence; he refused to take advantage of her unhappiness.

As he opened the door and stepped into the restaurant, he considered the conversation that had taken place only moments before, when he'd stared at Hilda and said, "Hilda, he's your husband. He's the man who kept me from bleeding to death."

"I never loved him, Lawrence," she said. "It was you I gave myself to, and it's still your face I see above me even when it's really his. I close my eyes and try to imagine you there." She'd stepped closer, but Shaw held her gently at arm's length.

"Stop, Hilda," he said. "Think about what you're doing. The two of you treated me back to health. I can't ride in here after all this time and watch you tear your life apart, not over somebody like me."

"Your coming here is only a part of it," Hilda had told him. "I've been coming to a decision for a long time. I'm leaving my husband. I can't spend the rest of my life living this pretense. . . ."

Shaw stepped inside the restaurant and

instinctively looked all around. Taking off his hat, he put Hilda and Dr. Hauler farther back in his mind and quickly appraised the half dozen customers on his way to a table in the rear corner facing the front door.

Across the street, at the corner of an alley running alongside the Fair Deal, Willow Creek's only saloon and gambling establishment, three men who had arrived in town the day before stood watching Shaw until he'd disappeared inside the restaurant. "So, what do you say, Mariner?" one of the three asked the other two as he nervously rubbed the palm of his hand on the top of his holstered Colt. "Is that Shaw?"

"Yeah, far as I can tell it's him. If it ain't he still looks like a hired gun from the ground up, far as I'm concerned," said Jess Mariner, not seeming at all concerned with whether or not this was Lawrence Shaw.

"Yeah, but if it's this man Shaw," said Otis Felts, "he *is* known as the fastest gun alive."

"By who?" said Mariner. He nodded toward the boardwalk along the dirt street. "These sodbusters and steermongers? Fuck Shaw." He spit. "In Chicago a new 'toughest man alive' pops up about every morning. He's usually boxed and stuck into the ground before noon." A thin, hard smile came to his lips. "Like as not, it was me or my pals who put him there."

Felts shrugged. "If Shaw makes you no difference, he don't me either."

"Then I did right, coming to tell Mr. Blank?" a young livery hostler wearing a frayed bowler hat asked Felts.

"Yeah, sure, Dick," said Felts, staring at the door to the restaurant. "You earned yourself four bits."

"Four bits!" said Dick Harpin. "I get that much currying some flea-bit hammerhead. I'm hoping to ride for the Frenchman. Can't you put in a good word for me?"

Mariner gave the young wannabe gunman a look and said, "As long as you're calling him Mr. Blank, I'd sooner not mention you to him, Dickie boy."

"I thought everybody calls him, Mr. Blank," said Harpin in his own defense.

The other two had turned their attention back to the restaurant door. "Only them with no better sense call him Blank," Mariner offered. "His name is *LeBlanc.*"

"Which is French for 'your ass is dead if you ain't careful what you say around me,' " said Felts, with a cruel grin. "So, if I was you I'd try to remember the man's name before I go trying to fill a saddle for him."

Mariner also gave a slight grin, drawing a big Remington from under his riding duster and checking it. "Maybe you ought to write it down somewhere and practice saying it some," he said to Harpin. Instead of holstering the big Remington, Mariner let it hang loosely in his hand. "Now what about this saddle tramp Shaw?"

"Want to let him finish breakfast first?" Felts asked. "He looked like he could use a good meal." He also lifted his gun from his holster and checked it. Then he slipped it back down in his holster, leaving it loose, the safety strap off the hammer.

"Hmmph. Nobody ever gave me a chance to finish breakfast," said Mariner. "Are you starting to get soft on me, Felts?"

"Soft?" Felts gave him a sidelong glance. "Stand here and watch the fur fly."

But as Felts started to take a step forward, Mariner stepped quickly ahead of him. "Whoa, now, I want this one. You just back me up if I need it." Taking the lead toward the restaurant, he said, "Lag to the side and watch through the window. This is going make some locals think twice before they buck up against us once the herd gets here."

"You want him, you got him," said Felts, staying a step behind Mariner. "I've got the window covered."

"What about me?" Dick Harpin asked.

"What about you?" Mariner replied.

"There's two windows. I've got this Uhlinger. I can help."

"Save the pocket gun for the Fourth of July, Dickie boy," said Mariner.

"Or go start a race with it," said Felts, neither of them looking back. "This is a Samuel Colt–size job." He idly opened and closed the fingers of his gun hand.

At his table in the rear of the restaurant, Shaw had placed his order for steak, eggs, potatoes, and mush, and had buttered a hot biscuit an elderly stoop-shouldered waiter brought to him on a clean white saucer. The waiter poured a cup of steaming coffee as Shaw stuffed his checkered table napkin down into the neck of his shirt.

Shaw bit into the soft biscuit just as he saw the break in sunlight at the window to the right of the front door. Felts stepped up and looked inside. "I see him," Felts said over his shoulder, squinting through the wavy pane of glass. "He's sitting straight-backed against the rear wall. Poor sumbitch is eating like the world's coming to an end."

"I got news for him," said Mariner, his thumb cocking the big Remington. "It is." He reached out, opened the door, and stepped into the open doorway, sunlight streaming in around him. "Lawrence Shaw!" he bellowed, the gun coming up, out at arm's length.

Upon seeing the gun and hearing the tone of voice, the patrons would have instinctively dived for cover. But there was no time. Before the customers could make a move two shots exploded from Shaw's Colt. One shot slammed Jess Mariner back out of the doorway and onto the street, his Remington flying from his hand. The other shot shattered the glass and flipped Otis Felts backward, the bullet punching through the bridge of his nose and out the back of his head, splattering blood on Dick Harpin.

The breakfast patrons sat in stunned disbelief. Shaw stood quickly and walked to the doorway, still chewing a mouthful of biscuit. His smoking Colt in his right hand, Shaw reached up, jerked the checkered napkin from his shirt, and dropped it on a table in passing. Seeing the old waiter standing in the service door with a coffeepot in hand, his mouth agape, Shaw said, "Keep cooking my breakfast. I'll be right back."

In the street, stooped over the body of Jess Mariner, Dick Harpin busily searched through the dead man's pockets and stuffed the cash and coin contents into his own. When Shaw appeared on the narrow boardwalk, his Colt still smoking in his hand, Harpin threw his grimy hands up and shouted, "Please don't shoot! I'm not armed! See?" He wiggled his fingers.

"You're the stable hostler," said Shaw, recognizing the seedy, disheveled young man.

"Yep, that's me, Dick Harpin!" he said quickly. "I'm taking *real* good care of your horses! I wasn't with them! That is, I was with them, but I had nothing to do with them coming after you!" he lied. "I warned them not to! I swear I did!"

"Sure you did," Shaw replied in a cynical tone. "After you told them about me and showed them where to look." As he spoke he walked forward and stopped with his Colt cocked and pointed down at the hostler's face. "Whatever you've got, give it up."

Harpin lowered his hands, opened his coat carefully, and took out the small Uhlinger pistol with his thumb and fingertip and dropped it on the ground. "I'd forgotten I even had it," he said sheepishly.

"Who are these men?" Shaw asked. From various points along the dirt street, bystanders ventured forward for a closer look.

"This one is Jess Mariner," said Harpin. Nodding toward the other bloody body lying in the dirt, he added, "That one is Otis Felts. They both work for the big French spread headed here."

"I see," said Shaw, gazing south at the rise of dust on the horizon.

"They came here last week to sort of check things out, I reckon," said Harpin, his hands still chest high.

"They don't look like drovers to me," Shaw commented, eyeing the dead men's clothes and hats, their well-cared-for holsters and shooting gear.

"They're not drovers," said Harpin. "The Frenchman who runs the spread, Mr. LeBlanc, has a small army of guards working for him. Word is there could be a range war once the big spread gets here."

Drovers or guards either one, Shaw realized there could be trouble once the spread arrived and the men found he'd killed two of their riders. "Get on your feet, hostler," he said, giving Harpin a nudge with his boot. "Go get the sheriff and bring him back here." Shaw looked all around, wondering why the town sheriff hadn't heard the shots and already come running.

"Our sheriff quit the day he heard about the big spread coming," Harpin said, lowering his hands slowly.

From the far end of the street, Shaw saw Dr. Hauler hurrying along, his black leather bag in hand. In the upstairs window of the hotel, Hilda Hauler craned her neck, watching Shaw amid the close-drawing crowd of onlookers.

Seeing Shaw stare toward the approaching doctor, Harpin said, "Doc Hauler is sort of overseeing everything here until we get ourselves a new sheriff."

"What was your part in this, hostler?" Shaw asked, turning his attention back to Harpin as the doctor hurried closer.

"Nothing, I swear!" said Harpin. But upon seeing that Shaw knew better, he quickly added, "All right, I admit I had talked to these two about putting in a word for me with the Frenchman. I've been looking for a new job. But that's all. I wanted nothing to do with trying to kill you."

Shaw turned away from him as the doctor pushed his way through the gathered crowd.

"Ask him for his gun, Doc," said an old man standing nearest to Shaw and Harpin. "That's what the sheriff would do first thing."

Doc Hauler gave the old man a quick glance. "That won't be necessary," he said. He stooped down to the body of Jess Mariner and checked for a pulse, finding none. "I'm certain that if Mr. Shaw wanted to shoot anybody else, he'd have already done so." Hauler walked a few feet away to Otis Felts and checked again for a pulse, in spite of the blood and brain matter lying strung out across the dirt. Straightening, he walked back to Shaw and asked bluntly, "What happened, Mr. Shaw?"

"This one came in the restaurant, called me out with a pointed gun. I shot him. The other one there I shot through the window." He gestured toward Felts. "I figured him for this one's backup."

"You shot him just because you *figured* he was backing this one's play?" the doctor asked, seeming puzzled by such a line of reasoning.

"Ask him," said Shaw, wagging his Colt toward Dick Harpin. "He was with them."

Before the doctor could ask, Harpin offered, "Yep, it's the truth, Doc. They come to kill him. I tried to stop them. They wouldn't listen."

"But still," said the doctor to Shaw, "you didn't know that before you shot him."

"Call it a strong hunch," said Shaw. "Had I waited to see what he intended, it wouldn't be me you're standing here talking to." He gestured toward the restaurant. "You can ask anybody in there. This was self-defense."

"I understand," said the doctor. He ran his fingers through his hair in worried contemplation. "But now I have to wonder what's going to happen when these men's friends get to town. They're part of that big European spread I told you about."

"So I heard," said Shaw. "I gave it some thought myself. My best hope is to be out of town before the herd gets up onto the grasslands."

"That would be wise," said the doctor. "I hoped you would look at it that way." The two looked south toward the wide drift of dust. "I calculate they'll arrive in three days, four at the most. Men like these two will be arriving ahead of the main body. So word of the shooting will start spreading anytime. I'll have these two taken to the spring-house behind the saloon until someone of authority comes for them."

"As soon as Rita has her baby and gets settled in, I'll be out of here, Doctor," Shaw repeated. "I told you, I'm not looking for trouble."

At the door of the restaurant the old waiter appeared and called out, "Your breakfast is ready, sir. Come and get it."

"Doctor, if we've got more to talk about, can we do it while I eat?" As he asked, his eyes moved past the hotel window, where Hilda Hauler watched them intently.

"Go ahead and eat your breakfast," said the doctor, his eyes and expression showing no sign of his having heard Shaw and his

62

wife talking earlier while he stood listening through the door. "Any talking we need to do will keep till later."

CHAPTER 5

By the time Shaw had finished his meal and begun sipping his second cup of coffee, the hotel clerk, a meek young man named Charlie Brewster, ventured inside the now-empty restaurant with his hands chest high. Before walking any closer to Shaw, he called out cautiously, "M-Mr. Shaw?" Upon seeing someone else standing inside the front door calling out Shaw's name, the old waiter disappeared quickly through the service door, his hands full of dirty breakfast dishes.

"Yes, what is it?" Shaw asked. He gestured the clerk forward. From the other side of the service door a crash of breaking dishware resounded.

Startled by the sound, the clerk stopped abruptly and said to Shaw in a fast, nervous voice, "Dr. Hauler said to tell you the young lady is giving birth."

"Obliged," Shaw replied. He stood and glanced toward the service door, dropping a gold coin on the table and picking up his wide-brimmed hat from an empty chair. He reached for a smaller coin with which to tip the clerk, but upon relaying the doctor's message the young man had already backed out the door and vanished.

Leaving the restaurant, Shaw glanced only in passing at the dark spots of blood on the dirt street and the bodies lying with their arms crossed on their chest in the bed of an open freight wagon. He walked along the boardwalk the distance from the restaurant to the hotel, feeling the eyes of store clerks and townsfolk on him each step of the way. Stepping out of sight into the hotel lobby, Shaw saw Charlie Brewster standing behind the oaken counter, catching his breath, wiping his sweaty forehead with a wadded handkerchief.

"Is . . . is there anything else I can do for you, Mr. Shaw?" he stammered. "If there is, please don't hesitate to ask."

Shaw only nodded his head slightly and climbed the stairs to the room. Before he could knock on the door, Hilda opened it for him expectantly and said quietly as she stepped aside, "She's awake; you can see her for a moment." In an even lower voice she added, "I heard the shots and saw the bodies. Thank God you're all right."

"Yeah, thank God," Shaw acknowledged in a wry tone. He took his hat from his head.

Rita heard Shaw's footsteps, even though he walked softly to the bedside, and she turned her face to him, nestling her blanket-wrapped newborn against her side. Her tired dark eyes glistened with tears. "Lawrence, here is our daughter," she said. "Come say hello to her."

This was not the time for Shaw to contest the baby's parentage. "A daughter," he said softly, bending over the bed and watching Rita pull the corner of the thin spread away from the tiny face.

"Isn't she beautiful?" Rita whispered.

"Yes, Rita, she is," said Shaw. He reached out with his fingertip and touched the child ever so lightly on its chin. Avoiding the tiny wandering eyes, he murmured to her under his breath, "Look at you, little darling . . . what on earth are you doing here? Your ma was expecting a boy."

"*Si*, I expected a man child," Rita said with a trace of disappointment in her voice. "I do not know what to do now that I see I have a daughter."

"You'll both do just fine, Rita," Shaw said, realizing even as he said it how great the odds were against it. He gave a glance toward Hilda Hauler, wondering if she had

66

just thought the same thing. "Jimmy Blaine's spread is not far from here," Shaw continued. "While you rest a day or two I'll ride out and speak to him."

"But I am able to ride now," Rita said, adjusting herself upward against the pillow at her back. "So is my baby."

"The doctor tells me it's a long day's ride. I think it best if I ride out first and make sure Jimmy is there," Shaw said, knowing that Blaine might not take kindly to the unannounced arrival of a woman and an infant at his door.

As if realizing that Shaw was right, Hilda Hauler stepped over to the bed using the pretext of adjusting the bedcover and pillows. "Mr. Shaw is right," she said gently. "You've gone through a long, hard labor. Rest is important for both you and your baby."

Rita gave her a dubious look that made Shaw wonder if perhaps she'd not really been asleep when he and Hilda had talked in the room earlier. "Is this what your husband, the doctor, will say?"

"Yes, it is," Hilda said softly, but with confident authority. "He will tell you that you must allow your daughter to rest for at least a day . . . two days would be even better."

"Our horses need some rest too," said Shaw. "Early tomorrow morning I'll ride out to Jimmy Blaine's. I'll ride back here the next day."

"You won't just ride away and not come back?" Rita asked, her voice sounding shaky and distrustful.

"Rita, you have my word," said Shaw, feeling Hilda's eyes on him.

Before Rita could respond, a commotion on the street below caused both Shaw and Hilda to step over to the window and look down. In front of a stage and telegraph office a dusty stagecoach slid to a creaking halt. Surrounding the stage, four horsemen circled and whooped and laughed loudly. "It's Henry McCarty and his pals. Or I should say Billy Bonney," Shaw corrected himself, watching Dr. Hauler hurry out onto the street to try to quiet them down, his leather medical bag in hand.

"Oh, dear!" said Hilda. "I hope Adrian doesn't get himself hurt!"

Shaw looked surprised to hear Hilda call her husband, the doctor, by his first name. From the bed Rita called out in a tired but excited tone, "It is Henry? It is *really* him?"

Shaw stared out the window at the horsemen and their billowing dust and said over his shoulder, "Oh, yes, it's him, all right."

"Then you must help me up!" said Rita. "I must go tell him he has become a father!"

Hilda looked back and forth between Rita and Shaw, confused, then said to Shaw, "But you said Jimmy Blaine is the father . . . ?" Her words trailed off as Shaw shook his head slightly, letting her know not to pursue the matter any further. "Oh . . ." She trailed off again, sounding no less confused.

"You're not going anywhere right now, Rita, not until you've rested," said Shaw firmly, seeing her start to take her arm from around the baby nestled beside her in order to get out of bed. "I'll tell Billy you're here."

Rita settled back into the bed. "Tell him he must come see me. Tell him he is a father. Tell him his daughter looks just like him."

"I'll tell him every word you said." Shaw put on his hat and turned to the door, saying in a wry tone, "And tomorrow I'll go tell Jimmy Blaine the same thing."

As Shaw opened the door to leave, Hilda stepped half into the hallway and asked him quietly, "Why are you going along with this, Lawrence?"

Shaw gave her a look. "Do you know what happens to most babies born to women in her profession?" Before she could respond, he whispered, "If they don't get burned out of the womb, they end up knocked in the head and thrown in somebody's hog lot."

Also whispering, Hilda said, "Yes, I know, but —"

"She needed my help to travel here, Hilda," said Shaw, cutting her off. "You see how she is. If I'd turned her down she would have come on her own, or tried to."

"But all this about telling two different men that they're the baby's father . . . ?" said Hilda.

"She's scared, Hilda," said Shaw. "She's just playing the long odds, hoping for a break."

"But it's ridiculous," Hilda said. "Neither of these men is going to fall for it. It's obvious she doesn't even *know* who the father is."

"That doesn't matter," said Shaw. "I had to either play along with her or turn her down. What would you and the doctor have done?"

"I understand." Hilda sighed in resignation. "Rarely do we hear of these women having a child . . . one that lives, anyway."

"But this baby is here, alive and kicking," Shaw said. "So I reckon it was meant to be." He offered a tired smile and added, "Who knows? Maybe Blaine or McCarty will take

70

one look into that little girl's eyes and his heart will melt. If either one of them convinces himself that she's his daughter, everybody will come out ahead."

"What about you, Lawrence?" Hilda asked. "Your heart didn't melt, did it, looking into that little girl's eyes?"

"I didn't look into her eyes," Shaw said. "But it wouldn't matter. My heart doesn't melt as easy as some." He stepped away, allowing her to shut the door behind him.

On the street, Dr. Hauler stood beside the stage, talking with the driver and shotgun rider while the Kid and his friends sat on their horses, looking on, their wrists crossed on their saddle horns. "I'll be honest with you, Doc: I never saw any 'pache, or any other Indians," said the driver, Scotty Hood, a wiry man whose curly red hair lay dust-coated beneath his battered hat brim.

The shotgun rider, Joe Hayley, cut in, saying, "But if Billy Bonney says him and his pals chased some away before they could ambush us, that's good enough for me any day!"

"Yep, me too," said Hood, "and we're both obliged for them doing it."

"Aw, hell, fellows" — the Kid grinned shyly — "don't go making a big thing of it.

71

We seen them lying in wait above a cliff, and knew right away what they was up to."

"Still, Mr. Bonney," said Doc Hauler, "that was very heroic of you and your friends."

"What are you getting at, sawbones?" the Kid said, flaring a bit at the doctor's words.

Hauler looked taken aback at the sudden change in the Kid's mood. "Nothing, sir! Nothing at all! I am simply trying to thank all of you for looking after our stage. It was very . . . uh" — he stalled for a moment — "very *kind* of you."

"We didn't do it trying to make ourselves look like heroes," the Kid said.

"Of course not," said Hauler. "I certainly didn't mean to imply anything of that nature."

"We only did what any good pilgrims would do," said Hyde Rudabaugh.

"Nothing more," Free Drink Stemlet added. "We saved these men's lives, then came on about our business. We ask nothing in return."

"That's right," said the Kid. Then, upon seeing Shaw walk toward the wagon from the boardwalk of the hotel, he gave a wide, crooked grin and said, "I'll be skinned and salted . . . if it ain't Fast Larry hisself."

"Howdy, Kid," said Shaw, stopping a few

feet away without touching his hat brim. "If you don't already know, I killed your friend Tommy Childers. But he came looking for it. He sided against me with Brady Katlin. I killed him too."

"I heard," said the Kid. He shrugged. "Tommy owed me eleven dollars. Otherwise I won't miss him."

"Then you and I are straight?" Shaw asked.

"As a string," said the Kid. "If we wasn't I expect I would be riding with the Katlins right now, hunting you down."

Shaw nodded and looked off along the trail. "Where are they?"

"Lost, if I had to guess," said the Kid. "Hell, we come upon you without trying." He chuckled and spit. "You remember Free Drink, Sturgis, and Hyde." He gestured toward the other three, who nodded and sat staring.

"Yep, howdy, fellows," said Shaw, touching his hat brim now that he knew how the Kid felt about his killing Childers.

"McBain and the Russian brothers told us you're traveling with a pregnant woman," the Kid said with a curious look.

"I was until today," said Shaw. "But she's not pregnant anymore. That's something else I wanted to talk to you about."

73

"Yeah?" the Kid asked, getting a wary look on his face.

"The woman is Rita Vargas."

"Sweet Rita," said the Kid. "Now, there's one worth drinking to. How is she?"

"She's good, Kid," said Shaw. "She gave birth to a little girl. She's asking for you to come see her." He gestured a thumb toward the hotel.

"I'll do that right now," said the Kid. He started to swing down from his saddle.

"I'd better tell you she claims you're the baby's father," said Shaw.

The Kid swung back into his saddle. "Obliged you told me," he said. "But I think she's confused me with somebody else."

"That's possible, Kid," said Shaw. "She's also saying it might be mine or Jimmy Blaine's."

The Kid looked down and shook his head. "Doves don't have babies. Didn't anybody ever tell her?"

"I suppose not," said Shaw. "But Rita's got one, and she needs a daddy for it . . . or thinks she does, anyway."

"Well, give her and Jimmy Blaine my best," said the Kid, turning his horse toward the saloon farther down the dirt street. "I'll just be ambling along now."

"You could go see her, Kid," said Shaw.

"It wouldn't hurt you."

"It wouldn't help me either," said the Kid. He gave Shaw a closer look. "Why are you traveling with her, anyway?"

"It's a long story," said Shaw. "She needed some help. I wasn't doing anything." He shrugged. "Here we are."

"Yeah, here we are," said the Kid, considering things as he gazed away for a moment. Then he said, "A little girl, huh?"

"Yeah," said Shaw, "a little bitty thing, pretty as a peach." He stared at the Kid expectantly.

"Well, hell." After a pause the Kid sighed and swung back down from his saddle. "Let's go take ourselves a look-see." Over his shoulder he said to Free Drink, Sturgis, and Rudabaugh, "Boys, set me one up beside yas. I'll be right there, if Fast Larry don't get me married off."

"No danger of that happening, Kid," Shaw said, the two of them walking toward the hotel.

Stepping up on the hotel boardwalk, the Kid stopped for a moment and said to Shaw, looking him up and down appraisingly, "You haven't said much about the Katlins hunting you. Are you that cool about it, or just acting the way the fastest gun alive has to act to keep up appearances?"

"I have no appearances to keep up, Kid," Shaw said. "The fact is, I just don't give a damn."

"Whoa!" The Kid feigned a surprised look. "Now, that is a dangerous position for you, Fast Larry."

"Do me a favor, Kid," said Shaw. "Stop calling me Fast Larry, will you? That's not a name I go by anymore."

The Kid looked surprised. "Why? After all it took to get yourself that name?"

"My own reasons, Kid," said Shaw, "same as when you wanted people to stop calling you Henry and start calling you William Bonney, or Kid."

The Kid stared at him for a moment, then shrugged. He reached out and opened the hotel door. "Sure thing," he said. "From now on I call you Shaw. Does that suit you?"

"Obliged, Kid," Shaw said, stepping into the small lobby of the hotel.

CHAPTER 6

Shaw smiled to himself as he watched the look on the Kid's face as he bowed over the bed and looked at Rita's baby daughter. "Can I touch her face before we go?" he asked, after he and Shaw had been there a few minutes longer than he had anticipated.

Rita smiled, trying to hide her fatigue. She had borrowed a brush from Hilda Hauler and hurriedly brushed the tangles from her long, raven black hair. "You can pick her up and hold her if you like." Her smile widened. "She is your daughter too."

The Kid's finger came away from the baby's cheek as if she'd bitten him. "I'd better not," said the Kid. "I'm not fit to hold a baby, let alone father one." He shot Shaw a glance that asked silently for his help.

"Not meaning to rush you, Kid," said Shaw, getting the signal, "but your pals are waiting for you."

"With you it is always your pals, Billy,"

Rita said, pouting a bit. "Is there no time for me and for your baby?"

"Rita," said the Kid as kindly as he could, "take my name off your list of fathers. If I ever decide to settle down and be somebody's daddy, it'll be my own choosing. . . ."

Even as he spoke, his tone of voice softened as he looked down into the baby's eyes.

"Kid," Shaw said quietly after a moment, "I can tell your pals you're going to be a while longer, if you want me to."

But the Kid stood only a second longer. Seeming to snap out of a deep train of thought, he said, "What? No, that's all right. I'm going."

Saying his good-bye to Rita, the Kid turned and walked out of the room with Shaw. Passing Hilda Hauler, who had stood by silently and now held the door, Shaw whispered just between the two of them, "The Kid's heart doesn't melt either."

On the boardwalk, the Kid turned to Shaw and said, "Damn. I wish you hadn't talked me into that." He nodded back toward the hotel, toward Rita's room, where the newborn infant lay nestled at her mother's breast.

"Kid, I don't recall talking you into anything," said Shaw. "I told you she's here, said she wanted you to come see her. The rest was all your doing."

"Yeah, I know." The Kid grinned, looking away along the dirt street. "That is a beautiful baby. Did you see the way she looked at me?"

"Yeah, I saw it, Kid," Shaw agreed, although he knew that all newborn babies looked at things about the same way. He wasn't sure a baby this young could even see clearly. *But what the hell . . .* Rita is a good girl," he said. "A man could do worse than her."

The Kid grinned, his mind going off in a different direction now. "I expect that settling with a dove you could always count on more than just home cooking."

"Forget it, Kid," said Shaw. "I'm talking about a wife and family. A daughter to start with — who knows, maybe more down the road. It might be a good fresh start for a man. You might want to grab on with both hands while you've got a chance."

"Oh? If it's such a good deal, maybe *you* ought to grab onto it with both hands," the Kid countered. The two walked toward the saloon across the street and a block down from the hotel.

"I had my chance at that kind of life, Kid," Shaw said in sad reflection. "I let it get away from me. It won't happen for me again. Rita and the baby coming with me would only end up harming them both." He thought about the wife he'd lost to violence. Even if he loved Rita, he would not expose her and the baby to his life.

Knowing what had happened to Shaw's wife, Rosa, the Kid fell silent for a moment. When he spoke again he'd changed the subject. "What about the Katlins?" he asked out of the blue.

"What about them?" Shaw countered. The two of them stared straight ahead.

"You know what about them," the Kid said. "They'll come here to kill you."

"I won't be here," Shaw replied quickly.

"All right," said the Kid. "But if it happens that you *are* still here, do you want any help?"

Shaw looked at him, a bit surprised. "I thought you and them rode together now and then."

"Yep, we have, if it suited both our situations," the Kid said. "But they ain't nothing to me."

"And I am?" Shaw asked, giving him a look.

"You and me have never wronged one another," said the Kid. "Between you and the Katlins I'd take your side, if you asked real polite-like."

"Obliged, Kid," said Shaw, turning his eyes forward again as they walked on, "but I fight alone."

"You and Cray Dawson fought together. I heard all about it," said the Kid. "They say he gained his big-gun reputation out of it."

It began to look to Shaw as though the Kid himself might be looking for such a big-gun reputation. "He and I fought together; that's true. But we'd known one another all our lives. Anyhow, it's something I only did once and will never do again," said Shaw.

"Why is that, Shaw?" the Kid asked. "Don't you trust me beside you when the going gets slim?"

"Kid, there is nobody I would trust as much as you if the going got slim," Shaw replied. "But it's a personal reason. Too personal to talk about."

"Damn *personal*. I'm rude as a cactus cushion," the Kid insisted. "Now tell me why."

Shaw hesitated, then said, "All right, I'll tell you, and maybe you can learn something from it. I fight alone because I figure every fight I have, I caused it."

"You must be a busy man, causing so much trouble." The Kid chuckled and shook his head. "That's the biggest crock of horse sh—"

81

Shaw cut him off. "Listen, Kid, I don't mean I start it every time some fool comes at me with a gun wanting to prove himself. But if I had never walked into this kind of life, that fool wouldn't come looking."

"Damn, Shaw," the Kid said with a grin. "Do you also walk on water, make it rain? You got anything to do with the sun coming up?"

"Don't make this into a joking matter, Kid," Shaw cautioned him. "You wanted to know, so I'm trying to tell you."

The Kid settled and said in a more serious tone, "What I'm saying is, you ain't responsible for everything that happens."

"I know, Kid," said Shaw, letting out a tightly drawn breath. "But sometimes it feels like it."

"And that's why you don't give a damn anymore who's looking for you?" He seemed to study the situation. "Damn, I'm going to have to get you drunk and get you bedded down with a dove pretty quick . . . get you cheered up." He patted his shirt pocket. "We might even smoke some of this Mexican locoweed."

"Naw, not me, Kid," said Shaw. "Not right now, anyways. I'll have a drink or two to be sociable. But I'm no fun to drink with these days. I carry a bottle in my saddlebags and do my drinking alone."

"Ain't you the pleasant soul," said the Kid with a narrowed gaze and a slight grin.

At the far end of the street, Bratcher McBain had ridden up onto the wide dirt street and saw Shaw and the Kid from behind as they walked toward the saloon. "Jesus!" He gasped as if he'd seen two dark apparitions.

Jerking back hard on the reins, he caused his horse to let out a loud whinny as he quickly turned the bewildered animal and rode away at a fast clip.

"What was that?" the Kid asked, both he and Shaw turning instinctively at the sound of the horse. Just as instinctively their gun hands were poised near the holstered revolvers.

Catching only a glance of the rider through a cloud of dust before he disappeared out of sight over a rise at the edge of town, Shaw let his gun hand ease back down to his side. "It's somebody who didn't want me to see him," he said. "I've had it happen before. First couple of times I thought there was something about me that scared horses."

The Kid saw a trace of a smile and realized this was Shaw's weak attempt at humor. "I wouldn't discount that possibility out of hand if I was you," he replied. Looking at Shaw closer as they stepped onto the boardwalk of the Fair Deal saloon, he asked, "How do you know it wasn't somebody who wanted to avoid seeing *me*? Why is it you think every stone rolls to your end of the table? I've marked a pretty wide spot myself all the way from here to New Mex Territory."

Shaw said, "Then suit yourself, Kid. It was somebody who didn't want to be seen by *you.*" The two stepped inside the saloon. "That's all right by me. I can use the rest."

The Kid chuckled and shook his head. "Shaw, no offense, but I have never seen a man so stuck on himself."

Shaw let it pass, taking a quick glance around the wide floor full of battered game tables, some covered with torn and soiled green felt and surrounded by straight-backed chairs. Only four of the tables were occupied. Other tables sat with empty bottles and shot glasses on them from earlier games that had broken up. Along the bar drinkers leaned in a row and watched the two through the mirror behind the bar. Shaw's leaving two gunmen lying dead in the street had been the bar talk of the day. Seeing him walk in with young William Bonney drew everyone's hushed attention.

"Down here, Kid, you and Fast Larry!" Free Drink called out from the far end of the bar, wanting everybody to know he was with the two gunmen, even though everybody knew he and the Kid rode together anyway. Then he called out along the bar, "All right, give my pals some room here! Don't hog the bar!" His voice sounded a bit dulled by rye whiskey.

Although the long bar offered plenty of room, the drinkers drew a little closer together to make space for the Kid and the famous gunman beside him. "We was just telling everybody about the 'pache we chased away from the stage, Kid," said Sturgis, he and Hyde Rudabaugh standing alongside Free Drink.

"That's enough about the Injuns, Sturgis," said the Kid. He held up two fingers toward the bartender as he and Shaw stepped up to the bar.

"Coming right up!" said the nervous bartender. He quickly set two shot glasses in front of them and filled them. Before Shaw or the Kid could raise money from their pockets to pay for their drink, the bartender said to Shaw, "First drink is on the house for you, Mr. Shaw." He turned his eyes to the Kid. "And, of course, you too, Mr. Bonney."

"Obliged." Shaw nodded, accustomed to having free drinks shoved at him.

The Kid grinned and looked a little surprised, enough to let Shaw know that he was *not* accustomed to such royal treatment. He looked at Shaw, who started to comment, but before he got a chance Sturgis said, "Go on, Kid; tell Shaw about the 'pache waiting to ambush the stage."

"I said that's enough about the 'pache," the Kid replied, looking a little embarrassed. "Shaw doesn't want to hear about that . . . it wasn't nothing."

Shaw looked at Sturgis and the others as he threw back his shot of rye, then said, "That's all right, Kid. Tell me about it."

"Yeah, go on and tell him, Kid," Sturgis said.

"Well," the Kid said with shy reluctance, "on our way here we was riding along some high ground overlooking the trail and we come upon a band of seven or eight 'pache lying in wait to ambush the stage."

"It was eight," Sturgis cut in.

"All right, eight," said the Kid. Warming to the tale, he gestured with his hand as he continued, "They were right down here on a cliff beneath us, and below them here come the stage, unawares."

"That stage didn't know what the hell was

fixin' to hit them!" said Sturgis, excited and drunk. He raised his glass and tossed back his drink. "Whooieee! Them bloodthirsty bastards!"

The Kid gave him a hard stare. "Am I going to tell this, or are you?" he growled.

"Sorry, Kid," said Sturgis, reaching for the half bottle of rye standing near his hand. "I just got kinda carried away."

"Anyway" — the Kid shrugged, his interest in telling the story starting to wane — "they didn't see us until we opened fire on them. Sturgis shot one; I shot a couple more. The rest took to the dirt like prairie dogs." He shrugged again. "That's all."

"I'm betting they was part of a larger body," said Sturgis. "Tell him how many more you figure there might have been waiting nearby! There could have been a hundred or more! It wouldn't have mattered to us!"

"Yeah, yeah," said the Kid, trying his best to end the conversation, again looking embarrassed by it. "That's enough of it. Let's drink and do ourselves some dove hunting." He looked at the bartender and said, "Hey, huckleberry, where's the women?"

"Only one around here is Nadine. She's prettying up for you fellows right now. I

87

expect she'll be down 'most any minute."

"Our pal Shaw gets first go at her, eh, Shaw?" the Kid said, grinning.

"I might pass on it, Kid," said Shaw, "but obliged for the offer."

"Whatever you say, Shaw," the Kid said loudly, raising his shot glass above his head in a toast. "Here's to Lawrence Shaw, the fastest damn gun alive!"

Shaw nodded and said quietly, "And to you, William Bonney."

"Listen, Shaw, about them Indians and the stage," said the Kid, leaning in close, his voice lowered just between the two of them. "I don't think we really killed any of them; mostly we just scared them away."

"I understand, Kid," said Shaw. "The main thing is they didn't get to ambush the stage."

"Yeah, that's right," said the Kid. He seemed to consider it for a moment, then said, "I can't say for sure they was about to ambush it . . . but it looked like they might have been. Sometimes an Indian story gets a little blown up when it's told. Do you see what I'm saying?"

"Yeah, Kid, I see what you're saying," said Shaw. He tossed back the rest of his drink and reached for the bottle of rye. "The whole world loves a good Indian ambush story."

"It ain't that we made it up, Shaw," said the Kid, looking embarrassed. "It's just that we sharpened its edges some." He grinned. "I expect you've done that some yourself, haven't you?"

"No, Kid," Shaw said flatly. "I've never told any of my own tales. Somebody else always does that."

"Oh . . ." The Kid nodded and stood in silence, staring down at his empty glass until the bartender refilled it. "Well, what the hell," he said finally, picking up his glass and raising it. "Who cares how the word gets spread, so long as somebody spreads it." His crooked grin came back to his face. "Here's to the Wild West, and all us boys game enough to take it on!"

CHAPTER 7

T. J. Katlin sat in his saddle at the edge of a clearing, staring out across a sweep of flatlands toward the thick, wide cloud of dust stretched across the evening sky. Beside him sat his brother Lane. Behind them sat Uncle Linton, Bratcher McBain, and the Russian brothers. They had been observing the cloud of dust as it drew closer to them for the past two days.

"Here's where we lose them," said Bratcher McBain, looking down at the hoofprints they'd followed from the shack along the west fork. The prints disappeared into a larger path of tracks running back and forth toward the large herd in the distance.

"One thing's for damn certain," said Uncle Linton, looking up from the many hoofprints and off toward the dust. "If Fast Larry has thrown in with the European spread, he'll be hard to flush out. They're hiring any gunman who'll work for them, is what I been hearing."

"What are you saying, Uncle Linton?" T. J. snapped at him harshly. "That we ought to forget about what Shaw did to brother Brady?"

"Hell, no!" said Uncle Linton. "I'm just stating the facts. If you want to ride in on the Europeans and throw down on them, I'm with you in it up to my elbows! Brady is my nephew just like the two of yas." He looked back and forth between T. J. and Lane. "Gawdamn it, boys, blood is blood, is what I always say. I'm willing to die for one of our own. But let's try to use good sense."

"Listen to him, T. J.," said Lane. "Uncle knows what he's talking about. If Shaw rode into the European spread, all we can do is bide our time and catch him when the rest of them ain't around."

"I hate lying back like a damn vulture and waiting for something to die," said T. J. "The son of a bitch killed Brady. I want to taste his blood the minute I see his murdering face."

"That's not real smart, T. J.," said Lane. "Suppose we get killed by the whole damn European spread? Then who'll get revenge for Brady, or *us,* for that matter?"

"I know," said T. J., cooling down and taking a deep breath. "I'll hold on and go along

91

with whatever you say, so long as we *do* get to kill the son of a bitch."

"Soon as we get a clear bead on him, T. J., he's dead," said Lane. "You've got my oath on it."

"Good enough, then," said T. J. He pulled his horse back sharply, spinning it in a restless half circle. "What the hell do you propose?"

"How's this for a suggestion?" a voice asked from the sparse woods behind them. "All of yas raise your hands away from your guns, real slow-like."

"What the . . ." Lane jerked his attention toward the sound of the voice and saw three mounted riflemen pointing their Winchesters at him, cocked and aimed.

"If I say it again, it'll be after one of yas hits the ground face-first," warned a rangy man wearing a long black duster and a thick red mustache. A tall, stained white Stetson sat atop his head.

"Raise your hands easy-like, boys," said Uncle Linton, staring hard at the three riflemen. Then, to the man with the red mustache, he said, "Unless you're Jesse by-God James, you're making a bad mistake."

"I heard mention of the European spread," the man replied, nudging his horse a step forward as the Katlin Gang eased their hands away from their guns. "I thought we'd best introduce ourselves and see what you fellows have on your minds."

"Our minds are our own damn business," said T. J., a sour look on his face. "Who the hell are you, and what's your game?"

"We're the ones who got the drop on yas," the man replied. "So let's start with who *you* are, and what's *your* game?"

Before T. J. could say something that might spark a gunfight, Lane cut in and said, "We're the Katlins. He's T. J., I'm Lane. These men ride with us. We're out looking for a son of a bitch who killed our brother."

"The Katlin Gang," the man said flatly.

"Yeah, that's us," said Lane, liking the fact that this man had heard of them. "I reckon word travels fast."

"I suppose." The man shrugged, as if unimpressed. "I'm Red Downing." He didn't bother to introduce Freddie Himbly and Joe Tate, two Texas gunmen riding with him. Nor did he make mention of two other Texans, Jack Priddy and Oscar Hogue, who remained out of sight, their rifles ready at port arms. "I ride front gun for the European spread. So I expect you can understand my concern, riding up and hearing my employer being discussed from inside a

93

blind spot." He gestured toward the surrounding woods.

"I've heard of *you* too, Red Downing," said Lane, becoming more at ease. "You used to be head security honcho for the Union Central Railroad." He grinned and continued, "Hell, you didn't hear us saying anything worth listening to. We're tracking a killer named Lawrence Shaw . . . wondered if maybe he's riding for the spread now."

Red Downing's eyes piqued with recognition. "You mean Fast Larry Shaw?" he asked.

"Yep, that's the son of a bitch," said Lane. "He killed our brother."

Red Downing lowered his rifle a few inches. "He's killed lots of brothers. I had no idea he was in this territory."

"He is, but he won't be once we find him," said T. J.

"What you heard was us wondering if he might have taken up with the European spread," said Lane.

"No, he's not with us," said Downing, already wondering if Shaw might have ridden to the territory to take the side of the settlers. "Why'd you think it?"

"We heard the Europeans are hiring gun hands," said Lane. "Figured it would be a good place for a man like Shaw to lie low."

A thin smile came to Red Downing's face. "A man like Shaw doesn't lie low for anybody."

"He does for us," said T. J.

"Then my hat's off to you," said Downing. He looked each of the Katlin Gang over in turn, as if sizing them up. "But you're right about one thing — we are hiring gun hands. Any of yas interested?"

"These men ride for us. I just told you what we're doing," Lane said, sounding a little testy about Downing offering his men a job right in front of him.

"Right, you did," said Downing offhandedly. He looked at the two big Russians and said, "What about you two big boys? You look like you could twist the nuts off a running grizzly."

"Tweetz nutz from grizzly bear?" said Jerniko, the oldest of the two, to his brother, Vladimir. They looked confused and murmured something in their native tongue. Then they said, "Ah," in unison, as if having cleared up the matter. "Katlins say *tweetz* nuts, we tweetz nuts." They stared blankly at Red Downing.

"I told you they ride for us," Lane said in a slightly stronger tone.

"No offense, Katlin," said Red Downing. "Part of my job is finding good help."

"Then good luck to you," said Lane. "Now, if your boys will lower their rifles we'll ride on."

Downing looked Lane up and down, then said, "I've got an idea. What say the six of yas ride for us awhile . . . just till we get settled into the grasslands?"

"Obliged, but we've got business to attend to," said Lane.

"Since you've heard of me," said Downing, "you're bound to know I have a reputation for getting folks to do what I want them to do." He gave a short, tight grin.

Lane bristled a little, but kept himself in check. "I have that same reputation," he said.

As if he hadn't heard him, Downing went on. "You see . . . the way things are going to shape up around Willow Creek, I figure any gun that ain't pointing away from us is going to be pointing at us once we get on the grasslands."

"Cattle wars ain't our game," said Lane.

Still not hearing him, Downing said, "If you boys are seen riding with us a day or two, then nobody on the other side is going to be looking to recruit you." He shrugged. "That shouldn't be a problem for yas, unless you're going to be *wanting* the settlers to recruit yas."

"We're not looking to be recruited," said Lane. "It's like I told you: we're out to avenge our brother's death. So we've got to tell you no."

A tense silence settled in while Lane Katlin stared into Downing's eyes and watched him ease the rifle back up to his shoulder and cock it again. "You might want to take a second and reconsider," Downing said quietly, breaking the silence. "You'd best keep in mind that I never take no for an answer." Raising a gloved hand, he gave a gesture that brought the riflemen out into the open, their Winchesters aimed and ready.

Lawrence Shaw rode his horse at a walk from the livery barn onto the dirt street and out toward the trail leading west of Willow Creek. Without turning to face the hotel window directly, he saw Hilda Hauler standing there watching him from Rita's room overlooking the street. But he gave no indication that he realized she was there. Instead Shaw kept his eyes straight ahead. At a turn in the wide street he rode away from the hotel, still feeling her gaze upon him.

"He is not coming back, you know," Rita said, seeing Hilda Hauler stare out the window with a look of longing in her eyes.

"Oh, I wasn't . . . That is, I didn't mean to . . ." Hilda turned quickly away from the window and from Rita's gaze, quite shaken that she had let her emotions reveal themselves so clearly.

"You do not have to pretend with me," Rita said softly. Her infant lay wrapped in a thin sheet, nestled comfortably in the crook of her arm. "I will say nothing of it to your husband."

"I'm certain there's really nothing to say," Hilda lied, nervously pulling back a loose strand of hair with her fingertips. "You need to get some rest. Mr. Shaw assured us he'll return after speaking to Mr. Blaine. We must take him at his word."

Rita gave a reserved smile, yet said bluntly, "You love him; I can tell."

"No, that's preposterous," Hilda said. "I admit Mr. Shaw is a captivating man. But I am a married woman, and I have no —"

"I can tell you have *known* him before," Rita said, cutting off the woman's string of nervous chatter. "A woman like myself can look at two people and know if they slept together." She pointed a finger and said, still smiling gently, "You and my baby's father have been lovers. Do not deny it to me. I can tell."

Neither denying nor confirming the accusation, Hilda said, "What do you mean, a woman like yourself?"

"I mean women like me who have laid down with many men," Rita said, jutting her chin a bit. "Too many men to mention."

"You have been a . . . a *prostitute*? Is this what you're telling me?" Hilda asked, trying to sound as if she hadn't already drawn such a conclusion on her own.

Rita sighed. "Yes, I have been a prostitute — a soiled dove, as they say. Do not act like you are surprised to hear me say it."

"All right, I won't," said Hilda. She turned back to the window and looked down to see Shaw ride away toward a distant hill line. "Now that we are being forthright with each other, let me ask you this." She watched Shaw ride on as she continued, "How can you even say that Lawrence Shaw, Jimmy Blaine, and William Bonney are the only ones who might possibly be the father of your child, if you have slept with all these many men?"

"Because they are the only three men who I cared enough for to allow myself to carry their child," Rita replied with stern conviction. "A woman knows whose seed her body has accepted." She looked down at the sleeping baby cradled in her arm. "Besides, my baby has a resemblance to each of these three men, and to no one else."

Hilda, not knowing how to respond, turned from the window and stared at her for a moment, then shook her head. "If you will excuse me, I must go now and make my rounds." She turned another glance out the window in time to see Shaw look back toward the town before he and his horse dropped out of sight over a rise in the trail. "The doctor will arrive shortly to check on you and the baby," she said, walking quickly toward the door.

On the trail, Shaw settled back into his saddle and gazed ahead, having looked back only long enough to see Hilda turn away from the hotel window and move out of sight. Now that Hilda had gotten over the shock of walking into a room and seeing him standing there, he hoped she would take the time to rethink the things she'd said to him. Dr. Hauler was a good man. *A far better man than you,* he told himself. Hilda was bound to see that she had no business with a gunman, a drifter like him. . . .

"Some other time . . ." Shaw said wryly, refusing to chastise himself at that moment. Impatient with himself, he gathered his

Seneca Falls Library
100
47 Cayuga Street
Seneca Falls, N.Y. 13148

reins into his right hand and sharply collected the horse beneath him. Rather than reflect grimly on his life and dwell on what he'd become, he nudged the horse up into a gallop along the flat trail and rode on until the trail rolled upward into a steep, rocky path leading into the hill line.

Following a meandering elk trail through a maze of broken rock and scrub pine and cedar, he rode in uninterrupted silence until the early afternoon. This was familiar land — *cattle land, land that men kill and die for,* he reminded himself. Looking around, he took in the majestic beauty of the land, yet he did so warily, seeing it through a translucent image of the dead and dying as they rose up bloodily from his violent past.

Fast Larry . . . ! he heard a voice cry out; and instinctively he felt himself half turn and reach for his Colt before realizing it was only the voice of some lost soul he had cast forever into the silent void. "Take it easy," he said to the horse, as if it were the animal beneath him and not himself who had reacted so suddenly to things unseen.

Settling himself, he rode on.

When the land leveled into a grassy valley beneath his horse's hooves, he guided the animal down a cut-bank and crossed the shallow, sprawling Little Blackfoot River. A half hour across the Little Blackfoot he rode the horse onto a sloping meadow of pale green grass and stopped when the meadow flattened and ran out into the rocky mouth of a narrow canyon.

"Sabo Canyon," Shaw said to himself, rubbing the horse's withers with a gloved hand as his free hand lifted his canteen by its strap. He uncapped it and sipped slowly. He took his time capping it, then looped it back around the saddle horn, knowing full well that he'd been watched from halfway down the sloping grassland.

From atop the rugged edge of Sabo Canyon, an old rancher named Claude Batson turned and called over his shoulder in a hushed tone, "Blaine, he's at the canyon. He's stopped and looking up toward us like he knows we're here! Come take a look! My eyes ain't the best."

Jimmy Blaine eased up from where he'd been sitting alone on a low rock with a cup of coffee in his hands. He rose to his feet, rifle and coffee cup in hand, and stepped over beside Batson. "Yeah, it's Shaw, all right."

"That's what I figured," said Batson. "But whoever it is, I saw that he's no newcomer." The two watched Shaw walk his horse back and forth, giving them a good look at him from both sides at a distance only the best of rifle shots could take advantage of. "He knows all the right things to do. He's accommodating. I'll say that for him."

Blaine almost smiled. "That's Shaw's way."

"Yeah, I remember it's his way," said Batson, "so long as he didn't come to do some killing. Want to wave him on in?"

"Yep, let's wave him in," said Blaine. "We'll ride down and meet him, feel him out before we take him in."

"Feel him out?" said Batson. "Hell, he's already killed two of the Frenchman's men."

"But that could have been over anything," Blaine said, staring out at the lone rider who sat easily in his saddle staring back at them. "Lawrence Shaw has always just killed somebody." He set his tin coffee cup on a rock, stepped into Shaw's sight, and waved his rifle back and forth slowly. "Let's go hear from him whose side he's on."

CHAPTER 8

After meeting and saying their hellos at the mouth of Sabo Canyon, Shaw rode back up with Jimmy Blaine and Claude Batson. Once back at their lookout, Blaine and Shaw sipped coffee while Batson stood a few yards away watching evening sunlight streak long across the rolling grasslands. They had talked enough on the ride up to assure Blaine that Shaw was not on the payroll of the European spread. Still, the matter of the looming range war came up again once they had their hands around hot tin coffee cups.

"I expect I knew right off that it wasn't your style, hiring your gun out against us small ranchers," Blaine said, almost apologetically.

"You did right to wonder, Jimmy," said Shaw. "A man who carries a gun for a living never knows who he'll have in his sights, or for what reason." Shaw sipped his coffee, then added, "But the fact is, I'm no longer in the business of selling my gun skills."

"I heard that too," said Blaine, "but I heard it off the wind, so I thought I'd better check."

Shaw felt at ease around folks like Blaine and Batson. These were hardscrabble cattle ranchers, not shifty-eyed gunmen out to claim themselves a reputation at the expense of his life.

"Yeah." Shaw smiled faintly. "Word travels fast, but it also travels loose. Except in this case. I have a hard enough time keeping my gun holstered these days without hiring it out and looking for trouble. Besides, once the other hired guns hear what happened in Willow Creek, I'll be lucky if they don't want to nail me on their wall."

Blaine nodded in the direction of Willow Creek and said quietly, "If it gets too hot for you down there, send word. Some of us will ride in and take a part."

"Much obliged," said Shaw, "but I always make my own stand."

"It wouldn't make you beholden to us, if that's what you're thinking," said Blaine. "That's not what I was trying to do."

"Trying or not, it would shape up that way, Jimmy," Shaw replied. "I have a hard time not taking your side as it is. I never liked the way these big spreads come onto an open range and push their weight around. I expect this Frenchman I'm hearing about is no different." He sipped his coffee and looked away for a moment. "I almost wish I hadn't shown up here when I did."

His words drew a curious look from Blaine. "How come you *did* show up here? This is pretty far off your graze, the best I recall."

Shaw looked down at his coffee cup and shook his head slightly. "Well, believe it or not I rode up here looking for you, Jimmy."

"Oh?" Blaine gave him an even more curious look, this time with a bit of concern. "Things are straight between us, like always, aren't they?"

"Yeah, we're straight, as always," said Shaw, dismissing any cause for concern. He knew how unsettling it could be for an honest man like Blaine to hear that Fast Larry Shaw was looking for him. Taking a breath, Shaw asked, "Do you remember a young woman named Rita Vargas?"

Blaine considered it for a moment, running the name through his mind and murmuring it to himself. "Yep, I remember her. A beautiful dove, as I recall." He stared at Shaw expectantly.

"Well, Jimmy," said Shaw, postponing the news no longer, "she's in Willow Creek. She sent me to tell you she wants you to come see her." When he'd finished he gave Blaine a flat stare, searching his eyes for any sign of his knowing why she might come looking for him.

"See *me*?" Blaine looked bewildered, drawing nothing from Shaw's gaze. "What for?"

"She just had a beautiful baby girl, Jimmy." Shaw wondered at what point, if any, Blaine might begin to make a connection.

"Oh? Well, that's nice . . . I reckon," Blaine replied.

A silence passed before Shaw gave him the rest of the information.

At the sound of Blaine's raised voice, Batson turned quickly from looking out across the fading sunlight and saw the young drover spring straight up from his seat on a low rock. Batson's hand tightened instinctively around his rifle stock. But then his hand relaxed when he saw Blaine lean backward and let out a gleeful howl toward the evening sky.

"Yee-hiii! Man, oh, man!" Blaine called out. "Me, a pa? Me, somebody's daddy? My, oh, my!"

"Easy, Jimmy," said Shaw. He stared at the young drover with a stunned expression, never imagining that Blaine might take the news in such a manner.

"Take it easy?" Blaine said loudly. "How can I take it easy? I'm a father! A *daddy*!" He waved Batson over toward them. "Claude, come listen to this! I'm a pa! I've got myself a baby daughter!"

"Jimmy, settle down! It's not a sure thing," said Shaw, trying to get him to listen to the whole story. "Rita says it's either yours or Henry McCarty's or mine."

"Oh . . ." Blaine slumped for a moment, but only for a moment. "So what, then?" he said, getting excited all over again. "It's two-to-one odds I'm a pa! That's better odds than I ever thought I'd have. I'll take them odds any day!" He spun on his heel toward Batson. "Are you hearing this, Claude? Can you see me being a *pa*?"

"That's *some* news, all right," said the old rancher, giving Shaw a strange, curious look, as if questioning Blaine's mental state. "But does that mean the woman and baby are going to be living here with you?"

Blaine hadn't yet considered that question. He turned to Shaw. "Are . . . are they, Shaw?"

Shaw just stared at Blaine for a second, at

108

a loss for words. Finally he said, "I don't know, Jimmy. Maybe that's why she wants you to come see her."

"You bet I'll go see her straightaway!" said Blaine. But as soon as he said it, he realized his situation and settled himself down. "I can't go just now. Can you tell her I'll be coming to see her and the baby real soon, Shaw?"

"Yeah, I'll tell her that," said Shaw. "That is, if it's true." He gave Blaine a questioning glance. "I don't want to get her hopes up if you don't mean it."

"Don't worry; I'll be there!" said Blaine. "Soon as one of the drovers shows up to relieve me here, I'm on my way! Tell her not to go anywhere until I get there. Tell her I want her and the baby to live with me at my place." He hesitated, then said, "I mean, if she wants to, that is . . . and, that is, if you and McCarty don't mind."

"No objection here." Shaw shrugged, still not understanding Blaine's elation. "The fact is, I'll be leaving Willow Creek as soon as I tell Rita I came here and talked with you. As far as McCarty, I don't think he'll care much one way or the other about being a father."

"He won't?" Blaine asked, appearing surprised at such an attitude.

"Jimmy, I've got to admit," said Shaw, "I'm not all that excited at the prospect myself."

"Then both of yas can rest easy," said Blaine, appearing satisfied. "I'll take up the slack and be a pa for all three of us."

Shaw sat, nodding slowly. Not knowing what else to say, he said, "Well, then, congratulations," and raised his tin coffee cup in a toast.

Before dawn, without benefit of a fire, Shaw ate a strip of cold jerked beef, a plate of leftover beans, and some lukewarm coffee from the blackened pot sitting amid the smoldering embers from the night before. He looked at Jimmy, who lay asleep wrapped in a blanket on the ground, his hat over his face and a worn saddle for a pillow. Jimmy had relieved Batson during the night, but now Batson was back on lookout, seated atop a rock, as still and silent as the stone itself.

"Hell, why not?" Shaw whispered under his breath, thinking about Jimmy's elation at having fathered a baby with a whore. "There's worse places in life. . . ." Shoving his fingers back through his hair, Shaw stood up, buckled his empty gun belt around his waist, and holstered the Colt he'd drawn

110

from beneath his blanket. He pulled on his boots and walked over to Batson.

"You leaving so early, Shaw?" Batson asked softly. "Don't you want to stick around and hear Jimmy's plans for being an all-around regular pa?"

Shaw gave a thin smile, hearing the good-natured mockery in Batson's words. "I've heard enough," said Shaw. "He'll be a good one, though; I'd bet on it." He straightened his hat on his head. "Tell him adios for me," he said. "I'm headed back to Texas."

"To Texas? You're going to miss one god-awful hell of a gun battle if you leave the territory so soon," said Batson.

"Yeah, I know," said Shaw. "That's what I'm hoping to do."

When he'd made his bedroll and saddled and readied his horse, he rode away before a thin mantle of sunlight pushed upward from the dark horizon. By midmorning he'd stopped on a high ridge overlooking the trail to Willow Creek. While he sat sipping water from his canteen, he spotted Hilda Hauler on the winding trail and watched her ride along in a single-horse buggy with its top down.

"Jesus . . ." Shaw murmured to himself, looking ahead around a blind turn in the trail. Having spotted the buggy from a

111

higher position, two riders had veered their horses off the trail into a stand of scrub pine and lay in wait for the unsuspecting woman. Shaw watched them raise their bandannas to cover their faces as he slipped his Winchester from its saddle boot. "Big mistake, boys," he murmured quietly.

In her buggy seat Hilda rounded the long upward turn and caught sight of the masked riders just as they lunged their horses forward, blocking the trail, one on her right and one on her left. Before she could make a move either to flee or to struggle, both men grabbed her horse's bridle at the same time and dragged the animal to a sudden halt. Hilda rocked forward with a gasp and almost flew from the seat.

"Who are you? What do you want?" Hilda shouted. Reaching down, she grasped the shotgun her husband kept beneath the seat, but before she could fully raise it, one of the men loosed her horse and rode up beside her quickly. He reached out and grabbed her by her forearm.

"Here, now, little lady, you won't need that," he said, leaning from his saddle and wrenching the shotgun from her hand. He held her firmly by her forearm.

"Please! I'm the doctor's wife!" Hilda said, struggling uselessly against his powerful grip.

"I don't need no doctor; do *you,* Blue?" he asked the other man.

"I'm fit as a fiddle," the other replied with a shrug.

"Let me go! I have no money!"

"Hear that? She's got no money," the man holding her arm and her shotgun said jokingly to the other.

"Aw, now, ain't that too bad," the other replied. "You shouldn't raise so much dust this time of the morning. What if there was hostiles lurking around out here?"

"Please, I have nothing for you!" Hilda pleaded.

"Now, that ain't exactly true, is it?" said the one holding her forearm. He flung the shotgun to the ground and jerked her toward him. "Come on; we'll take us a little ride togeth—" His words stopped as a rifle shot ripped down through his chest and rolled him from his saddle, his hand flying limply from her arm.

Hilda screamed as the report of the rifle shot caught up to itself, and blood stood as if suspended for a second in a fine red mist above the empty saddle. The man holding her horse screamed as well, and had to turn it loose and back his animal away lest the spooked buggy horse drag him from his saddle as it took off along the trail.

The next rifle shot hit the other man high in his left shoulder and spun him from his saddle like a broken top. He hit the hard, rocky ground and rolled off into the stand of scrub pine from which he'd appeared. On the trail, the two men's frightened horses raced away in one direction. Hilda's buggy horse bolted away in the other.

From the higher ridgeline, Shaw slid the Winchester into its boot and punched his heels to his horse, sending it down a thin, steep elk path toward the trail. By the time his horse had touched its hooves to the trail, Hilda had brought her buggy horse under control and turned the rig back. She sat trembling, staring at Shaw from seventy yards away, the reins gripped tightly in her hands.

"Lawrence," she whispered in a breathless tone, too far away for him to hear her.

Shaw nudged his horse into a gallop, giving a quick glance toward the dead man lying with his bandanna twisted away from his slack jaw. On his way to Hilda he looked all around for the other man. But he saw no sign of him other than a large splotch of blood where he'd slammed to the ground and rolled away.

"Oh, Lawrence!" Hilda cried in a tense

voice, her whole body shuddering violently. "Lawrence!" She reached her arms up toward him, letting the buggy reins fall from her trembling hands as he neared her. "Lawrence!" Tears streamed down her cheeks.

Shaw swung his horse up to the buggy, swept her up into his arms, and cradled her against his chest. "Shhh," he whispered near her ear. "They can't bother you. They're gone . . . you're safe. I've got you, Hilda." He pressed her face to his chest and rode the horse in a wide circle around the trail.

When he'd circled back to the buggy to let her down, she resisted and clung to him. "No, Lawrence, hold me," she whispered tearfully. "Please hold me."

"I'll hold you," Shaw said, his cheek warm, his lips searching until they found her mouth. As if something had snapped inside him, he swung off the saddle and down into the open buggy with Hilda wrapped in his arms, both their lips feverishly at work.

In moments she lay naked on the buggy seat in the heat of the sun. "Oh, yes, Lawrence! Yes," she said breathlessly.

Oh, Jesus, no . . . ! Shaw told himself, even as he shed his clothes and laid his Colt beneath the seat. "This is so wrong, Hilda," he said to her, watching her pale breasts rise and fall. *What the hell are you doing . . . ?*

Yet even as he spoke aloud to her and silently to himself, he knew he was powerless to stop. Suddenly he had to have her. He moaned as her hands reached out and closed tightly around him. Nothing else mattered, he told himself as he grasped the folded-down buggy top and raised it above them, blocking out the sun and shutting out the rest of the world.

CHAPTER 9

Shaw gave no thought, as he lay naked beside Hilda Hauler in the leather-cushioned buggy seat, to the second man he'd shot. Hilda dozed against his chest, her arm over him as if to make sure he wouldn't slip away from her. This wasn't right, he reminded himself; but it was the same thing he'd told himself over and over while they'd spent the rest of the morning making wild love to each other with reckless abandon. *You never learn. . . .*

Feeling her breathing softly against him, he ran his hand down her long silken hair, picturing how she'd let it come undone earlier after first shedding her clothes. This was a warm, beautiful, giving woman, Shaw told himself, looking down the length of her. Why the doctor didn't see it and realize it and attend to her every need was beyond Shaw's understanding.

But then, perhaps the doctor did see it.

Perhaps he did attend to her needs. For all Shaw knew, Hilda could be lying. It wouldn't be the first time . . .

He took a deep breath and let it out slowly, knowing that soon she would awaken, and there were things he had to say and make clear. What had happened here today would have to forever remain their secret. She would have to go home to her husband and pretend this never happened, he would tell her, lest she get the wrong idea and think there would be a place for her in his life. His life . . . ? What a cruel, bitter joke to call this his *life.*

To keep his thoughts from slipping into the darkness, he reached his hand down and gently lifted her sleeping face toward his. Even in her slumber she anticipated his lips wanting hers, and her mouth opened slightly, welcoming him. But before he could place his lips on hers, the soft click of a horse's hooves coming toward the buggy caused him to freeze and listen intently. It flashed through his mind how he had ridden past the blood splotch on the trail and had not looked for the body to make sure the man was dead.

Damn it! he cursed himself. This was not like him. He knew better than to leave anything to chance.

The sound of the hooves moved slowly closer to the buggy until he could almost picture the horse stopping a few yards away. Silently he lowered his right hand beneath the buggy seat, took the Colt, and raised it, his thumb lying poised over the hammer. Outside the raised top he pictured the wounded man slipping down from his saddle and stalking forward.

Now . . . ! Shaw told himself. In one motion he sprang upright in the buggy, throwing back the top with his left hand, his right coming out at arm's length, cocking the Colt, ready to fire. But it was not the wounded man facing him, but rather two middle-aged women in long dresses and riding bonnets. They screamed long and loud at the sight of Shaw standing naked, facing them from less then twenty feet away.

"Aw, my God!" Shaw shouted beneath the piercing screams. He started to duck down out of sight, but before he could Hilda sprang up beside him, terrified, her naked breasts cradled in her arms. Thinking quickly, Shaw stepped in front of Hilda, blocking her from view.

"Get out of here, both of you!" Shaw bellowed. He could feel the women's wide eyes go up and down him. One threw her hand over her mouth and gasped as she leaned closer and tried to get a look at the cowering Hilda. "Right now!" Shaw demanded, feigning as if he were about to fire the Colt in the air.

"Hurry, Clora! He's a *madman*!" one of the women screamed, shoving and coaxing the other to turn their buggy and drive away. In a flurry of dust, screams, whip cracking, and horse nickering, the small rig spun almost on one wheel and fishtailed away along the trail toward Willow Creek.

Jesus . . . ! Shaw turned away, took Hilda in his arms, and sank with her onto the leather buggy seat.

"Do . . . do you think they saw me?" Hilda asked, trembling again.

"I don't know, Hilda," said Shaw, "but they were bound to recognize the doctor's buggy."

"It's not his buggy," Hilda said. "It's a livery rental. His buggy is having new spokes put on. Oh, thank God for that!" she said in a quavering voice.

"Maybe they won't say anything, even if they did see you," said Shaw. "Some people keep their mouths shut to keep from causing trouble. Who are they?"

"Oh, God, one is Clora Helms, a deacon's wife," said Hilda, sinking her forehead into the palm of her hand and shaking her head

120

slowly. "The other is Mattie Spriggs, a spinster — our church organist."

"Good God, I should have shot them," Shaw said.

"No, Lawrence, you couldn't do that!" Hilda gasped.

"Of course not," said Shaw with a sigh. "Maybe your husband won't hear about it, though. Sometimes a town can keep something like this under their hats."

"I have never seen such a town," said Hilda, her head still resting in her palm.

"Neither have I," Shaw admitted.

"What am I going to do?" Hilda murmured, more to herself than to Shaw.

Shaw pulled his duster up around both of them and sat holding her. After a moment of silent contemplation, he said gently, "Hilda, I want you to know that this life I live is no fit place for a woman. It's no fit place for me, except that I chose it, and now I'm stuck with it."

"Please stop, Lawrence," Hilda whispered. "The life you lead has nothing to do with my situation."

"No, I have to say it," Shaw persisted. "I know how much you care about me, and I know it would be easy for me to take advantage right now, the way you're feeling. But I can't let that happen. I'll go into

Willow Creek and face whatever is waiting there. But you can't come with me when I leave. You're life is there. I won't allow you to —"

"Will you *please* stop it, Lawrence?" Hilda said in a stronger, more insistent tone. "I've got a serious problem. I don't need you to tell me I can't come with you. I wasn't going to ask. I'm no fool. I see the sort of life you live."

Shaw looked puzzled. "But in Rita's hotel room you said you love me —"

"I know what I said," she cut him off again. "But that was then, and this is now. I *wanted* you, and I've had you. Heaven forbid that this little indiscretion cost me my marriage."

Shaw just looked at her.

"Please," she said, averting her eyes from his, "can we just get dressed and go? I still have to finish my rounds out here. These people are depending on me."

Shaw watched her step into her undergarments and wiggle them into adjustment. When she had pulled her dress on and began buttoning it, she turned a glance to Shaw, who still sat in the same position. "Well, come on," she said. "Why are you just sitting there?"

"This isn't your first indiscretion, is it?"

122

Shaw asked flatly.

"This is the first time I've been caught," she said shamelessly. "Now let's get moving. If those two old biddies saw your handiwork they might bring the whole town out here." She gestured toward the body lying alongside the trail.

His handiwork? Shaw nodded and looked away, feeling he'd been used, yet unable to describe in just what way.

"All right." He stood up and began to dress. "But you have experience with other men, yet you have no idea how your husband is going to act if he finds out about us?"

"Yes, something like that," Hilda said, her fingers working with her hair as she spoke, twisting it into a long plait and circling it atop her head, a pin between her teeth. "I know this is going to hurt him" — she took the pin from her teeth and slipped it through the gathered bundle of hair — "but I'll just have to see how things go. I know he has had his suspicions before." She sighed as if something had just crossed her mind. "If he does take this badly, please promise me you won't . . ." Her words trailed off.

"Won't what, kill him?" Shaw responded. "I'll try not to." He stopped and stared at her again, seeing a slightly different woman than he had only a few hours ago, and different by far from the Hilda Hauler he'd talked to in Rita's hotel room. "If he asks me about this, I won't insult him by denying it happened. No man wants to be made a fool."

"I understand, Lawrence." Hilda gave him a pleasant smile and cupped his cheek in her hand. "But be strong for me . . . for both the doctor and myself. Help me work my way through this."

Work her way through this . . . ? Shaw stared at her again for a moment, then said, "I'll do what I can."

He finished dressing silently, cursing himself for having gotten involved with this woman. As it turned out, Hilda Hauler was just one more unfulfilled woman wanting to sleep with the fastest gun alive. One more thing he should have seen coming, he told himself, sitting down and pulling on his boots.

"What about the bodies?" Hilda asked, putting on her high-topped shoes beside him. "Will you just leave them lying where they fell?"

Did he detect a tone of disdain? "Yes," he said sharply. "I don't owe them anything. They meant you harm; I killed them. Let the critters and bugs handle the burying."

He picked up his hat and stepped down from the buggy. "Burying is not among the *services* I provide." He put on his hat, gathered his horse's reins, and swung up into the saddle.

"Lawrence, Lawrence." Hilda sighed, catching the implications in his voice, as if taking stock of both of their mood and manner. "I'm sorry. I didn't want things to turn out this way. I wanted this to be something we could both remember from now on."

"Oh, it's *that* in spades," Shaw said. He pictured himself buck naked, aiming his Colt in the faces of the two upstanding churchwomen.

"Yes, it is *that* indeed," said Hilda, standing in the buggy, having taken up the reins. She offered a coy smile. "I'm sure it's made a lasting impression on Clora and Mattie."

Shaw studied her eyes, and found them no less warm and sincere than they had been before. He allowed himself a thin smile in return. What the hell — who was he to judge her, he asked himself, or to feel used by her? "We should have pulled off the trail," he said.

"Yes, we should have," she said, seeming willing to take her share of the blame. Looking into his eyes, she hesitated for a second, then said, "Lawrence, when I told you I love you, I meant it. I still mean it. But things feel different now. Things always feel different when the lovemaking is completed. Before, I thought I loved you enough to give up my husband, our life in Willow Creek." Her smile took on a sad quality. "But that's not true. Will you forgive me?"

"There's nothing to forgive," said Shaw. "We did what we did. Now that our fires are cooled, we'll have to go back and face up to it, see if we can undo it."

William Bonney and his pals stood drinking at the bar when four riders from the European spread walked inside the saloon and stopped and looked all around. Seeing the four in the mirror, the Kid called out without turning to face them, "Don't be shy, gents; come on in. We're a peaceable bunch here, till it comes to cockfighting and faro."

The man standing forward of the other three wore a thin mustache and a flat-crowned hat with part of a Cheyenne war dressing stuck into its band. He gave a shrug of his shoulder, indicating that he couldn't care less how peaceable the crowd was, and walked halfway to the bar and stopped again. The other three followed two feet behind him.

"I'm inquiring about the shooting that just took place here," he said, turning his eyes from one card game to the next, then to the few drinkers along the bar.

The Kid, Free Drink, and Sturgis turned now and faced the men, looking them up and down. The Kid gave a crooked drunken grin and said, "Just took place *here*?" He gave a bewildered look around the saloon. "I didn't hear nothing. . . . You mean right here where we're standing?"

"This one is a funny man," said one of the three standing behind the leader. He stepped forward, a young, tough-looking man not much older than the Kid. "Let me settle his stew, Oakley."

"Settle my stew?" The Kid chuckled, giving the young man a hard stare, but with the same grin.

But the leader, a hired killer named Merlyn Oakley, raised an arm, as if he were used to having to stop the young gunman from starting trouble. "Easy, Tallow. We came here for a reason. Let's stick to it."

"I will if funny man will shut his funny mouth and keep it shut," said Sid Tallow, staring hard at the Kid.

"Uh, Tallow," said Oakley, a cautioning tone coming to his voice, "this is Henry McCarty, the one I told you about."

Tallow blinked, but made no other show of concern. "He needs to show some manners. A man comes in a strange place, he don't want to hear fun poked at him."

The Kid ignored Tallow and said to Oakley, "I'm not McCarty anymore, mister. I'm William Bonney now. Maybe you ain't heard, riding drag, staring up a cow's ass."

Oakley grinned, flat and mirthlessly. "Just like that, you change your name?" He snapped his fingers.

"Yeah, I outgrew it." The Kid shrugged.

"The other name got too hot for you is my guess," Tallow said in a sour tone.

"Is he going to stop talking without one of us sticking something sharp in his belly?" the Kid asked Oakley, ignoring the young gunman.

"I'd like to see one of yas try!" Tallow growled, once more stepping forward, once more stopped by Oakley's raised arm.

"Maybe later," the Kid said to Tallow, dismissing the matter. At his side Free Drink's hand had tensed a bit, but now relaxed, as if the Kid had given him a signal. "Pals," the Kid said to Sturgis and Free Drink, "meet Merlyn Oakley, the former captain and *pride* of the Hoboken Police Department." He gestured a hand toward the Cheyenne war dressing in his hatband

128

and said, "He took that off the body of a Cheyenne warrior, I heard." He paused for a second, as if giving it some thought, then said, "Or was it an old Cheyenne squaw? I never can remember." He grinned and said, "Either way, it was a feather in his cap."

Oakley gave the same flat, mirthless smile, unprovoked by the Kid. "Let's save the introductions, Kid," he said. "I heard what happened here. Where's Shaw?"

"Don't know the man," the Kid said flatly. "You never will either, if you know what's good for you. The gunfight was your men's doing; I can tell you that."

"Thought you said you don't know the man," Sid Tallow cut in.

"I don't," said the Kid. Then without missing a beat, he said to Oakley, "Shaw never starts a gunfight. But he's a good hand at ending them. Are you gunning for him, or offering him work? I heard the spread is hiring guns."

"I'm here to find out the particulars," said Oakley. "If Shaw is in the right, he's got nothing to worry about."

"Lucky him." Free Drink snickered.

Oakley looked at him, then back to the Kid. "As far as gun work, what about you and your pals? Are you interested in hiring out for a while, at least until we get settled into the grasslands?"

"Not me," said the Kid. "I've got spending money to last awhile. I don't much like the big spreads, anyways."

Oakley started to say more, but the sound of hooves pounding down the middle of the dirt street caused him and the others to turn toward the saloon door. "Damn, what's this?" asked Tallow, all of them watching the buggy streak past with the two church-women inside, each holding a hand atop their riding bonnets.

CHAPTER 10

William Bonney, his pals, and the four men from the European spread stood in front of the saloon and watched townsfolk gather around the door of the doctor's office. Before the dust had even settled from the buggy racing along the dirt street, Dr. Hauler walked out of his office and headed toward the livery barn. As he passed the saloon the Kid called out, "Doc, what's the commotion?"

Hauler gave the Kid and the others a glance without stopping and said, "It's nothing to worry about, gentlemen."

Free Drink grinned, watching the doctor walk by. "Good thing he said something, I was starting to worry already."

From the doctor's office, Hyde Ruda-baugh stepped out of the door and came ambling along the dirt street toward the Kid. "Now we'll hear the whole of it," the Kid said. "Hyde can pluck gossip out of a passing breeze."

Beside the Kid, Merlyn Oakley said, "About that shooting between Shaw and our men. Did you see it firsthand?"

"Yeah," the Kid lied, looking Oakley in the eye, straight-faced. "We all saw it. So did half the town. The ones eating breakfast, anyways."

"And everybody called it self-defense?" Tallow asked, cutting in.

Still ignoring Tallow, the Kid said to Oakley, "It was sure enough self-defense. If I had to sign a courthouse affidavit, that's the way I'd call it. What about you, Free Drink, Sturgis? Self-defense?"

"Nothing less," said Free Drink.

"Straight as a string," Sturgis said, raising a hand as if swearing an oath.

Tallow gave them a dubious look, but before he could comment, Oakley gestured him and the other men inside the saloon. Following him through the doors, one of the gunmen, a Missourian named Dubbs Hawkens, said to him under his breath, "Do you believe anything these saddle tramps said?"

"Oh, hell, no," said Oakley. He stepped to the bar and looked back out the door where Hyde Rudabaugh had just stepped onto the boardwalk. "Besides, it doesn't matter. We

132

can't have a big gun like Shaw hanging around loose. Once the herd moves into the grasslands, either he's got to be with us, or we've got to kill him." He offered his same flat, lifeless smile. "It's good that we already have this shooting as an excuse."

Out front of the saloon, the Kid gave Rudabaugh an expectant look as the aging outlaw stepped up stiffly onto the boardwalk. "Well, let's have it."

"Have what?" Rudabaugh gave a sly grin.

"You know what," said the Kid.

"The buggy, damn it," said Sturgis. All three of them drew in closer around Rudabaugh.

"All right, take it easy," said Rudabaugh, taking a step back from the three. "The women heard some shooting and came upon a body lying beside the trail," he said in a lowered tone of voice. "They found a buggy they thought was empty, but when they rode over to it a man and a woman jumped up, both of them naked as apes and the man pointed a gun at them!"

"Naked, huh?" said the Kid, considering it. "A dead body by the trail . . ."

"Yep," said Rudabaugh, "and as rattled as these two women are, it sounded like the man might've pointed more than a gun at them."

The Kid chuckled quietly, picturing the scene in his mind. "This has Shaw's brand stuck on its hip, sure as hell."

"That's what I thought too," said Rudabaugh.

"Anybody seen the doctor's wife today?" the Kid asked slyly.

"You mean Shaw and the doctor's wife?" Free Drink asked in an astonished tone.

"The woman is a real fine looker, Free Drink," said the Kid. "It's almost worth getting shot just to get her to attend you."

"Oh . . ." Free Drink fell quiet for a second, seeming to be weighing the information.

"It struck me funny that the doc ain't mentioned this to nobody," said Hyde Rudabaugh. He gestured a hand toward the townsfolk gathered in front of the doctor's office. "Had I not been there getting some medicine whipped up for my sore bones, I'd never have heard about it."

"Finding a dead man that close to town ain't no small thing. You'd think he might want some folks riding out there with him," Sturgis cut in.

"Yeah, that's curious," said the Kid, rubbing his chin as he looked off toward the livery barn. "But you'd best keep your mouths shut about this around Oakley and his men till we see what comes of it."

"I wouldn't say nothing about *nothing* to anybody riding for the European spread," said Free Drink. "Far as I'm concerned, we can side with the settlers and ranchers once the shooting starts."

"Naw," said the Kid, "this is their war. I'm keeping my beak out of it." He nodded toward Oakley and his men inside the saloon. "If Shaw shows up and needs some help with these baboons, maybe I'll throw in with him." He grinned as if giving it second thought. "Then again, maybe not. It might be fun just to stand back and watch the fastest gun alive in action."

"Whatever you say, Kid." Free Drink shrugged. He adjusted the dagger in his coatsleeve. "I'm still ready to stick somebody anytime you say the word."

"I know that, Free Drink, and I'm much obliged," said the Kid with a grin. They watched the door to the livery barn open and saw Dr. Hauler nudge a big bay out onto the dirt street at a walk. "There he goes. . . ." The Kid and his three pals stood watching attentively. They touched their hat brims toward the doctor as he rode past them and headed out of town. "I just know in my gut that Shaw has something to do with this," the Kid surmised.

Shaw had hitched his horse and walked more than a mile and back inside a stretch of pine woodlands while he awaited Hilda's return. At the edge of the woods a good distance away he gazed in reflection at the weathered part-stone plank house standing on a rise above a wide turn of a shallow running creek. In front of the house cattle stood strewn out, milling all along the wide creek bed. More cattle stood scattered across rolling grasslands between the creek and a distant cliff line.

He looked at the land and cattle and reminded himself that these were the things men lived and died for in this harsh, majestic land. These were the things that he himself would have lived and died for had fate not stepped in and sent his life in its present direction. Which was no direction at all, he told himself bitterly.

The pastoral scene before him had once been his life in Somos Santos, Texas. The lay of the land was different; the size and shape of the house was different; yet, in the long, peaceful shadows of evening, here before him lay the life he'd led. Or the life he would have led, he quickly reminded himself, had he only had the good sense to stay home with his wife, Rosa, and enjoy it.

Stop it! he demanded, not wanting to hear the cruel, torturing inner voice that always managed to find its way into his brain. His wife, his home, whatever he'd once had was gone, and never coming back. For all intents, being gone was the same as never having happened. He had memories, he told himself, seeing Hilda walk out of the house and step up into the buggy — memories and nothing else. He turned to his saddlebags, took out the bottle of whiskey, uncorked it, and took a hot, strong drink.

Having nothing might be the best thing for a man like himself, he thought, feeling the whiskey spread across his chest. All he had to worry about was this horse and himself. He had no family to lose; hell, he'd already lost it. He threw back another drink as if to both soothe and punish himself. No home . . . it was gone. No possessions . . . everything had slipped away from him somehow while he wasn't looking.

Damn it, you've got it made, Fast Larry, he told himself with dark sarcasm. He watched the buggy roll slowly toward him as he drank. *Look at this. . . .* Beautiful women, respect, a reputation men were dying — yes, actually dying — to claim. What was it he had he longed for in life that he hadn't gotten? Nothing that he could think of, he told himself. He corked the whiskey bottle and put it away inside his duster pocket. Life had its costs as well as its rewards, he'd come to learn.

So stop being a fool and take what's offered, a looser and more relaxed voice said through his warm whiskey glow, seeing Hilda draw closer along the trail. "It's all you get," he whispered to himself.

"Lawrence? Are you all right?" Hilda asked, slowing the buggy to a halt. She took a quick glance back over her shoulder to make sure no one at the house could see them.

Shaw led his horse forward and said, "I couldn't be better." He stopped beside the buggy and nodded along the creek where it narrowed and flowed into the sheltering pine woodlands. "I found a deeper spot dammed off in there. It looks like a perfect place for an afternoon swim." He gazed into her eyes. "Got time for a swim?"

She looked into his eyes, sensing both his need and his urgency as she considered his invitation. She knew that once they returned to Willow Creek they would never be with each other again. She wouldn't deny that in spite of all the trouble awaiting her at home she was not sorry for what they'd done; and she had to admit to herself that she still wanted him. After a silent moment she sighed quietly and said as if in resignation, "Yes, lead the way. I'll follow you." She let her hands and reins fall loosely to her lap and sat back in the leather seat in submission.

Shaw turned and walked inside the wood line, leading the buggy horse in one hand and his horse in the other until the rig stood well hidden beneath a rich green canopy of pine. "We'll walk from here," he said softly, lifting her down from the buggy easily.

"Whatever you say, Mr. Shaw," she said. "I'm all yours until we ride back to Willow Creek." She parted her lips to his.

"Then let's not waste time," Shaw whispered, determined to quiet the demons inside his head. He kissed her long and deep, until they both felt each other's blood quicken.

"Yes, please, let's go," Hilda whispered with sudden breathless abandon. With their arms encircling each other's waist, they walked in silence to a short cut-bank along the creek, Shaw leading his horse behind him.

As he took off his riding duster and spread it on the ground, Hilda stepped out of her dress and undergarments and moved to him. "Here, let me help you," she whispered, barely keeping her passion in check. Naked, she unbuttoned his trousers and loosened his shirttail. Shaw dropped his loosened gun belt to the ground, raised a foot, and began pulling off his boots, even as Hilda's mouth found his and they kissed hungrily.

Deeper inside the woods, a small party of Ute Indians watched the couple in silence until, after a few moments, they lost interest. Their elderly leader turned to another elderly man beside him and said in their native tongue, "She is the medicine woman from town. The man with her is not one of the ones who shot at us."

"She carries medicine for gunshot wounds in her medicine bag," said the other old man, stretching upward looking for her buggy in the direction from which Hilda and Shaw had walked into the woods.

"It is not good to bother her right now," the leader replied, eyeing the lovemaking with detachment. "I saw no medicine bag in her hands."

"It is in her buggy," the other said, still searching in the direction where Hilda and Shaw had hidden the horse and buggy. "We must find her buggy while they are busy rubbing together."

"After what those white men did to us, give me a gun and I will shoot them both," a teenage boy said to the old men in a lowered voice, averting his eyes from the naked white couple on the spread riding duster.

"You want a gun? Here is a gun," said a wounded elderly man with a bloody rag pressed to his shoulder. "Take it and kill them both or else be silent about it from now on."

The boy took the battered six-shooter and passed it back and forth in his hands. "I am not afraid to kill whites," he said, jutting his chin. "Why should I not kill them before they kill us?"

"I told you, these two are not the people who shot at us," said the leader. "This is the doctor's woman."

"The whites are all the same," said the boy. He held the gun at his side and slipped away in some underbrush toward the two lovers.

When they had finished making love and lay in each other's arms for a moment on the spread riding duster, Shaw finally rolled over onto his back and looked upward through the towering pines. "And here is where we have to end it," he said in a tone of regret. He took a breath and let it out. "I suppose we should have left it where it lay earlier."

"No." Hilda rose onto a knee above him. "This is a better place to end it. Here, in the soft evening light, in this gentle, beautiful place."

"Yes, I suppose it is," said Shaw, not wanting to discuss it. The aching sadness that had overcome him earlier upon looking out at the house and the cattle along the creek came back to him now. He sat up and looked at the swirling water lying before them. "Take your swim and let's go," he said. "It'll be dark before long."

Seeing his mood turn downward, Hilda stood without another word, walked down the few feet to the creek, and slid into the waist-deep water. Shaw reached down into his duster pocket and took out the bottle as he watched her dip water up in her palm and pour it gently over her firm breasts. These were the spoils due to him from his world, he told himself, tipping the bottle toward Hilda's wet, naked breasts.

"Salud," he murmured under his breath; and he threw back a long drink and leaned back on an elbow. If he could stay drunk, maybe he could better appreciate what his world had to offer. Being sober was the problem, he decided in a wry surge of

142

whiskey wisdom.

"Aren't you coming in with me?" Hilda called out, hoping to lighten his spirits. She cupped her wet breasts softly with both hands and turned half away from him, smiling coyly at him over her shoulder.

Shaw stared at her broodingly and took another long drink. For the next few silent minutes he watched her, feeling the whiskey glow move across his mind once again and settle his dark thoughts. She stepped onto a rock where the water was only knee-deep. "Come on; I want you to wash my back," she said.

"Jesus!" he whispered, watching her raise a long, shapely leg and run her hands along it, washing herself. He placed the cork back into the bottle and palmed it down tightly. The sight of her stirred him again. "Why the hell not?" he asked himself, rising to his feet.

CHAPTER 11

No sooner had Dr. Hauler found the buggy beneath the pine canopy than he had followed its wheel tracks into the woods. And there sat her medicine bag. He stepped down from his horse, picked up the leather bag, and walked on into the woods, leading the horse behind him. Moments later, when he'd caught sight of his wife as she stood up naked and walked down to the creek, he sighed deeply, let the horse's reins fall from his hand, and stalked forward quietly, like a man in a trance.

Why, Hilda? he asked her silently, seeing her bathe herself with her hands — part bathing, part playful seduction, he noted.

At twenty yards he stopped for only a moment in the cover of a downed pine, long enough to touch his fingertips to his eyes and raise the five-shot German revolver from his waist. He had no idea what he was about to do. He'd made no plan. He was not a killer. What was the gun for? He wasn't sure. But he knew Shaw. A gun was what this man would understand — the only thing he would respect. He looked at the gun and walked forward, raising it at arm's length, pointed at Shaw's naked back. *I once saved your life, Shaw!* he would say when Shaw looked around. *Now I'm taking it!*

There, that was his plan, he told himself, walking forward, seeing a look of shock and fear on Hilda's face as she looked past Shaw and saw him advance toward the gunman.

On the duster, Shaw had just stood up and pitched the bottle aside, feeling the effect that both the whiskey and the sight of Hilda standing wet and naked had on him. She smiled, welcoming him, her eyes offering more of herself.

"Take all you can get," Shaw whispered to himself. Yet, as Shaw took a step forward, he saw Hilda's smile disappear.

Her face took on a shocked look, and her eyes stared past him to the clearing in the woods behind him. "Lawrence! Look out! Adrian, no!"

Shaw spun on his heel and caught a glimpse of Dr. Hauler just as he made a dive for his holstered gun lying on the duster. But even as his hand closed around the Colt and brought it up in play, it was not Dr. Hauler he aimed at, but rather the young Indian who had stood up less than fifteen feet behind the doctor and let out a war cry. Shaw saw the battered revolver aimed and cocked at the doctor's head. He made his decision even as the doctor began firing round after round at him.

Shaw's Colt bucked once in his hand. The sound of it seemed to bring all other sounds of gunfire to a halt. Dr. Hauler's German pistol slumped toward the ground. His free hand went to his right ear, feeling warm blood running from his missing earlobe. But behind him the young Indian let out a cry. At the same second he had fired the revolver, the gun flew from his hand in a spray of blood and broken gunmetal.

Hilda screamed and ran out of the water, slipping and falling on her way, cutting her forehead on a rock. But she wasted no time scrambling the rest of the way to where Shaw lay on his duster, his free hand clasped to his lower left side, a red trickle of blood running through his fingers. "Oh, God, Adrian! You've shot him!" she cried out, wiping a hand across her bloody forehead.

Adrian Hauler turned, his mouth agape. He saw the Indian youth bowed at the waist, grasping his bloody right hand. Hauler looked at the gun on the ground at the young man's feet, and without hesitation pointed his revolver at him. "Don't move!" he shouted, his other hand clasped to his nicked earlobe.

"Get his gun, Adrian!" Hilda shouted, huddled naked over Shaw, blood running down and dripping from the tip of her nose.

"I'm all right, Hilda," Shaw said calmly, his voice and demeanor hardly affected by the bullet wound in his lower left side. "Go to your husband." He nodded toward the doctor, who stood with an uncertain look on his face, the gun still pointed at the Indian, but the barrel starting to slump toward the ground.

"Are . . . are you sure?" Hilda asked. "You're shot. He shot you." She seemed stunned by the doctor's behavior.

"Yes, I'm sure." Shaw nodded. "He's shot too." But Shaw grabbed her arm before she went running away from him. "Put something on first," he said firmly.

"Oh, yes!" Hilda snatched her dress up from the ground and hurriedly pulled it on as she ran to her husband. "Adrian, are you all right?" she said, trying to keep her voice from trembling. She wiped her bloody forehead again, feeling the knot that had already risen.

The doctor had lowered the gun and stepped over to the wounded Indian boy, setting the medicine bag on the ground at the boy's bare feet. "We'd better take a look at the hand."

Seeing that her husband appeared to be in a state of shock, Hilda grabbed the revolver from his hand and pulled him away from the medicine bag. "Here, let me look," she said in an icy tone. "You've done plenty already. You shot Lawrence Shaw."

"What? Oh, no," said the doctor, turning his eyes toward Shaw. "I'm . . . so sorry."

"Go see what you can do for him," Hilda ordered, realizing she would have to take charge until her husband regained his composure. "And check your ear." She jerked a roll of bandage dressing from the leather bag and shoved the bag into the doctor's hands, causing him to choose between dropping either the bag or the gun to the ground.

"Oh, my!" The doctor let the gun fall. He pulled out a clean handkerchief, held it to his nicked ear, and hurried over to Shaw, his wits coming back to him. "I'm sorry, Shaw. I didn't come here to shoot you," he said. "Although I can't say exactly what I *did* come here to do." He pulled Shaw's hand away from his side.

Shaw had managed to pick up the bottle even with the gun in his right hand, his left hand pressed to his wound. He pulled the cork with his teeth and blew it from his lips. "No apologies, Doc, please," he said. "I feel like the worst son of a bitch in the world for doing this to you." He threw back another long drink of whiskey.

The doctor heard the whiskey slur in Shaw's voice. Instead of answering he nodded, took the Colt from Shaw's hand and laid it aside, and examined the wound closely. After a moment he sighed. He reached around behind Shaw and found the exit wound. "This is going to hurt," he said calmly, in control of himself. He drew back his thumb and jammed it hard into the bloody open wound.

Shaw bit down on his lip in pain to keep from crying aloud. "Jesus, Doc! What the hell was that for?" He gasped.

"That's for screwing my wife," said Hauler, still talking calmly, seeing Shaw wince in pain. "Now, let's get this wound dressed and get you to Willow Creek. The bullet went through clean enough, but we need to be mindful of infection."

"I can't be laid up, Doc," Shaw said. "I've got to keep moving. I was only going back long enough to see Rita and to clear things up with you."

"Clear things up with *me*?" said Hauler, looking up from the wound as he made a bandage and pressed it into place. "I can't imagine how I ever popped into your mind, as busy as the two of you were." He looked with disgust at Hilda's undergarments and shoes lying on the ground next to the duster. He looked over at Hilda, who stood finishing up with the young Indian's hand. Then he shook his head and looked back at Shaw. "You are not her first infidelity, you know."

"I . . . I thought maybe there'd been other —" He didn't get to finish his words.

"No, indeed. Not by a long shot," Hauler continued. "So don't consider yourself too special. I'm afraid my wife is a very unhappy, unfulfilled woman." He picked up Shaw's shirt from the ground, ripped it quickly and expertly into shreds, and drew a length of cloth around Shaw's waist. He tied it firmly over the bandage. "I have every right to send her packing —" His words stopped short as he looked away and seemed to consider the consequence such an action would bring. "I'm afraid I love her far too deeply ever to do something like that." He looked ashamed to admit that he loved a woman so much.

Shaw took another long drink and offered Hauler the bottle.

"No, please," said the doctor, nudging the bottle and Shaw's hand away from him. He took a deep breath and said quietly, just between the two of them, "Be honest with me, Shaw. Do you love her? I mean, do you love her the way I do?"

"No," Shaw said flatly. "I don't love her, Doc." He paused. "But I lied to her. I *told* her I loved her. None of this was her fault. I caused it to happen. Don't blame her."

The doctor seemed to not to hear Shaw's defense of his wife as he continued attending the wound. "You saved my life, Shaw," he said. "Saved me even while I tried my best to kill you."

Shaw dismissed the matter. "If you had tried your best to kill me, I would be dead right now. Don't try to make me into something noble. I'm a no-good son of a bitch."

"Nevertheless, you saved my life," said the doctor.

"And you once saved *my* life," said Shaw. "You deserved better than this from me."

Before the doctor could respond, Hilda called out in a tense voice, "Adrian! There're more Indians!"

Shaw and the doctor looked over at her

151

and the young Indian and saw four more of his group come into sight like wispy apparitions arising from the woodland floor.

"Easy, Doc," Shaw said. He reached over and picked up his Colt, then used the doctor's forearm to help him to his feet.

"Yes, of course," said the doctor, "I've seen these Utes before. They're quite harmless, I'm certain."

"Yeah, except for the one who just tried to shoot you in the back," Shaw replied cynically. He saw the young man back away from Hilda and join his people, holding his bandaged hand to his chest.

Seeing Shaw limp forward with the Colt in his hand, the doctor right beside him, the leader called out, "We come to you for help. I carry a white sign of peace!" He waved a small gray handkerchief back and forth slowly in his gnarled hand.

"That one is in bad shape," said the doctor, his eyes going instinctively to a younger man wearing a poultice of leaves and rags on his bloody chest. The elderly leader held the wounded man's arm draped across his bony shoulders, helping him along.

"They must need help badly to come to us. They usually keep to themselves," the doctor said sidelong to Shaw. "I'd better get to him."

Shaw didn't try to stop the doctor, seeing that Hilda had already stepped forward to help the wounded man. Instead he limped forward in a short circle, Colt in hand, able to cover the doctor and his wife while the two healers went about their work.

In a moment the doctor looked up from where he and Hilda had laid the wounded man on the ground. The rest of the Indian band had settled onto their haunches and sat watching intently. Looking all around at the changing evening light, Hauler said, "I'm afraid we won't make it back to Willow Creek before dark, Shaw. We'll make a camp and head back first thing in the morning."

Shaw nodded in agreement, but he dreaded the awkwardness of the three of them camped together overnight. "Jesus," he murmured to himself, shaking his head, "the doctor, his wife, and the man he caught her making love to."

Among the Indians, the leader heard what the doctor said to Shaw, and he gave orders to his people, sending them off to gather firewood. While the Utes searched the woodland floor and brought in deadfall pine and spruce for a fire, the old leader ventured over to Shaw and squatted down beside him. "The doctor says he must take my grandson to town to get a piece of gunmetal out of his hand."

Shaw sighed. "He can't get to it out here?"

"He says the metal is stuck against the bone that makes his fingers move. To remove it he needs another kind of knife that he left in town," the Ute said.

"That's all right by me," Shaw replied, more concerned with spending an awkward night camped with the doctor and his wife than with the young wounded Indian. "But your grandson best mind his manners — make sure he doesn't decide to shoot somebody in the back. What did he mean by that, anyway?"

"We were set upon by white men," the old Ute said. "We were hiding from a coach. The white men might have thought we wanted to rob it." He guffawed. "When have the Ute people ever robbed a white man's coach? Never, that is when."

"I understand," Shaw said, knowing nothing else to say. He sat in silence, picturing William Bonney and his pals and their alleged Apache attack.

After a few silent moments had passed, the old man reached out a weathered closed fist and gestured for Shaw to hold out his hand and accept its contents.

"I'm not in much of a trading mood," Shaw said, yet he held out his hand anyway

154

and watched the old man pour a few colored wooden beads and tiny freshwater shells into his palm. "What are these for?" he asked.

"To fix the mind and spirit," the old man said in a matter-of-fact tone.

"Obliged," Shaw said flatly, "but they'd have to be a lot stronger than they look." As he spoke he began idly pouring the beads and shells back and forth from one hand to the other.

The old man watched. After another moment of silence, seeing that Shaw wasn't going to make an offer in return, the old man said, "Got any tobacco?"

Shaw remembered the bag of chopped tobacco still in his shirt pocket from after the shooting with Katlin and Tommy Childers. He stopped pouring the beads and sand long enough to take the bag from his pocket and pitch it into the old man's waiting hands. "Help yourself," he said. "I seldom use it."

The old man nodded, stuck his fingers and thumb into the bag, and lifted out a pinch of dry, finely chopped smoking tobacco. But instead of rolling a smoke, he stuck the tobacco into his jaw and worked it down into a wet wad. He stuck the bag inside his ragged shirt.

"Keep it then." Shaw shrugged and went back to pouring the beads and shells from palm to palm, staring off into the woodlands, where the rest of the Utes were gathering fuel for a fire.

"I am happy you chose only to wound my grandson," the old man said after a spit of tobacco juice.

"Yeah? That would have been a hard shot. What makes you think I was only trying to wound him?" Shaw replied, pouring the beads and shells.

"I saw you shoot," the old man said with confidence. "You only *meant* to wound him. Otherwise he would be gone from this world." He spit again.

Shaw turned a questioning eye to him. "What else did you see? How long were you and your people in those woods?"

"Long enough to see what a man and woman want no one to see if they belong to someone else," said the old Ute. He gave a knowing glance toward Dr. Hauler and Hilda, then looked back at Shaw.

"Jesus . . ." Shaw looked away from him, red-faced with embarrassment. His hands continued pouring the beads and shells back and forth, a little faster now.

The old Indian studied his face closely and continued talking. "I have heard the name Shaw," he said, watching Shaw pour the beads and shells. "You are powerful among the white men."

"Powerful?" Shaw gave a dark chuckle. His pouring of the beads and shells stopped. "Feared . . . hated . . . cursed and despised maybe. But I wouldn't say *powerful* . . . unless you think being a low, cheating, no-good murdering son of a bitch is being powerful."

The old Ute looked at Shaw's hands, seeing them clenched and lying on his lap. "There are men who do only bad things, but because they refuse to see the bad they do, they go on doing it, thinking the world is wronging them."

"Yeah, I know the type," said Shaw. "The boneyard is full of them." His hands started again, slowly pouring the beads and shells back and forth.

The Ute nodded and stared closely at Shaw from the side while Shaw watched a fire begin to flame up amid a pile of gathered twigs and limbs. "There is another kind of man who sees only the bad he does, and because he does not see any good, he thinks there is no good in him."

Shaw sighed and stopped pouring the beads and shells back and forth. "I bet you're getting ready to tell me that I am

157

that kind of man. That I probably am a good enough man, but that I've just done some bad things that I refuse to forgive myself for?"

The old Ute stared quietly at him.

"That's what I thought," said Shaw, taking the Ute's silence to be agreement. "Well, in that case you'd make a good preacher," said Shaw. "Trouble is, I've heard all that kind of talk before." He gazed at the doctor and his wife, the two of them working side by side in some warm, holy act of kindness — helping life to sustain itself. Seeing them made him take a deep breath and appreciate *goodness* . . . something he recognized and often longed for; yet something that tortured him because he felt there was none inside him.

He stopped pouring the beads and shells and reached his hand sidelong to the old Ute. "Here," he said. "Maybe you'd best give these to somebody who deserves them. My mind and spirit are as fixed as they're ever going to be."

The old Ute held his weathered hand beneath Shaw's fist and caught the beads and shells as Shaw poured them. "Don't think I'm not obliged," Shaw said without facing him. "Maybe I'm just too far gone to even give a damn about it."

158

"Yes," the old Ute said, "I think that is it." He took the bag of tobacco from inside his shirt and laid it back on Shaw's lap, as if to keep something of this man's would be to summon the same sort of darkness upon himself. "I will save these for the living," he said softly, shaking the beads and shells in his hand.

■ ■ ■ ■

PART 2

■ ■ ■ ■

CHAPTER 12

No sooner did Early Lee Springer and a black rancher named Belan Foley arrive at the lookout post to relieve Jimmy Blaine, than a smaller cloud of dust rose up from the rocky hillside beneath them. Foley's Appaloosa gelding had thrown a shoe and picked up a stone bruise on the ride up. While he inspected the gelding's hoof, Blaine saddled his claybank dun and prepared it for the trail. Batson and Springer stood watching the dust until they saw four trail hands from the European spread ride into sight with seven head of cattle they'd flushed out of the rocks and gullies.

"Damn it, that's *my* cattle!" shouted Claude Batson.

"Are you sure?" Springer asked.

"Hell, yes, I'm sure!" said Batson, already stomping over toward his horse, his rifle gripped tight in his glove hand. "I'd recognize that brindle-backed bull of mine anywhere. I'm going after him!"

"Hold up just a minute," said Foley, standing up from beside his Appaloosa. He shouted over to Blaine, "Jimmy, you'd best come take a look at what's going on here!"

"I'm coming, Foley," Blaine replied. Having already heard their conversation, Blaine led his horse over quickly to where Batson had jerked his saddle up from the ground and flung it over his horse's back. Before saying anything to Batson, Blaine looked down and saw the cattle being pushed along the trail toward the large cloud of dust above the coming horde of men, horses, and cattle. "That's his bull, all right," Blaine said with a sigh of regret.

"Dang it, Claude," said Springer, "you knew this big spread was coming. Why didn't you pin that bull till they cleared out of here?"

"Because that bull goes where he damn pleases," said Batson, snapping a pull on his horse's cinch and dropping his stirrup. "He always has; he always will. I couldn't see him bow and curtsy to this bunch."

"Hell, I knew you'd be hardheaded about all this," said Springer. He jacked a round into his rifle chamber. "Wait up till I get saddled." He looked at Blaine. "You go on about your business in Willow Creek. Me

164

and *Hardhead* here will take care of this. Foley can't go. These rocks will ruin his horse."

"I'm headed that way anyway," said Blaine. "I'll ride down with yas." He looked at Foley and said, "You'll have to rest your horse here a couple of days before walking him home."

"I hate letting you down," Foley said to Springer and Batson.

"You've never let us down, Foley," said Springer. "Take care of your horse. We'd best get started."

Blaine stared sternly at Batson and said, "This doesn't have to turn into a fight. They had no way of knowing whose cattle they were." Even as he said it, Blaine knew it wouldn't stand with Batson. He only wanted to offer a chance for some cooler reasoning.

But Batson would have none of it. "Horseshit," he said, swinging up into his saddle. "Those cattle are too far ahead of the herd to have strayed up, 'less they was running like *elk*!"

"All right, I know it," Blaine admitted. "But let's go down with cool heads and see if we can't get them back without bloodshed." He stepped up into his saddle and swung around beside Batson.

"I thought you was in some all-fired hurry

165

to get to Willow Creek?" said Springer, climbing into his saddle and laying his rifle across his lap.

"I am," said Blaine, "as soon as we get this settled."

"We all three know this is just the start," said Batson, his temper cooling a little as the three turned to the thin path leading down to the trail. "These sons of bitches are going to draw in any free-range cattle that step into their path. They can call it what they want; it's nothing but plain stealing."

"Keep your cool," Foley cautioned. "It's hard to argue over unbranded cattle."

"Are all your cattle branded, Belan?" said Batson. "Hell, no, they're not," he answered sharply before Foley could reply. "That's what separates us from the lowlanders. We know what cattle's ours without marking them. We're the ones come up here and made something of this territory. We do all the work; they run their cattle up here to eat our grass. There's nothing *right* about it."

"I agree with you, Claude," said Blaine, "but Foley's right. Let's not forget ourselves. This is free range for everybody, including the big syndicate spreads."

"Yeah, and they're the worst thieves of

all," said Springer. "They run on foreign money, hire the cheapest cowhands they can pull up from across the border, and spend the real money on gunmen to bully their way along."

Batson spit and then said, "They fatten their cattle on American grass, then sell their herds to the American market." He shook his head. "Sometimes I think this country is run by lunatics."

"Then the question is, how do those lunatics all end up so rich?" Springer said wryly, giving a wink. "I'm thinking we're the ones who are crazy. . . . We're the ones who put these trifling, lying, lousy sons-abitches in office."

"Easy, now, both of yas," Blaine cautioned as they rode down onto the trail at a sprightly pace. "Don't get all stoked up and primed for a shooting. The law *does* give them the right to be here, whether we like it or not."

Springer said flatly, "When the law is wrong, there is no law."

"They forfeited any legal right when they rustled my bull off his graze," Batson added, staring ahead toward the dust rising from the hillside.

Seeing the two getting out of control again, Blaine shook his head and raised his rifle from its boot. "Boys, I'd be obliged if you don't get me killed before I see my baby daughter."

"We won't," said Batson, as if speaking for himself and Springer.

But moments later, when the three rode onto the flatlands, and drovers from the European spread looked back at the sound of their horses' running hooves, Batson raised his rifle from his lap and shook it threateningly.

Stopping on the trail while the seven head of cattle trudged slowly forward, the leader of the four riders — a gunman, Bertrim Sipes — said to the man nearest him, "Well, now, look who's coming here, Shoats. We've got ourselves some local figures." He rested his hand on the bone handle of his holstered Colt. "I bet they're going to be *real* upset over us rounding up our strays."

"Yep, that would be my guess too." Bobby Shoats spit and lifted his rifle from across his lap.

The other two, both Mexicans, gave each other a guarded look, seeing the three riders coming toward them at a hard gallop. *"Señors,"* said Jorge Sontage, "my brother, Ramon, and I both know these cattle are too far ahead to be our strays. This is the kind of thing that creates tension. We did not hire on to shoot people."

"You've got to be the most long-winded Mexican I ever seen," said Sipes. "Whoever it was taught you to speak American English wasn't doing nobody a favor." He raised his Colt from his holster threateningly, and cocked it as he spoke. "Do I need to teach you how *not* to speak it, real quick-like?"

Ramon Sontage cut in, saying, "Excuse my brother. We are not gunmen, not men of respect like yourselves."

"Don't go begging off on us, Ramon," said Shoats, giving him a dark stare. "You mighta hired on to romance cattle, but if we work up some shooting, you better grab something and commence shooting too." He jacked a round into his rifle chamber one-handed. "Else we'll start thinking you ain't our friend."

Ramon raised a hand in submission and fell silent, he and his brother watching the three riders ride nearer, coming slowly down the last few yards and then spreading out on the trail.

Blaine called out from thirty feet away, "Hello, the trail." Then, without waiting for a response, he said, "You boys have some of our cattle there."

"Hello, yourselves," said Sipes. He slipped his Colt back loosely into his holster. "I believe you're mistaken, mister. These are strays from our herd. We're drovers, part of a large herd up from —"

"We know who you are, and *what* you are," Batson cut in bluntly. "That's my bull going there." He pointed a gloved finger toward the animal. "Two of those steers are mine, and the rest belong to a neighbor named Farlin Clemons."

"Gentlemen, it's a good thing you said something," said Sipes with a flat smile. He sidestepped his horse, putting a few feet between himself and Shoats. The two Mexicans also moved away from each other, both wearing worried looks on their faces. "I looked them over good and found no brand of any kind. Did I miss something?"

"You didn't miss anything," said Batson. "They're not branded. The steers won't be branded till I ready them for market. The brindle bull needs no brand; everybody knows who he belongs to."

"Then we have a problem," said Sipes, his smile going away from his face. "We've got both branded and unbranded in our herd. Now, how will we know which are ours and which are yours?"

"Because I just told you," said Batson.

"How close is your herd?" Blaine asked, hoping to keep the exchange civil.

Sipes only shrugged. "Not too far," he said. "Why do you ask?"

"Because if it's as far away as that cloud of dust says it is" — he nodded at the looming dust in the distance — "it's not likely these cattle could have strayed this far off and ahead of the herd."

"You've got a point there," Sipes said in a cordial tone. "These two fellows just said the same thing." He gestured toward the Mexicans. "But I just told them, without a brand, who knows? They could be yours, they could be ours, they could be running wild."

"Mister, there ain't an animal there that didn't originate here in these high grasslands," said Batson, "and you and us all know it."

"I repeat, we do have a problem." Sipes seemed to study the matter for a moment, tapping his fingers idly on his bone-handled gun butt. Finally he said, "I believe I know the way we can settle this in a civilized manner."

Blaine let out a tense breath without anyone noticing and sat more at ease in his saddle. "Let's hear it," he said in a polite yet firm tone.

"First of all," said Sipes, "where *are* our manners?" He looked at Shoats, then back at Blaine. "Gentlemen, I'm Bertrim Sipes . . . this is Mr. Bobby Shoats." He didn't bother introducing the two Mexicans.

Blaine spoke grudgingly, unable to decide whether Sipes was being polite or only mocking them. Removing his hat, he introduced himself and the other two in a tolerant tone. Then he asked, "What were you going to say?"

"Oh, yes," Sipes said. "You mean about how to settle this." He nodded toward the distant cloud of dust. "Ride with us to the herd and we'll let our boss, Mr. LeBlanc, settle it for us. We'll even invite you to stay for tonight's fixin's."

"I don't need your boss to settle this for me," said Batson. "These are my cattle. Your boss has no say-so up here. He ain't the law."

"That's where you're wrong, Mr. Batson," Sipes said, his expression turning dark. "Wherever Mr. LeBlanc goes, he *becomes* the law. He hired me and Mr. Shoats here to make sure of it." Turning to Shoats, he said with a look of disappointment, "I just knew they weren't going to like my idea."

"Me too," said Shoats.

"Hell, that wasn't an idea worth —" Batson started speaking but never got to finish his words. Sipes's Colt came up too fast to

172

be seen and fired a bullet straight through his heart.

Reacting quickly, Blaine swung his rifle up from his lap and fired. But his shot went wild and struck Ramon as Sipes's second shot slammed high into his side and sent him rolling backward from his saddle.

Early Lee Springer's rifle never made it up from his lap. Bobby Shoats's Colt fired twice, both shots hitting the man in the chest. The rancher slid down his horse's side and fell over dead in the dirt. "Get your brother up into his saddle and get moving, Jorge," Sipes ordered. "If he can't ride, I'll put him out of his misery."

Hurrying, Jorge did as he was told. Ramon groaned as Jorge raised him to his feet and helped him get a foot into a stirrup. "I . . . I am bleeding so badly, *mi hermano,*" he said, reverting to his native tongue in his anguish. "I don't think I will live."

"Please, Ramon, you must live!" Jorge pleaded, whispering as he shoved him into his saddle. "These men will kill us too! We must get back on our horses. I will give you my shirt to hold against the bleeding!"

"Demasiada sangre . . . demasiada sangre," Ramon murmured as he pushed himself upward with his brother's help and sank onto his saddle.

"What did he say?" Sipes asked, punching out the smoking shell from his Colt, replacing it expertly, and, with one swift motion, slipping the gun into his holster.

Adjusting to his saddle and holding the reins to Ramon's horse, Jorge said quickly, "He said he will be all right, *señor*! He said for me not to worry!"

Sipes looked at Shoats, cocking a questioning eyebrow.

"He said there's too much blood, or some such mumbo jumbo as that," said Shoats, his smoking Colt wagging loosely in his hand.

"Shame on you for lying to me," Sipes said to Jorge.

"Por favor, señors!" said Jorge. "I will take care of him! Don't worry; we will both be able to do our jobs!"

"What do you think, Shoats?" Sipes asked.

"I think they're both more trouble than they're worth," said Shoats, raising the Colt and firing it as he spoke.

"Damn it, Shoats!" said Sipes, giving a dark chuckle as he watched Jorge flip from his saddle to the ground, his grip on his brother's reins causing Ramon to spill into the dirt beside him. "Never shoot a Mexican when you're this far out from camp! Now look who has to drive these stinking cattle."

Shoats blew smoke from the tip of his pistol barrel and holstered the weapon. "Aw, hell, it was just good practice. They couldn't have done much anyway, one half-dead, the other fretting over him." He smiled. "We'll tell LeBlanc that these Sabo Canyon boys ambushed us on the way back to camp. That ought to keep the European boys and the locals at one another's throats and keep us both on the payroll for a long time to come."

"Whatever you say then," said Sipes. He turned his horse and nudged it along behind the traveling cattle. "But if these animals start spreading out and wandering away, I'm not doing a damn thing to stop them." He grinned, nodding toward the bodies as he rode past them. "I've done my day's work."

CHAPTER 13

Jimmy Blaine had no idea how long he'd been lying in the dirt when he awakened to the feel of the dun's wet tongue on his cheek. His face rose and fell with each long, relentless lick. "Oh, God . . ." His voice trailed off, yet the sound of it caused the dun to chuff low in its throat and stare at him for a moment before giving him a sound push with its muzzle.

Blaine rolled onto his wounded side and felt the pain shoot through him. "Whoa, Sonny," he murmured to the dun. Clasping a hand to his bloody, dirt-crusted side, he struggled onto one knee and waited for a moment. Then, taking the dun's dangling reins in hand to steady himself, he pulled himself to his feet and looked all around.

"Aw, Claude," he whispered with sorrow. "Early Lee . . ." He shook his head slowly at the sight of both men lying dead in the dirt. "I can't even bury you ol' waddies," he said in a hurt voice. "I . . . I got to get on to town."

Although Blaine's voice did not rise above a rasping whisper, Ramon, lying in the dirt a few feet away, heard it, and turned over and clawed the ground toward him. "*Señor, por favor* . . . help us," he pleaded.

Help you . . . ? I'll kill you. . . . Blaine's hand felt around on his empty holster before he realized his gun had fallen from his hand. Weaving back and forth in place, his hand clamped to his side, Blaine searched all around on the ground, then staggered a few feet and lowered to one knee again and scooped up his Colt.

"*No, señor,*" Ramon moaned. "Don't shoot. We are not gunmen, my brother and I. . . ."

Gesturing the Colt toward the bodies of Springer and Batson, Blaine said in a weak tone, "Could have fooled me." He cocked the Colt and tried to steady it in his hand.

"*Señor,* I beg of you . . . think before you pull the trigger. What did my brother and I do? Are we not wounded ourselves?"

"Not enough," said Blaine, pulling the trigger and watching a blast of dirt kick up only inches from the wounded Mexican's face. "Damn it!" He steadied his hand with

177

determination and fired again. Still, he missed.

"We are *inocente,* innocent, *innocent!*" Ramon cried aloud, his voice muffled, his head lowered behind his encircling forearms. *"Por favor!"*

The effort of holding the gun up and making the shots caused Blaine's gun hand to fall limply to his side. He saw the other Mexican lying faceup, his mouth agape, his eyes staring blankly into the hot afternoon sun. "All right, on your feet then," he said to Ramon, relenting as he realized the two Mexicans had to have been shot from their saddles by the same men who shot him and his friends. "I can't seem to hit nothing anyway."

Ramon struggled upward, one of his loose boots coming off in his effort. His wounded side had caked itself with dirt and thick, pasty blood, enough to stop the bleeding for a while. He pressed his hand to the wound as he looked around and saw his brother's tongue and dead eyes baking in the hot sun. "Oh, no! Poor Jorge," he said, trying to keep from sobbing aloud.

Blaine watched him stagger over and collapse at his dead brother's side. With trembling fingers he shut Jorge's eyes and mouth, closed his brother's loose shirt in front, and

178

brushed dust from his chest.

Blaine swayed and almost lost his footing. Seeing Ramon look up and all around, then at the other bodies as if searching for something, Blaine said, "We're in no shape to bury anybody, if that's what you've got on your mind."

"But the critters, *los buitres y los coyotes*!"

"I'm sorry about vultures and coyotes," said Blaine. "But they'll be eating our innards too if we don't get to town and get help."

"Oh, Jorge, Jorge," Ramon whispered. "I cannot bear to leave you this way."

"Suit yourself," said Blaine, though he understood the man's feelings toward his brother, "I'm going on." He spotted his hat lying on the ground a foot away, stepped over, stooped down stiffly and picked it up, and slapped it weakly against his chaps. "There's your horse and your brother's."

"Will you help me put him over the saddle and bring him along?" Ramon asked.

Blaine looked at Springer and Batson lying in the dirt and took a deep breath. "I hope we don't fool around and die ourselves out here. I've got a baby girl I want to see."

"But this is my brother . . . these are your friends," said Ramon.

"I know it," said Blaine. He let the reins

drop from his hand and said to the dun in a weak voice, "Stay right here, Sonny; we're going to try to load everybody up." He'd started walking unsteadily toward Ramon and his dead brother when he heard his name called out from fifty yards away. He turned toward the sound of the voice, a hand pressed to the deep, throbbing, pulsing pain in his wounded side.

"It's me, Foley! Don't shoot!" said the black rancher. He stood with the sun to his back, waving his rifle back and forth.

"Foley . . . thank God." Blaine sank back down to the ground and waited for Foley to arrive.

"I saw the whole thing from up there," Foley said, coming up to him with a canteen. The stone-bruised Appaloosa limped along behind him. "I'm sorry I couldn't get here sooner!" He helped Blaine turn up a long drink of water. Then he stepped over to the Mexican and handed the canteen to him. "You two never had a chance," he said to Ramon.

Blaine gave the Mexican a look, letting him know the black man had just removed any doubt about what had happened. "We've both got to get to town," he said to Foley.

"I can't push the Appaloosa," said Foley.

"But I'll get you two going and stay behind you as close as I can."

"There could be other riders from the big spread along this trail," Blaine warned him.

"Then they'd best be as ready as I am," said Foley. "Let's get you two up and out of here. I'll bring in the dead."

Henri LeBlanc sat on the large, overstuffed armchair inside the open tent, feeling a cool evening breeze blow in from off the mountain range. Beside him Otto Perls sat experimenting with rolling an oversize cigarette, having wet two rolling papers and stuck them together. Watching the German for a moment, LeBlanc said, "If you knew how stupid you look, I am certain you would stop what you're doing and smoke your pipe."

Undaunted by LeBlanc's critical remark, Perls laid a line of chopped tobacco in the cupped paper and began twisting it all together carefully into a fat cigarette. Loose tobacco spilled out of both ends. Without looking up, the German cattleman said with a thick accent, "If I am living wid cowboys, I will larn de cowboys' ways."

"Don't plan on living with them much longer," said LeBlanc. Looking away, he shook his head again, then loosened his necktie and pulled his collar open. "As soon as we get this herd fattened on free-range grass, I will abandon this wasteland and return to a civilized country."

Still engrossed with rolling the large cigarette, Perls didn't answer. But when the whole thing came undone as he raised it to his lips to lick it, he cursed half in English and half in German, *"Verdammen* it to *Hölle!"*

"I see you are learning to swear like these uncultured fools," LeBlanc noted. Seeing the endless difficulty the German had rolling the oversize smoke, he added, "Get done with it; here they come." He gazed at the Katlin gang as they approached the open tent. "I want your attention when we talk about what to expect once we get into these grassland valleys."

"Sohn eines Weibchens!" the German cursed, wadding the faulty, crumbling cigarette up and throwing it away.

"Uh-oh," said T. J., "he just called somebody a sonsabitch."

"Who'd he call a sonsabitch?" asked Bratcher McBain, getting defensive at the sound of the German cursing as he and the Katlins drew closer to the tent. He walked three feet behind T. J. Katlin, Lane Katlin, and Uncle Linton. Behind McBain walked the Russian brothers, Vladimir and Jerniko.

"I reckon he speaks to whoever the boot fits," T. J. said with a short, tight grin. But as they had walked to the tent he'd seen the German struggling with the oversize cigarette. Stepping beneath the sheltering top of the open tent and up to the Frenchman and the German, T. J. and Lane Katlin stopped and took off their hats. "Afternoon, gentlemen," T. J. said confidently. He reached out and picked up the bag of tobacco and rolling papers from Perls's lap before the German could stop him. "Let me give you a hand with that, pardner."

Perls turned to LeBlanc in protest. "Vat does he mean wit dis 'partiner'?"

But the Frenchman didn't answer. Instead he rested his large, bearded chin in his hand and stared intently, watching T. J. wet two rolling papers with his tongue and stick them together. T. J. shook out a healthy amount of tobacco into the cupped paper.

"Watch this now," he said with a smug grin. He rolled the cigarette up tightly, licked the edge, sealed it, then ran the fat cigarette in and out of his mouth, wetting it and making it stick together. His thumbnail caused a match to flare up. "Stick it in your mouth and puff it," he said, pushing the damp cigarette so close to Perls's lips, the

German's face recoiled back from it.

"Vat dis means, 'purf et'?" he asked Le-Blanc, who sat staring with a sour expression.

"He means, *hauch es,*" said LeBlanc, translating the word *puff* into perfect German.

"Oh, *hauch es,*" Perls said. He took the cigarette, but upon feeling the dampness of saliva, he stuck it down into his coat pocket and said, "*Danke,* another time perhaps."

T. J. chuckled darkly under his breath and shook out the burning match.

"If you two are through, let's get down to some serious talk," LeBlanc said firmly in good English. He raised a hand and waved Dick Harpin over from a spot where he sat waiting farther back in the open tent.

"Well, I'll be damned," said Lane Katlin to T. J. and the others. "It's that livery hostler from Willow Creek."

"So, you men know each other . . . that's good," said LeBlanc, as if he already knew it. "Harpin came all this way just to tell us about Shaw killing Felts and Mariner. He also wants to ride with us, volunteer his guns for us against the ranchers and settlers when the time comes." He shot Harpin a sharp glance. "Isn't that right, Harpin?"

"Absolutely, Mr. La . . . La—"

"It's LeBlanc, you damn fool," T. J. cut in.

"Yes, sir, Mr. LeBlanc," said Harpin. "I want to volunteer my gun. . . . I'd also ride for pay, if you'd let me, that is."

"We'll have to see," LeBlanc said with a toss of a thick hand.

"But didn't you already send some of your best men to check things out in Willow Creek?" T. J. asked LeBlanc, eyeing the hostler with disgust. "What do we need this ass kisser for?"

"We've got too many men stretched between here and Willow Creek," said LeBlanc. "This has me concerned." He held up another thick finger as he named names. "There's Merlyn Oakley, Sid Tallow, Hawkens, and Reardon. They went to check on Lawrence Shaw for me. They're not back yet."

"No disrespect," said T. J., "but you shoulda sent us. We want Shaw dead worse than anybody you could send."

"Don't worry, you're going to get your chance," said LeBlanc. Raising two more fingers he said, "I sent Bertrim Sipes and Bobby Shoats out with a couple Mexicans to bring in some local cattle, to make up for the ones we lost on the way up here." He shook his head. "They're not back yet." He looked from one pair of eyes to the next as

185

he continued, "There's a gunman in the midst of things named Fast Larry Shaw. I understand you men have a personal reason to want to kill this Fast Larry?"

"We do," said T. J. Katlin. "Shaw killed our brother."

"Ah, I see," said the Frenchman. " 'The code of the West' is what you call this, eh?"

The Katlins looked at one another. "I don't know about any code," said T. J. "But when we run into Shaw, he's a piece of dead meat. You won't need to concern yourself with him anymore."

"I'll soon have too many of my top guns in Willow Creek checking on this Fast Larry," LeBlanc mused, almost as if thinking out loud. "What happens if we get in a shooting war with the ranchers in Sabo Canyon?"

"You'd be in a hurting situation, that's what," said Lane. "Who knows, maybe Shaw and the ranchers have put their heads together and come up with this whole plan to get all your men looking for Shaw while the ranchers get together and scatter this big herd from here all the hell back to Texas?"

LeBlanc listened to the Katlins talk, weighing their words and considering their merit.

"So, how about it, boss?" T. J. asked, getting more familiar with the big Frenchman. "You sent some of your top men to check out Shaw and you haven't heard squat. Why not watch the Katlin Gang in action?"

"I'd still like to have a big gun like this Fast Larry Shaw working for me," said LeBlanc, letting them see he wasn't going to give in easily. "What happens after you men kill him? You ride on; I'm still left with the ranchers in Sabo Canyon to deal with." He shook his head. "I don't know. . . . It might be better if I ride in and make Fast Larry Shaw an offer in person, try to win him over to my side."

"Mr. LeBlanc," said Lane Katlin, seeing that T. J. hadn't gotten very far calling him boss, "I give you my word, once we kill Shaw, we'll stick with you until you pick up and leave these grasslands come spring. Your enemies will be Katlin enemies."

LeBlanc took out a long cigar from his coat pocket and snipped the tip off of it as he seemed to consider what to do. Sticking it in his mouth, he raised his brow as if summoning one of the Katlins to give him a light.

"Right here, boss, allow me," said T. J., snapping another match to life with his thumbnail and holding it out. "My brother

187

seldom gives his word to any man. But once you've got it, you can haul freight cars on it. It can't be broken."

LeBlanc looked back and forth between the two brothers as he puffed on his cigar. "Get Red Downing," he said with authority. "I'm setting up a well-guarded perimeter around this herd." He took another long draw on the cigar and let it out slowly.

"You heard him, McBain!" Lane commanded, turning with a harsh stare toward the aging gunman. "Go find Red Downing!"

"I'm going to ride along to Willow Creek myself," said LeBlanc. "It's time to let the local ranchers know we have arrived. We'll have to see what happens once we get there." He turned to the German. "Why don't you ride along too, Herr Perls? This could make for a nice holiday for you, something for you to tell your investors about back in Dresden."

"*Ja,* I vould like dat!" The German shook his head and spread a brisk smile. "But vat aboud dis William the Child we have heard so much bad tangs aboud? Vill he not be dere also?"

"You mean Henry McCarty, known of late as Billy the Kid," said T. J. with his dark chuckle.

188

"Hell, don't worry about the Kid," said Lane. "We both know him. He rides with us sometimes. He won't step in when we kill Shaw. If he does, we'll swat him out of the way like a fly. Right, men?" He looked around at the others. All of them nodded and mumbled in agreement.

Vladimir raised a big fist in the air and twisted it back and forth, saying boldly, "If Katlins say so, I will tweest off his nutz like I would a grizzly bear!"

"Ouch!" said T. J., giving his brother Lane a look as he laughed and threw up his hands in a joking gesture.

"See, Mr. LeBlanc," said Lane, "this is the kind of help we can offer."

LeBlanc listened to T. J. and Lane Katlin sell him on giving them a free hand in dealing with Lawrence Shaw, until McBain returned with Red Downing. "You sent for me, Mr. LeBlanc?" Downing asked, eyeing the Katlins.

"Yes, I did," said LeBlanc. "Prepare for a ride into Willow Creek right away. I want to get a feel for what's going on there. I haven't heard anything from Okaley."

"Oakley is a former detective, Mr. LeBlanc," said Downing, still eyeing the Katlins, "not some saddle bum looking to shoot somebody in the back for his next meal. I'll

189

wager he's met and sized up every gun in town. He'll know how to take care of anybody he thinks ain't on our side . . . including this Fast Larry Shaw."

"Indeed," LeBlanc murmured, rolling the cigar in his lips in contemplation. "Nevertheless, we're riding into Willow Creek. I want to give Herr Perls a look at what's involved in this cattle industry."

CHAPTER 14

Along the boardwalks in Willow Creek, eyes turned toward the heavily loaded buggy as it rolled along the dirt street toward the doctor's office. At the buggy's reins sat Dr. Hauler, his ear covered by a bloodstained bandage. Next to him sat Hilda, a compress covering the welt and the cut on her forehead. In the rear buggy seat sat an Indian youth, his hand held up, wrapped in a thick white dressing.

Following the buggy, Shaw sat slumped in his saddle, leading the doctor's saddle horse by its reins. He wore no shirt, only his grass-stained duster. Beneath the open front of the duster a bloodstained bandage covered his lower left side. A bullet hole showed plainly on the crown of his Stetson.

From in front of the saloon the Kid and his pals watched the buggy roll past them. He tipped his half-full beer mug toward Shaw in a welcome-back nod and said quietly to his pals standing around him, "Now there goes a story I can't wait to hear."

"That Indian looks familiar," Sturgis commented. "Don't you all think so?"

"Not to me, he don't," Rudabaugh said bluntly.

"Me neither," said Free Drink, giving Sturgis a guarded look, letting him know not to mention it again.

"I hope Oakley and his men aren't seeing this," said Rudabaugh. "Fast Larry Shaw ain't looking none too spry right now. I wouldn't bet on him heads-up in a gunfight right now."

"It's *Lawrence* Shaw from now on," the Kid said, correcting him.

"Yeah, I meant Lawrence," said Rudabaugh.

"Oakley and his men are all late sleepers," the Kid continued, speaking sidelong to him. "It was midmorning yesterday before any of them rode in from their camp." He watched Shaw and the buggy roll on, Shaw having given him the slightest nod.

"Besides," the Kid added, looking out in the direction where Oakley and his men had made camp outside of town, "I think Oakley understands that Shaw's killing those two jaybirds was a fair shooting. Fair is fair, even in Hoboken."

"Ha," said Rudabaugh. "Let that French-man give him an order and watch how quick him and his mugs try to put Shaw in the ground."

The Kid's grin went away. "Well, that's a different thing altogether. He's a paid gun sure enough. If he takes the man's money, I expect he'll do what he's paid for."

"Hell, yes," said Sturgis, "and so would I, if that was what I agreed to. Wouldn't you, Kid?"

"You know damned well I would," said the Kid. "That's why I'm careful what I agree to." He swigged his beer and gazed out along the dirt street, hooking his free thumb into his duckcloth trousers.

Rudabaugh, Free Drink, and Sturgis looked at one another in silence. Finally Rudabaugh spoke for all three. "Uh, Kid," he said, "we been mulling things over between us, and we're thinking maybe —"

"Mulling things over?" the Kid said qui-etly, still staring out in the direction of Oak-ley's camp.

"Yeah, that's right," said Rudabaugh. "See —"

"Not with me you haven't," said the Kid in the same tone of voice.

Rudabaugh tried again. "No, but we sort

of thought it's time we —"

"Does that seem right to you? All three of yas talking, not including me in it?" the Kid asked.

"Aw, hell, Billy, it ain't like we was cutting you out, talking behind your back," said Rudabaugh. "We just jawed things over, and thought maybe it was time to move."

"That's what you came up with, huh?" the Kid said.

The three looked at one another. "You have to admit, Kid, it's gonna get wild and woolly around here most anytime," Rudabaugh offered.

Still looking away, the Kid sucked a tooth and said quietly, "I thought we liked it wild and woolly."

"Well, we do," Sturgis cut in, seeing that Rudabaugh wasn't getting anywhere. "But a range war ain't a place to be unless we're on somebody's side . . . making something off it, you might say."

"So, you want to take sides?" asked the Kid. He finished his morning beer and set the empty mug on the saloon's windowsill.

"Not so much that as maybe just getting our knees in the wind, get on down to Ruidoso," said Rudabaugh.

"Yeah, where they fiesta day and night," said Free Drink. "You got to admit things is a mite heavy around here."

"Fiesta suits me," the Kid remarked, as if considering things.

A silence set in for a moment while the three looked at one another again. "So, that's it then?" Free Drink asked at length. "We put ourselves south of here, see how much ground we can throw behind us?"

"I'll be back in a spell," the Kid said solemnly. He pushed himself from the front of the saloon building and walked away toward the doctor's office without reply.

"Well, hell," said Rudabuagh, "that didn't go nowhere, did it?"

"Not that I can see," said Free Drink.

Sturgis said, "What is it about Shaw being around that gets him loco?"

"He wishes he *was* Lawrence Shaw," Rudabaugh speculated, watching the Kid walk toward the doctor's office.

"Watch your mouth," said Free Drink. "Billy's all right who he is."

"Hell, I don't mean nothing *bad* saying it," said Rudabaugh. "But he wishes folks looked at him the way they look at Shaw. To tell the truth, so do I sometimes. Being called the fastest gun alive ain't no small thing, any way you cut it."

"Yeah, well," said Free Drink, sounding a little too defensive of the Kid, "Billy's still young. Maybe someday they will."

Sturgis cut in. "You heard what Billy said — he don't believe there's such a thing as the fastest gun alive."

"Just because he doesn't believe there *is* one doesn't mean he wouldn't want to be *called* one," said Free Drink.

On the street, the Kid walked directly to the doctor's office, where he stepped onto the boardwalk and reached for the doorknob. But before he could open the door, Shaw, who had seen him coming through the front window, opened the door from inside, stepped out, and closed the door quickly behind him. The Kid looked him up and down and said, "What happened to you, Shaw? Have you gone off and gotten yourself shot?"

Shaw gestured him away from the door and limped down off the boardwalk, a protective hand held close to his wounded side. "I knew you would ask me that, Kid," he said, looking a little embarrassed. "That's why I met you at the door."

"Oh . . . ?" The Kid looked at Shaw's bandaged side, then suspiciously at the door to the doctor's office. Looking back at Shaw as if he'd suddenly figured out what had happened, he said, "Doc Hauler shot you, didn't he?"

"That's right, he did," Shaw said, lowering his voice between the two of them. "But it's all settled. There's no bad blood between us."

The Kid gave him an incredulous look, noting the bullet hole in his hat and the thick grass stains on his riding duster. "The man shot you in the gut — tried to kill you — and you have no hard feelings? What's he doing still alive? Did you at least rip his ear off?"

"No," said Shaw. "The Indian boy took a shot at him, meant to kill him, but I stopped him, caused him to only clip off the doctor's earlobe."

"And the Indian's hand?" the Kid asked, trying to put the scene together as he heard how it unfolded.

"I winged his gun hand. That's what kept him from killing the doctor," said Shaw. "Hilda slipped on a creek bank and hit her head on a rock when the doctor shot me."

The Kid shook his head, as if taken aback by Shaw's story. "I'm trying to see all this play itself out," he said, again looking at Shaw's stained duster. "The doctor caught you and his wife together —"

"It's a long story, Kid," said Shaw. "Picture it the way you want to, only keep quiet about it."

"You've got my word. But it *was* over his wife, wasn't it?" the Kid probed. "We all saw the two women ride in like they'd seen the end of the world coming. We watched the sawbones ride out alone. I figured something like this."

Shaw just looked at him for a moment before answering. "Yes, it was over her, Kid. But I don't want to talk about it anymore. It's over and done. Now it's best forgotten." As he spoke he turned and ambled toward the mercantile store on the next block.

The Kid walked along with him, uninvited, stifling a laugh at Shaw and his predicament. "Where are you headed now?" he asked.

"To get a shirt, a hat," said Shaw. "Then I need to see Rita and tell her what Jimmy Blaine said. Then I'm getting something to eat. I didn't eat last night. Too much on my mind, I reckon."

"What did Blaine have to say? Is he as pleased as we are about being a daddy?"

"Kid, Jimmy Blaine is happy as can be, and proud to be that little girl's father," said Shaw. "He made me ashamed for not feeling the same way. He's a good man. Said he'll take in Rita and the baby, if you and me don't object."

"Well, speaking for myself," said the Kid,

"I don't. What about you?"

"I wish I did feel that way," said Shaw. "I wish to God Rita and that precious little baby meant so much to me that I couldn't think of nothing else. I wish I was a starry-eyed, grinning fool for the both of them. That's the way life ought to be." He paused and let out a breath. "But . . . it isn't."

"Anyways, I'm glad to hear that about Blaine," said the Kid. "I always said he's a good man." Changing the subject quickly, the Kid said, "There are four men here from the big spread, wanting to know about the shooting."

"Obliged for telling me, Kid," said Shaw, taking the hint. "What are they asking?"

"The usual stuff," said the Kid. "Me and my pals told them it was a straight-up gunfight."

"Think that will do it for them?" Shaw asked, looking toward the saloon.

"I know a little about the honcho, a fellow by the name of Oakley, used to police in New Jersey," said the Kid. "He'll kill anybody for the right amount, but he's not stupid. He won't put himself too far outside the law in front of witnesses if he can help it."

"Good information, Kid; obliged again," said Shaw. He stepped stiffly onto the boardwalk in front of the mercantile store. "I'm going to get dressed, see Rita and the baby, get something to eat, then get out of Willow Creek."

"I understand." The Kid nodded. "It might look to some like you're running, but I know you're not. I've never seen so much trouble stick to a man's boot heels in my life as it does to yours."

Shaw turned and looked at him. "It never lets up," he said. "It's like this everywhere I go. I used to think it was because of my reputation with a gun. . . ." He paused for a second, recalling himself and Hilda, and the way he had wronged the doctor who had once saved his life. "But other times I think it's just that I'm a no-good son of a bitch who deserves everything that happens to him."

"Damn," said the Kid, "I've never seen a man blame himself as bad as you do. I think you'd best get over to the saloon with me and my pals and get some whiskey in you, smooth out some of the rocks in your trail." He offered a grin, but it didn't take. "We'll celebrate Jimmy and Rita's new life together."

"I'll come by, Kid," said Shaw, not sounding very sincere about it. "I'll have a drink with you before I leave."

The two parted at the door to the mercantile. Shaw went inside and picked out a new red wool-and-linen shirt and put it on in the stockroom. The store owner wondered but didn't ask about Shaw's bandaged side, or the fact that he wore only a riding duster from the waist up. He stood back and watched above his spectacles as Shaw tried on four hats without finding one that fit.

"I'm afraid we're out of the larger sizes right now, mister," said the store owner. "But we've got a new shipment on its way."

Shaw only nodded and put the fifth hat back on a peg and walked to the counter. "How much for the shirt?" he asked, putting his bullet-punctured hat back atop his head.

Across the street in the saloon, Free Drink and Hyde Rudabaugh looked out above the bat-wing doors and watched Shaw leave the mercantile and walk to the hotel. "He's got a shirt on," Free Drink called over his shoulder to the Kid, standing at the bar.

"Ain't he a treat to watch?" the Kid said with a chuckle. Raising a shot glass full of rye as if in a mock toast to Shaw, the Kid said, "Here's to the wild frontier, and the bold men who come to tame her!"

When Shaw knocked lightly on Rita's door and stepped inside at her beckoning, he found her sitting in a large rocker, holding the baby in her lap, rocking back and forth slowly. "You have come back," she said, keeping her voice not much above a whisper. She looked pleased.

"Yes, and I have good news," said Shaw, taking off his hat before Rita had time to note the bullet hole. "I spoke to Blaine, and he's on his way."

"Oh . . ." Rita responded. Shaw wasn't sure what he read in her eyes.

"Yep, and he couldn't have been happier when I told him he's a father," said Shaw.

"Really?" Rita perked up, appearing a bit surprised by the news. "And he is coming soon?"

"Just as soon as somebody showed up to relieve him, he said." Shaw smiled. "Said tell you not to go anywhere, that he'd be here. And he meant it, Rita," he added sincerely. "He said tell you that he had plenty of room for you and the baby."

"Oh . . . then this is good news. Jimmy will provide a home for me and our *bebè*," she said, glancing down at the infant sleeping peacefully on her lap.

Shaw saw a sad expression come to her eyes, and he stepped forward and said, "Rita, I thought this would make you happy. Jimmy Blaine is a good man — a far better father than either Billy Bonney or I will ever make."

"I know he is a good man," said Rita, changing her sad expression instantly. She smiled. "I will love Jimmy like no man has been loved," she said, suggestion flickering in her dark eyes. "And I will make him a fine wife in every other way as well."

"I know you will, Rita," said Shaw. "I have faith in you and Blaine both."

"But not enough for you to be my husband, my baby's father," Rita said softly yet pointedly, revealing the source of the sadness he'd detected a moment ago.

"Rita, we've been through this. . . ." Shaw let his words trail off.

Rita sighed. "I know." She paused, then said, "Please do not think I am ungrateful and that I do not know Jimmy Blaine is a good man. But I will say this now, and never say it again in my life — I wish it was you or Billy who would take me in and make a life for us." She looked down and shook her head as if ashamed for having said it. "What is wrong with me that I say such a thing? Am I a bad woman, Lawrence?"

"No," said Shaw, "you're a woman who has made her share of bad moves in life, but that can always change, if you want it to."

"Then tell me, please," she pleaded, with tears welling in her eyes, "why do I feel this way?"

"I don't know why," said Shaw. Shaw thought about Hilda and how she'd so easily made herself available to him, and how for a reckless moment she'd seemed willing to throw aside a good man like Dr. Hauler for a down-at-the-heels gunman like himself. He thought about his dead wife, Rosa, and what a fine woman she'd been. Had he failed her? Of course he had; and he knew that his failing her was the thing lying deep and dark inside him, eating him alive mind and spirit. "Damn, I just don't know," he repeated softly, stepping back and turning toward the door. "I wish to hell I did."

CHAPTER 15

"There he goes," said Sturgis, looking out above the bat-wing doors. "The fastest gun alive just walked out of the hotel and is headed for the restaurant. Want me to trail him? See what he has for breakfast?"

The Kid, ignoring Sturgis, swung the bottle of rye off the bar and looked it over with distaste. In his other hand he looked at the empty beer mug in the same manner and said, "How can a man stand here drinking this snake-head poison and this yellow horse piss when there's enough tequila and mescal to swim in down in *Nuevo Mèxico*?"

"Now you're talking, Billy!" said Free Drink, moving up beside him at the bar, getting excited at the prospect.

"What about *viejo Mèxico*?" Rudabaugh asked. "We'd get more for our money there, less cold weather too."

The Kid shrugged and slid the empty mug across the bar to the waiting bartender.

205

"New Mexico, old Mexico — hell, I don't care. Anyplace beats this place. Willow Creek is starting to make me restless."

"We can have our horses up and be in our saddles in five minutes!" said Free Drink, looking around at the others for support.

"I say we ought to get to doing it," said the Kid. He picked up the full beer the bartender slid to him. He took a shot of the strong rye and then a sip of beer and cursed under his breath. "In a minute," he grumbled beneath a whiskey-beer belch. Looking into the mirror along the wall behind the bar, the Kid watched Merlyn Oakley and his men walk in single file and line up along the bar beside him.

"I heard Shaw is back in town, Bonney," Oakley said in a gravelly voice, sounding as if he wanted to see if the Kid would try to lie about it. He laid a rifle up on the bar.

"He is," the Kid said in a firm, sharp response.

Oakley blinked, seeming surprised by the Kid's straightforwardness. "Did you warn him I'm here?" he asked.

"I did," the Kid replied in the same manner. "Why wouldn't I? You said you weren't out to kill him if it turned out the shooting was fair. Did you mean it, or was you just getting everybody's guard down?"

"I don't expect your guard ever comes down, Bonney," said Oakely. He gestured for the bartender to set him and his men up with a shot of whiskey. He seemed at ease. "Besides, I did check around. It was fair."

"I'd say it was *more* than fair." The Kid grinned crookedly. "Your pals Felts and Mariner got what they had coming to them, interrupting a man's breakfast, ambushing him in the midst of his hoecakes and eggs. Shaw gets real testy at mealtime," he added, implying that he and Shaw were on close enough terms that he knew Shaw's habits and moods.

No sooner had the Kid finished speaking than three gunshots exploded from the direction of the restaurant where Shaw had gone to eat. Everyone along the bar spun on their heels toward the shots. "Uh-oh," said the Kid. "I think you're getting ready to see what I mean!"

"Shaw's at the restaurant!" Tallow said to the other two, standing beside Oakley. "Let's go!"

"Damn it," said Oakley, seeing Tallow head across the floor. "You heard me say that Felts and Mariner was a fair fight! Don't call Shaw out for it!"

"Anything you say, boss," said Tallow in a sarcastic tone. Shoving his way through the bat-wing doors, he disappeared in the direction of the restaurant. Dubbs Hawkens and Bo Reardon, who had instinctively started to follow Tallow, stopped and stood looking at Oakley for advice.

"Let him go," Oakley growled. He tossed back his shot of rye and ran a hand across his lips. "I'm tired of riding herd on that hothead. He wants to build himself a reputation, he can do it by himself." He picked up his rifle off the bar. "We ain't running to keep up with his sorry ass."

The Kid and his three pals had already hurried past Oakley and his men and walked quickly along the street toward the restaurant. In the street out front, a body lay in almost the same spot where Jess Mariner had fallen the day he and Otis Felts came to kill Shaw. "I'll be damned; look at this!" said the Kid, hurrying along the street.

On the boardwalk in front of the restaurant, he saw Shaw jerk a cloth napkin from his collar and use it to blot his mouth. Shaw continued chewing a bite of crisp jowl bacon. Seeing men approach him from the direction of the saloon, and having been tipped off by the Kid that there were men looking for him, Shaw turned his smoking Colt toward them and watched them separate and come to a halt.

But not the Kid. The Kid spread his hands in a show of peace and continued forward. "Whoa, Shaw, it's me, all right?"

"Yeah, Kid, you come on over," said Shaw. Looking past the Kid at the others, he said with a narrowed gaze, "But I don't like being crowded, especially after a shooting."

"Who's this?" the Kid asked, looking down as he passed the body in the street. They saw an older blood-encrusted bullet hole in the dead man's shirt. Three fresh wounds had formed a thick puddle of blood on his chest. He'd died wearing a shocked expression.

Shaw shrugged and swallowed his food. "I thought I'd killed him and another man out there." He nodded toward the distance, where the two men had stopped Hilda Hauler.

Oakley, who walked wide around the body, stood facing Shaw from across the street. He called out, "His name is Blue Phillips. Him and another fellow were coming from Cheyenne to go to work for us."

"I've heard of Blue Phillips," Free Drink whispered to Hyde Rudabaugh and Sturgis, the three standing back where the Kid had left them in the street. "He was a wicked sonsabitch with a six-shooter."

"Not today he wasn't," Rudabaugh whis-

209

pered in reply, watching Shaw answer Oakley.

"*Us*, meaning the European spread I've heard so much about?" Shaw called out in reply. His Colt was still in hand, and his eyes watched Sid Tallow peripherally, seeing him advance in slow steps as if sneaking up on him.

"That's right, Shaw," said Oakley. "But they never showed up. Whatever happened to them is no skin off my back."

"This is Oakley, the man I told you about," said the Kid just between himself and Shaw. "He says he's good with your shooting Felts and Mariner too, but watch him. He's gotten awfully agreeable overnight."

"Obliged," Shaw whispered.

Oakley continued, saying, "I don't know what you've heard about the European spread, but you might consider hiring on yourself." He gave a flat grin. "We're getting more shorthanded by the day."

Shaw only stared at him, not sharing in his attempt at humor. "What about the one who thinks he's slipping up on me?" he asked the Kid quietly.

"That one thinks he's lightning on a stick. Oakley has given up trying to keep him reined in. Watch him close. He wants your rep."

"I wish I could give it to him," said Shaw. But even as he spoke the words, he flicked his Colt effortlessly in Tallow's direction, cocking it. "Next step toward me I'll open your head," he said to Tallow. The man jerked to a halt, stunned to realize that Shaw had been watching him all along.

But Tallow recovered quickly and wasn't through yet. He gave a show of his open hands, but still kept them close to his gun belt. "You don't own the street, Shaw. I go where I please."

Shaw only stared, letting the young gunman know that he had no more to say on the matter.

"Hear me, Shaw," Tallow called out. "I said you don't own the street."

Shaw ignored Tallow. From up the street, Dr. Hauler came loping, leather bag in hand, putting on his coat as he ran. To the Kid, Shaw said, "It's getting too crowded out here. I'm going to turn and walk inside. Why don't you come with me?"

"Sure thing." The Kid let his hand relax on the butt of his double-action Colt, looking pleased that Shaw had invited him along. He said in an authoritarian tone to Free Drink, Rudabaugh, and Sturgis,

"Watch things out here, boys, while me and Shaw go indoors a spell."

Inside the empty restaurant, the owner had started out the kitchen door with a cleaning rag and a bucket of soapy water. Seeing Shaw and the Kid, he turned with a sigh of resignation and walked back through the service door. The Kid looked all around at overturned tables and chairs abandoned by the breakfast crowd. Then he looked at three large, dripping splatters of blood on the front and side walls, where Blue Phillips had spun around in a circle, moving backward as the shots hit him. On the boardwalk lay the front door that Phillips had busted off its hinges as the shots drove him through it to the street. "Three shots?" the Kid said, as if wondering why it had taken so many.

"Some die quicker than others," Shaw said grimly. As he spoke he punched out the three empty shells from his Colt's chamber. Letting the brass shells fall to the floor, he replaced them with three fresh rounds from his holster belt.

The Kid watched, understanding why Shaw had wanted to get off the crowded street — he needed a chance to reload. But still, Shaw had invited him along, the Kid reminded himself. He liked the way Shaw did things, liked the way he didn't bother

212

explaining himself. *I'm going to turn and walk inside. Why don't you come with me?* The Kid smiled, recalling the way he'd said it. Shaw knew how to live the life of a big gunman.

"Aw, hell . . ." Shaw suddenly murmured under his breath, seeing Hilda Hauler come in through the service door and walk toward him quickly. The Kid turned, saw her coming, and turned away as if he hadn't seen her. "Hilda," said Shaw, "what are you doing here?"

"I . . . I heard the shots from Rita's room, and I saw the man lying in the street. It's him, isn't it? One of the men who accosted me?"

Shaw caught her by her forearms and held her back from him. "Yes, it is — it *was*. But you can't be here, not after all that's happened."

"I saw him and I got so scared," said Hilda. She struggled until Shaw gave in and let her push herself against him. "What if he had killed you? Is there no end to this?"

From the open doorway the doctor stepped in and saw Hilda and Shaw in what appeared to be an embrace. "My God, Hilda," he said in disgust, "apparently *no*, there doesn't seem to be any end to it!" he answered her.

"Jesus, Kid, get her out of here," Shaw said to the Kid, who hid his face and stifled a laugh at Shaw's awkward predicament.

"That won't be necessary," said the doctor in an icy tone. "She needn't leave on my account. I am aware that my wife is unable to control herself whenever you are around, Shaw. I can only accept it . . . as any civilized man must do."

Hilda had stepped back from Shaw and turned toward her husband. "Adrian, it isn't as it appears. I only came here because I saw that the man in the street is one of the men Lawrence saved me from on the trail — the ones I told you about, or *tried* to tell you about."

Staring away from her, the doctor said, "Pardon me for finding it hard to listen to you at the time, having found the two of you cavorting naked on a creek bank!"

The Kid covered his mouth with a hand and kept his face bowed toward the floor. But the doctor, catching a glimpse of him, said before thinking, "And you, Mr. Bonney, will be happy to know that I treated one of the alleged Apache warriors you kept from attacking the stagecoach."

"The hell are you talking about, alleged?" the Kid asked, his mirthful expression vanishing from his face.

"Nothing, Kid, forget it," Shaw cut in quickly, not wanting to see things turn ugly. He knew the Kid could have a hair-trigger temper. He didn't want to see the doctor catch the brunt of it.

But the Kid wouldn't turn it loose. He stared hard at the doctor. "Explain yourself, sawbones," he demanded.

The dark look in the Kid's eyes alone was enough to stun the doctor for a moment. He realized he'd stepped on a rattler's back. "I mean . . . one of the Indians you shot. He was not an Apache. . . . He was a —"

"That's enough, Doc. Take your wife and go," said Shaw. "I'm tired of seeing you two every time I turn around." He stepped between Dr. Hauler and the Kid and gave Hilda a shove and a bawdy slap on her behind. "It's been fun getting to know you again, sweetheart," he said, "but now I want you and your doctor husband out of here!"

With a mixed look of hurt, humiliation, and indignation on her face, Hilda stumbled a bit, but caught her husband by the arm and hurried him out the open door, feeling both gunmen's eyes on them. She stopped for only a second, long enough to turn and say, "What have I done? What kind of an animal have you become?"

"The kind who saw what I wanted and

took it! But I've had my fill of you. Now *get!*" Shaw shouted, hoping his rejection would hurry them both away.

It did.

Shaw looked at the Kid and saw him staring cold and hard at Dr. Hauler and his wife, appearing to be on the verge of going after the doctor. "Let him go, Kid," Shaw said quietly. "What the hell do people like that know about this world men like you and I live in? I've learned it's best to overlook them and go on about my business."

"Yeah, I expect you're right," said the Kid, still staring after the couple as they hurried away. "What do they know about men like us?" After a pause, he shook his head and chuckled with a crooked grin. "Let's go get a slug or two of rye." He looked at Shaw. "Think a couple of hosses like us can make it from here to the saloon without getting into trouble?"

"We can sure give it a try, Kid," said Shaw, breathing a little easier, knowing the doctor and Hilda were safely out of the way. He would never forgive himself for treating Hilda that way. But that was just one more thing he'd never forgive himself for, he thought. At least the Haulers were still in one piece. That was more than he could say

for some people whose lives had brushed
up against his.

CHAPTER 16

After having a drink with the Kid and his pals, Shaw washed down a sliced pork sandwich and two pickled eggs with a mug of beer at the bar. "Kid, I'm obliged for you and your friends' hospitality," he said, wiping his mouth on a clean cloth napkin the bartender had brought him.

"You needn't rush off," the Kid said. "Stick around a day or two and ride south with us."

"I've overstayed myself as it is," said Shaw. He thought of the trouble he'd played a part in between the doctor and his wife, and of how rudely he'd ended up treating poor, beautiful Hilda after taking advantage of the couples' unhappiness. "I want to get out of here before I cause any more trouble."

"Hell, you didn't cause trouble," the Kid said. "Trouble caused *you.*" He sounded a little drunk on the shots of rye he'd been tossing back ever since the doctor had made the remark about the wounded Indian not being an Apache.

"I let it happen." Shaw stepped away from the bar. "Sometimes that's the same thing as starting it."

The Kid only shook his head. "Suit yourself then," he said. He and the others raised a hand toward Shaw as he walked away. "Adios," the Kid said.

"Keep a tight bark on," said Free Drink. Rudabaugh and Sturgis only nodded.

Outside the saloon, Shaw stepped up into his saddle and turned his horse toward the south trail without looking toward the doctor's office or up toward Rita's hotel window, where Hilda might be standing. In front of the hotel he saw Oakley and his men looking in his direction; but he'd felt no threat from them since the shooting. Shaw touched his finger to his hat brim when Oakley gave him a respectful nod. He didn't trust Oakley, but he felt this was the kind of man who would act against him only if directly ordered to do so.

Riding at a walk along the dirt street, Shaw saw the owner of the restaurant hold a sign against one of the planks he'd put up to hold the broken front door in place until it could be repaired. The sign read: CLOSED UNTIL FURTHER NOTICE.

The owner held a nail against the sign with one hand. In his other hand he held a hammer ready, but upon seeing Shaw riding out of town, he appeared to consider his action for a moment. Then he lowered the sign and leaned it against the front of the building and gave Shaw a wary smile. Shaw nodded and rode on, glancing down for only a second at the dark bloodstain in the dirt where Blue Phillips's body had landed.

Shaw rode on, glad to be leaving, feeling curious eyes on him from both sides of the street. But no sooner had he gotten to the rise at the edge of town than he saw the wounded Mexican sitting wobbly in his saddle, leading Jimmy Blaine's horse up onto the dirt street. "Whoa," Shaw murmured, bringing his own horse to a halt. Blaine lay slumped forward in his saddle.

"*Señor,* I did not do this . . ." the Mexican gasped, looking far too pale around his eyes and mouth.

"I understand," said Shaw. He nudged his horse quickly over to Jimmy Blaine. "Jimmy! Can you hear me?" He raised Blaine upright in his saddle and saw his bloody, mud-encrusted wound.

Blaine grasped Shaw's forearm and tried to focus his weak eyes. "Is Rita still here?" he rasped. "Is my baby . . . all right?"

"Take it easy, Blaine," said Shaw. He leaned him forward again in his saddle to keep him from falling and took the reins from the Mexican, saying, "You take it easy too. I'll get you both to the doctor."

"There is . . . more dead coming," Ramon managed to say as he slumped forward, letting Shaw take over.

"More dead?" Shaw looked back along the trail, seeing no one.

"Foley's bringing them," Blaine murmured.

Shaw didn't ask any more questions. He led the two horses back along the dirt street into Willow Creek toward the doctor's office. On his way past the restaurant, he saw the owner look at him sadly and pick up the sign and reach for his hammer and nails.

The same eyes that had looked at him with curiosity on his way out of town now looked with even more curiosity as he returned leading the two wounded men behind him. Seeing him from in front of the hotel, Merlyn Oakley and his men stepped into the street and came forward, recognizing Ramon. "Keep your distance," Shaw cautioned the gunmen, placing a hand on his holstered Colt. "I'm taking them to the doctor."

Oakley stopped a respectful distance away

and called out, "The Mexican works for the spread." He looked at his three men. "Do any of you know his name?"

The men only shrugged. "He's got a brother he rides herd with," said Tallow. "That's all I know." As he spoke he moved closer.

But before Shaw said anything, Oakley grabbed the back of the young gunman's coat and jerked him backward. "You heard him. Stay the hell back and give him room."

By the time Shaw stopped his horse in front of the doctor's office, the Kid and his pals had noticed the townsfolk moving along the street and had walked out, seen Shaw returning, and now followed along behind him. "Shaw never stops, does he?" the Kid commented with a slight chuckle.

In the hotel window, Hilda Hauler and Rita stood side by side, Rita with the baby asleep in her arms. "That is Jimmy Blaine, my baby's father!" Rita said with a look of concern. "I must go to him! Help me down the stairs, *por favor!*"

"I . . . I don't think I should be there right now," Hilda replied hesitantly, not wanting to explain things to this woman.

"Then hold my baby for me! I must go," Rita insisted.

Hilda sighed. "Let me get you a shawl.

We'll all three go. I'm sure Mr. Blaine will want to see his daughter."

At the doctor's office, Shaw had stepped down from his saddle and begun helping Blaine down when Dr. Hauler stepped out onto the boardwalk. "My goodness!" said the doctor upon seeing the wounded men. Wasting no time, he hurried over and helped Ramon down from his saddle, into his office, and into another room, where he did his surgical work. "Well, Mr. Shaw," he said coldly over his shoulder, "I see you're *still* in our lives. I should have thought that after that little incident at the restaurant, you would be moving on."

"I was moving on, Doctor," said Shaw. "I don't want to be in Willow Creek any more than you want me here."

"That is impossible to imagine," the young doctor said wryly.

Shaw looked back over his shoulder before speaking, to make sure the Kid hadn't stepped inside with them. "Look, Doctor, I said those things to get you and Hilda out of there this morning before William Bonney emptied his gun in your belly over your Apache remark."

The doctor didn't respond. He helped Ramon onto a gurney, pressed him down onto his back, and opened his bloody shirt.

223

"If one good thing came out of it, I believe those hurtful remarks you made to Hilda have finally opened her eyes. She is a good woman in spite of what is going wrong between us. She didn't deserve you treating her that way."

"I know it, Doctor," said Shaw, resigning from trying to explain his actions any further. He took Blaine's arm from over his shoulder and helped him down onto another gurney beside the Mexican. "Once I see that Blaine is all right and hear what happened to him, I'll move on. I know this is no place for me and the trouble I bring with me."

"You like talking about how trouble follows you around, don't you?" said the doctor. He stepped away and picked up a pan of water and a washcloth. "I expect it's much easier for you to blame your trouble on some sort of predestined fate, rather than take the responsibility."

"I don't call it predestined fate, Doctor. I know I've brought on my own fate . . . the way I've lived, the path I chose."

"Do tell," Hauler commented wryly.

Shaw spoke as he watched the doctor open Blaine's shirt and look closely at the dark, bloody wound. "I don't blame anybody; I'm just stuck with it," he continued. "I wish I'd never ridden into Willow Creek and caused you and Hilda all this trouble, but I —"

"Kindly cease the familiarity of calling my wife by her first name," the doctor said, bristling.

"Excuse me," said Shaw. Even as he apologized he stopped and looked all around for another washcloth and water pan. He stopped looking when the front door opened and closed. He heard the sound of two women's footsteps as they walked across the floor.

Hilda entered the room first. She stopped and assessed the situation for a moment, giving Shaw only an awkward indirect glance. "I'll take over from here," she said crisply, unbuttoning her dress sleeves and rolling them up a little past her wrists. She stepped over to a shelf full of supplies against the far wall and came back with a pan and cloth.

"Oh, Jimmy!" said Rita, moving in closer to Blaine's gurney. "Can you hear me? Can you see me?"

"Where's . . . where's the baby?" Blaine managed to whisper without opening his weary eyes.

"She is right here," said Rita. She held the baby out for him to see. "You will be so proud of her, as I am." Blaine raised a blood-encrusted hand and let it lie softly against the blanket-wrapped baby. Shaw stood watching.

At the other gurney, Hilda said to her husband, "May I?" But then, without waiting for a response, she picked up a metal water pitcher near his side and poured water into the clean empty pan. Their eyes met for only a moment before she turned away from him and toward Blaine's gurney. Shaw noted to himself that the couple had shown no animosity, no bitterness in their eyes toward each other. Seeing it made him feel a little better. He stepped away from the doctor and his wife and moved closer to Blaine. "Who did this to you?" he asked quietly. But he already had a strong hunch who had been involved.

On the boardwalk in front of the doctor's office, the Kid stepped up to Shaw as soon as Shaw closed the door behind himself. But before the Kid asked him anything, Shaw gestured him to the side and said, low enough that Oakley and his men couldn't hear him, "Blaine says some riders from the big spread did this. Belan Foley saw the whole thing. He's on his way with the Mexican's brother, Batson, and Early Lee Springer strapped over their saddles."

"So, it's started already," the Kid said, seeming to perk up at the prospect of trouble having arrived.

"So it seems," said Shaw. "I told Blaine I'd ride out and take Foley a horse. His horse is nursing a stone bruise."

"Want some company?" the Kid asked, looking around at Oakley and his men, who stood watching them talk.

"Sure," said Shaw, "only maybe you ought to ask your pals to stay here and keep an eye on Blaine and the Mexican while we're gone. If things are heating up, I don't want to leave them here unprotected." He glanced toward Oakley, then back to the Kid. "The Mexican and his brother ride for the big spread, but it looks like the gunmen turned on them."

"Aw, yeah," said the Kid, "all the gunmen riding for the big spread must be busting to get a fight started so they can show the Frenchman how valuable they are."

The Kid pulled on a pair of leather riding gloves as he and Shaw stepped down from the boardwalk. He gestured for Free Drink, Sturgis, and Rudabaugh to gather around him, and quietly said, "I'm riding out with Shaw to meet another rancher on the trail. Keep an eye on things until we get back."

"You mean on these woodpeckers?" Free

Drink rightly interpreted. He shot a dark glance at Sid Tallow and said to the Kid, "I'll stick him a few times in his belly if you want me to."

"No, Free Drink," he said, "don't go sticking anybody while I'm gone." He turned and walked toward his horse at a hitch rail out front of the saloon. "See?" he said, giving Shaw a crooked grin. "Even my pals are busting for a fight."

Watching the Kid and Shaw mount their horses and ride out of town, Oakley said sidelong to Dubbs Hawkens and Bo Reardon, "Ease out of sight; then get your horses and follow those two. I want to know what they're up to. I'd hate to think this business has already turned into a shooting war and we don't know it yet."

"What about me?" Tallow asked.

"No, you stay with me. I'll be needing your gun if these saddle tramps start acting up."

Tallow gave a smirk. He looked toward the three ragged New Mexico Territory outlaws, liking the idea that Oakley might be in need of his gun skill.

CHAPTER 17

Not wanting to worsen the Appaloosa's stone bruise, Belan Foley had traveled on foot all the way from where he'd loaded the bodies of Jorge, Springer, and Batson on their horses. When he first spotted the two riders coming into sight around a turn in the trail, he tightened his grip on the rifle in his hand; but upon recognizing Shaw and seeing the saddled spare horse tagging along behind him, Foley breathed a sigh of relief and stopped in the trail.

"I see Blaine and the Mexican must've made it to town all right," he said as Shaw and the Kid arrived and turned their horses sideways to him. Shaw handed him the reins to a strong-looking buckskin barb.

"The doctor was patching them both up when I left," said Shaw. "Blaine was talking some. . . . He got to see his baby daughter."

"Then I expect he's a happy man," said Foley. He lifted his hat brim enough to wipe a faded red handkerchief across his brow. "He told you what happened then?" Foley gestured toward the dead.

"Yep, he told me," said Shaw. "He said you saw the whole thing."

"I sure enough did," Foley replied with a concerned expression. "I guess we shouldn't be none too surprised. We've been figuring something like this would happen once the big spread got here."

Shaw offered him a canteen of water, but Foley turned him down. "Obliged, but I got water." He patted his gloved hand on the barb's side. "What I've been needing is transportation." He looked back at Shaw and asked pointedly, "Are you going to be siding with us when it comes to a shoot-out?"

Noting the rancher had said *when,* not *if* it came to a shoot-out, Shaw replied, "It's not my intention. But I won't stand by and see good people get shot down for no reason."

"Listen up," the Kid cut in. He turned his horse quickly and saw Dubbs Hawkens and Bo Reardon ride into sight before they realized they'd been seen and heard. "Oakley's men!" the Kid shouted, snatching his Winchester from its boot.

"Wait, Kid!" said Shaw. "They are only

following, seeing what we're —"

Shaw's words were cut short by the roar of the rifle shot. The two riders had already slid to a halt in the trail when the shot kicked up a blast of dirt and rock and caused Hawkens's horse to rear up and twist back and forth out of control. Bo Reardon gigged his horse out of sight into the cover of rock alongside the trail; but as Hawkens's horse touched down it bucked high and sent its rider shooting forward into the dirt.

"Damn, Kid," Shaw growled, snatching his Colt from his holster as shots from Reardon whistled past them. "They wasn't going to do anything. They weren't expecting to run into us! We spooked them!" He fired two shots into the rocks to hold Reardon's fire while he, Foley, and the Kid took cover off the open trail.

"*Yeeehiii!* Let 'er rip!" shouted the Kid, paying no attention to Shaw. He fired round after round into the rocks, seeing Reardon duck down and cease firing.

Scurrying to his feet, Hawkens abandoned his horse and ran for cover, firing his Colt wildly over his shoulder. The Kid and Shaw both returned his fire and watched him dive out of sight into the rocks, joining Reardon. "Come on, Foley, before they start shooting again!" said Shaw, hurrying the rancher along, the limping Appaloosa slowing him down.

Behind a large boulder, Hawkens looked at Reardon while he reloaded his six-shooter. "These sonsabitches," he said. "I'm glad this happened. Now we can quit acting polite and get down to some serious killing. That's what we're getting paid to do, eh?"

But Reardon didn't reply. He only stared at Hawkens with a distressed look on his face.

"What the hell's wrong with you?" Hawkens asked, clicking his revolver shut, having finished reloading.

"I'm . . . shot," said Reardon, having to swallow a hard knot in his throat before finishing his words. He raised his hand slightly away from his inner thigh, where a ricochet from the Kid's rifle fire had sliced deep, opening a large artery. Blood shot out and splattered all around on the rocks and ground.

"Damn," said Hawkens, "that's a lot of blood. Are you going to be all right?"

"I don't know," said Reardon. His face looked white and drawn. He clamped his hand back around his thigh to slow the flow of blood, but it only caused it to gush out in a braided stream between his fingers.

232

"How much blood can a man lose . . . ?"

"Hell, I never thought about it . . . a few bottles full, I reckon," said Hawkens. He untied a bandanna from around his neck and handed it to the wounded man. "Here, stick this in it, or else tie a tourniquet around it. Make it stop."

"A few bottles full?" said Reardon, looking more and more pale and concerned. "Big bottles, small bottles, or what?" His voice turned shaky.

Hawkens stared at him in worried contemplation. "I don't know . . . but, pard, you ain't looking so good."

"A lousy damned ricochet," Reardon murmured, and closed his eyes. "That's what done it. . . ." His words trailed off.

"Shit, give it here; I'll do it," Hawkens growled. He snatched the bandanna from Reardon's bloody hand and quickly tied it around the man's thigh. He stuck his gun barrel beneath the tourniquet and twisted, tightening it. "Damn it to hell!" he said, watching the pumping blood slow, but not stop. "They're going to pay for this, Bo, the dirty sonsabitches! I promise you they will!"

From their cover behind a pile of loose rock and brush, Foley turned his face away from his aimed rifle resting in the fork of a dried scrap of pine, and asked Shaw, "Do

233

you think they skinned out of here?"

Shaw looked at Hawkens's horse standing off to the other side of the trail. "On one horse? I doubt it."

"Something's sure quieted them down," the Kid commented, his rifle lying across the top of a rock. "Hey, in the rocks . . . you two regulator snakes!" he called out. "Come on out with your hands held high." He gave Shaw a glance and grinned.

"All right, I'll come out with my hands high," said Hawkens.

Looking at Shaw again, this time in surprise, the Kid said in a lowered voice, "I didn't think he'd do it. Hell, I was only joshing."

"So is he, Kid," Shaw said in a serious tone.

Hawkens sprang from the cover of rocks and ran toward them, screaming and firing his Colt until Shaw stood straight up and fired a single shot.

The dead gunman fell faceup, a bullet hole in the center of his forehead.

"Good shot!" the Kid said. "I get the other one, though."

Shaw just looked at him, realizing that every move they made out here was going to draw them deeper into the coming range war.

"All right," the Kid called out toward the rocks, "your pal is dead. Stand up and face me one on one. Let's get it done." He lay his Winchester down and stood up in the open, his hand poised near his Colt Thunderer.

Sitting slumped against a rock, Shaw shook his head, sighed to himself, and said, "Kid, get down before you get yourself killed."

"No, I'm good with this, Shaw," the Kid replied. His eyes focused on the place where he'd seen Reardon take cover, his fingers fidgeting near his Colt. "Stand up, Bo Reardon. I'm sending you straight to hell."

"Jesus," Shaw murmured to himself.

"Kid," Foley called out, "*please* get down! We don't want to lose nobody else out here."

"I want to do this," the Kid said with determination. He started walking slowly forward.

"Either the man is dead or else he's gone," Shaw said to Foley, standing slowly and following the Kid.

Foley followed Shaw's lead and stood up slowly, his rifle cocked and ready. The three spread out as they covered the twenty-yard distance and eased warily around the large boulder where Reardon had taken cover.

"Well, I guess that's that," said the Kid,

looking down at Reardon, who lay as if asleep on a wide circle of bloody ground.

"Yeah, that's that, all right," Shaw repeated, stepping forward and kicking a gun away from Reardon's hand out of habit. He slipped his big Colt back into his holster, realizing the furor this could cause in town.

"Hey, Shaw," the Kid asked, his expression turning cross. "Have you got a mad-on over what I did, firing a warning shot at these two? Because I'm thinking if I didn't, they would have . . . and it might not've been a warning shot if they'd had one of us in their sights."

"No, Kid," said Shaw, letting go of any blame he might have held for the Kid having started the fight. "I've got no mad-on at you. These boys hired in for a fight. I expect nothing was going to stop it anyway." He looked back across the sky in the direction of Willow Creek. "Let's go tell everybody what happened out here . . . see how it sets with everybody."

"It will set the way it *is,*" said the Kid. "If the Frenchman or anybody else don't like it, they can step forward and take it up."

"I know, Kid," said Shaw. He turned and walked back toward his horse. "I'd be foolish to expect it any other way."

"I swear, Shaw," said the Kid with a

chuckle, following him toward the horses to help load up the dead, "you can be the gloomiest man I ever seen." He spread an arm toward the bodies on the ground and the dead lying strapped over their saddles. "Look at these poor sumbitches! All they got to look forward to is a faceful of dirt or a coyote supper."

"Let's not talk right now, Kid," Shaw said over his shoulder, "all right?"

LeBlanc and Otto Perls rode at the head of the column of armed men bound for Willow Creek. Behind them rode Red Downing, Dick Harpin, and the same four California gunmen who'd been with Downing when he had met the Katlins on the trail and brought them to camp. Behind Downing rode the Katlin brothers and their men. When the riders met the small string of cattle coming toward them, they moved to one side and watched Bertrim Sipes and Bobby Shoats ride into sight.

"Well, well," LeBlanc said to Herr Perls with a flat grin, "it appears I've begun regathering my wayward gunmen."

Seeing LeBlanc and Perls, Sipes and Shoats nudged their horses into a trot the last few yards and slid them to a halt as the cattle plodded on along the trail. "Mr. Le-

Blanc! Mr. Perls!" said Sipes, greeting them. But then to Red Downing and his men, he said, "We sure are damn glad to see all of you!"

"What's up, Sipes?" Downing asked, pushing his horse up beside LeBlanc. He could see that Sipes had serious business on his mind. Looking around, he asked, "Where's the Mexicans?"

LeBlanc contented himself to sit back, listen, and observe for the time being.

"Jorge and Ramon are dead!" said Sipes. "We got jumped by some gunmen on the way back from Sabo Canyon with these cattle."

"Did you get a look at them?" asked Downing.

"Oh, yes, we even got their names before the fight broke out," said Sipes. "But they're nothing to worry about now; they're dead too. We was just afraid we'd run into more of them on our way to camp! There's lots of small ranchers and settlers in Sabo Canyon, every damn one of them up in arms over us being here, these men told us."

LeBlanc, deciding he had heard enough, cut in and asked Sipes, "Where are Jorge's and Ramon's bodies?"

"Right along the trail where we left them," said Sipes. "We figured we'd better not

238

waste time burying Mexicans when we could be hit by more ranchers anytime." He looked at Downing. "Did we do right, Red?"

"Yep, as far as I'm concerned, you did," said Downing. He gave Sipes and Shoats a questioning look and said, "But I'd like to see these bodies before I go making any snap judgments."

"I don't blame you a bit," said Sipes. "Just stay on this trail; you'll come to them. Soon as Bobby and me get these cattle to the herd we'll turn back and join you."

LeBlanc intervened, saying, "I will send the Katlins to take the cattle on to camp. You two ride with us. We are going to Willow Creek."

"Willow Creek?" Sipes mused. "Well, then — hell, yes, me and Bobby wouldn't miss this for nothing."

In the rear, having heard LeBlanc, T. J. Katlin whispered to his brother Lane, "What the hell did he say? Send us back? Why can't he send them Californian sons-abitches?"

"Easy, brother," Lane whispered in reply. "We might start out taking the cattle back to camp. But damned if we're going to get this close to Shaw once again and not take a hand in killing him."

At the lead, LeBlanc called out to the Kat-

239

lins and gestured them up front.

"Here we go," said Lane to T. J. "Now don't argue."

"Not me," said T. J. "I'll follow your lead. Let's get the cattle out of here and get rid of them."

In moments the Katlin Gang had taken their orders from LeBlanc without a whimper. The six of them fell in around the cattle and kept them moving at a steady pace while LeBlanc and the others moved on along the trail. In the afternoon, LeBlanc and his men circled the spot where the bodies had been left lying in the dirt.

"Well, now . . ." said Downing. He looked all around at the dark bloodstains and saw a handprint where someone had pushed himself up from the ground. "It looks like somebody lived through the carnage." He looked at Sipes and Shoats and motioned with a gloved hand toward the hoofprints leading off toward Willow Creek. "At least we're all headed in the same direction."

LeBlanc said to Sipes, "Did you not make sure these men were dead before you left?"

"Well, we saw them fall, Mr. LeBlanc, and Bobby and I aren't known for having to go over our work once it's done. We are professionals, and like I said, we didn't know how many more might be swooping down from the rocks."

"It could be a problem if these men made it to town alive," said Downing.

"Oh?" said LeBlanc. "Not if our men here swear to what they have told us." He gestured a thick hand toward Sipes and Shoats. "If we find these men alive in Willow Creek, we would be justified to hang them for what they have done, would we not? For attacking my men, for killing two of my drovers?"

"Well, yes, that's true enough," said Red, "if the law will stand still for it."

"The law?" said LeBlanc. "Harpin tells me that there is only a doctor who is attempting to keep the law in Willow Creek until a *real* lawman can be appointed."

"That's true," said Dick Harpin. "All the doc is doing is sort of keeping check on things. He's no gunman, nobody to worry about." He grinned. "Hell, we could hang half the town; he couldn't stop us."

"There, gentlemen," LeBlanc said smugly, "we will be the law." He turned to Otto Perls and said, "Herr Perls, it appears that you might get to witness a real frontier hanging. Wouldn't that be something worth seeing?"

Perls gave him a stunned look and finally said after a moment of deliberation, "Yas . . . dat vould be most interesting."

241

■ ■ ■ ■

PART 3

■ ■ ■ ■

CHAPTER 18

Ever since Shaw and the Kid had left town, and Reardon and Hawkens had gone to follow them, Oakley had been talking to Sid Tallow about the best way to go about killing a big gunman like Shaw. "I don't see any reason I couldn't just call him out, pop a couple of bullets in him, and be done with it," Tallow said. "If you ask me, I think everybody has cut him too wide a cloth."

"I have thought that very same thing myself," said Oakley, keeping the young gunman's confidence up. "I just never told anybody."

"Yeah?" As Tallow spoke he slipped his Colt from his tied-down holster and spun it masterfully back and forth on his shooting finger. "You ever seen me shoot?"

"Yes, a time or two, remember?" said Oakley.

Tallow shook his head. "Naw, I mean have you ever seen me really shoot? I'm not talking about those two Chinamen or that drunken half-breed down in Kansas."

Oakley smiled at him in a fatherly way. "If you put it that way, no, I expect I haven't seen you really shoot." He passed the tall bottle of rye whiskey back to Tallow, encouraging him to take another drink. "But I've always known you was good with a gun. That's why I've always asked for you to ride with me when the Frenchman sends me out." The two of them stood in front of the saloon, watching the trail Shaw and the Kid had taken.

"Yeah?" Tallow tossed him a glance, still twirling and back-twirling the Colt.

"Oh, yeah. Yes, indeed," said Oakley. "I trust you more than any man out here. I've never said this, but if I had a son, I'd want him to be just like you."

"No kidding?" Tallow looked proud. He stopped twirling the Colt and slipped it back into his holster.

"The absolute truth," said Oakley. "Now, based on my experience administering the law, let me tell you what I think's the best way to kill Shaw." He nodded toward a window on the second floor of the building housing the restaurant. "A man positioned up there with a Winchester has a far better chance of killing Shaw quick and clean than

246

he would facing him down in the street. He wouldn't have to worry about Bonney and his pals turning on him no sooner than he got his killing done."

"But I can take Shaw straight up," Tallow insisted. "And I can take William Bonney and his girlie-looking pal to boot."

"Bonney and Free Drink?" said Oakley. "Hell, I have no doubt you can. But why do it that way? Why take a chance on even getting yourself nicked?" He nodded again toward the window. "Take my word for it, Sid — this is the best way."

"But if I killed Shaw," said Tallow, "I would want to be able to claim doing it . . . take the big-gun reputation away from him the minute his eyes close."

"You'd still get it," said Oakley. "Oh, at first maybe folks would say you ambushed him. But give that story time to circulate around a little, and everybody will forget how you killed him . . . but they'd never forget the fact that you *did* kill him."

"Hmmm . . ." Tallow gazed up at the window, then out along the trail. He took another drink and smiled to himself.

Inside the saloon, Free Drink, Sturgis, and Rudabaugh drank whiskey and stared out at Oakley and Sid Tallow above the bat-wing doors. "There's a certain kind of sonsabitch

247

that I always think if I don't kill, he'll be the one who kills me, sure as hell," said Free Drink. He tossed back his whiskey, let out a hiss, and said, "Them two are both that kind of sonsabitches."

"We promised Billy we'd have no trouble with anybody before he gets back," Rudabaugh cautioned him.

"That was no promise," said Free Drink. "That was more like a wishful expectation we all three placed upon ourselves."

"Well, whatever it was, we made it," said Rudabaugh. "I'll not be the one to break it."

"Yeah." Free Drink sighed. "Me neither. If it was anybody but Billy, though . . ." He shook his head slowly.

It was late afternoon before Shaw, the Kid, and Foley came riding in, leading the dead on their horses behind them. "Damn," Oakley growled under his breath, seeing the bodies of Hawkens and Reardon riding facedown over their saddles. "Trust those two idiots to go get themselves killed!" He and Tallow eased back out of sight and stood watching from the corner of an alley.

With a crowd of onlookers gathering behind them, Shaw, the Kid, and Foley stopped in front of the doctor's office. "See if you can get a wagon or buggy ready to roll. If Blaine is able to travel, slip him out of town tonight after dark."

"I hear you," Foley replied quietly as Dr. Hauler walked out the door, throwing on his suit coat, and stepped off the boardwalk.

"How is Blaine, Doctor?" Foley asked before the doctor began to speak.

"He's resting right now, Foley, but he's going to be all right," said Hauler. He stared at the dead with a grim expression. "This is all we need," he said, recognizing the bodies of Batson and Springer. He looked at the Mexican, then at the two regulators who had been with Oakley in town the past few days. He looked coldly at Shaw with accusation in his eyes. "I suppose I shouldn't be surprised. What happened, Shaw?"

"These two regulators followed us all the way out. They ran into us by surprise and a gun battle commenced." He shrugged.

"We won," the Kid cut in.

"Of course," said Hauler, sounding a bit sarcastic. "I suppose it goes without saying that they fired the first shots?"

"One of us fired a warning shot when we caught them following us," Shaw replied, not wanting to give anything up, but mindful that the doctor was also acting in a legal capacity on the town's behalf.

"And I suppose you are the one who fired the warning shot?" asked Hauler.

"You suppose wrong, sawbones," the Kid cut in again, not allowing Shaw to be put on the spot for something the Kid had done. "*I* fired that shot." He looked all around for Oakley and Tallow, not seeing them. Still, he called out loud enough for everyone around to hear, "I fired it . . . and I kept on firing. The truth is, I killed both these regulators — in self-defense, that is."

"What about it, Foley?" the doctor asked, implying that Foley was the only one of the three he could trust to tell the truth. "Was this a case of self-defense?"

"Yes, it was self-defense," Foley stated firmly, avoiding the details, "and there's going to be a lot more self-defense going on around here before it's over." Looking around, he added, "With all due respect, Doctor, you don't want to be asking too many questions until this thing with the European spread gets settled. I know you're committed to upholding the law here till we get a sheriff, but you might want to take back that commitment and stick to treating the ill and infirm. Lord knows there are going to be plenty of them for you."

"I take my commitment seriously, Foley," the doctor said firmly, looking at Shaw as he spoke. "If someone else will step forward, I'll gladly step down."

A tense silence passed. Finally Foley said, "I'll take it over, Doctor. This town knows me . . . knows I'll do my best to uphold the law —"

Dr. Hauler cut in, "Use your head, Foley. All we need is for the Frenchman and his men to hear that a local rancher is in charge here! My goodness. That would only add fuel to the fire."

Foley backed his horse up a step, the Appaloosa on a lead rope backing with him. "This is one fire won't need no fueling," he said. "If you don't need me, I'll be on my way to the livery barn. My horse needs tending." He looked at the Kid and Shaw. "Obliged, both of you." He said to Hauler, "Tell Blaine I'll be by later to look in on him."

"Unless you need a statement from me about what happened, Doctor," said Shaw, "I'm on my way."

The Kid looked surprised. "You're leaving? Right now? Just when things are starting to get fun around here?"

"Not my kind of fun, Kid," said Shaw. He touched his hat brim as he turned his horse in the dirt street and started to ride away.

Free Drink, Sturgis, and Rudabaugh had

251

hurried over from the saloon and gathered to one side, watching and listening. "Hey, Billy," said Free Drink, seeing Shaw turn to leave, "if he's going south why don't we ride with him, get the hell out of here while we can?"

The Kid said quietly to Free Drink, "He ain't going nowhere."

"Like hell he ain't," said Rudabaugh. "He's getting smaller every step. I could stand to get out of here myself, get on across the border and lie low awhile."

Gazing up the dirt street, watching Shaw, the Kid perked up and said with a crooked grin, "I told you: Now watch this — see how easy it is to get into trouble when you're the fastest gun alive."

In front of the saloon, Shaw stopped in the middle of the street and looked down at Merlyn Oakley, who had stepped out of an alley and stood facing him. Seeing the look on Shaw's face, Oakley raised his hands up away from his gun butt and said, "Whoa, Shaw! This is nothing like that! I didn't come to call you out. I just walked out to ask you what happened to Hawkens and Reardon."

"Why didn't you walk out here when we rode in?" Shaw asked bluntly. As Shaw spoke, he kept a close watch in his peripheral vision on the open window above the restaurant, where a pair of curtains swung lazily in an afternoon breeze.

"Easy, Shaw," said Oakley. Shaw watched him take a step back and raise his hat brim for no apparent reason. There it was — a signal if he'd ever seen one! Oakley's hand made the slightest start toward his holstered pistol. Shaw's Colt streaked up from its holster too fast to be seen, and fired. But the shot wasn't at Oakley, whose hand moved even quicker now.

Shaw's first shot still resounded as he fired again, this time sending Oakley backward. Before he could even raise the tip of his gun barrel from his holster, the former police detective fell dead in the dirt, as above the street shattered glass, flapping curtains, and a broken window frame spilled forward, with Tallow's body falling in the midst of it.

The Kid blinked as if in awe as the fusion of glass splinters and bloody flesh rolled down the metal-roofed overhang and tumbled to the ground. "Damn!" he said down to Free Drink and the others. "And you want to leave all this?" His horse crow-hopped nervously beneath him. But he reined it in, nailed his boots to its sides, and sent it racing down the middle of the street toward Shaw.

Shaw half turned in his saddle, his Colt coming around at the pounding sound of the horse's hooves. "Damn, Shaw, you sure know how to fill a day!" the Kid said, sliding his horse up beside Shaw. He looked down at the bodies in the dirt. "The old rifle backup, eh?" He shook his head. "What made a man like Oakley think a man like you would fall for something like that?"

"I don't know, Kid," said Shaw. "But it looks like everything I do here is causing trouble that somebody else is going to have to clean up after I'm gone."

"Yep, it does look that way," the Kid said, not allowing himself an I-told-you-so smile toward his pals, who came running up to them.

From inside the restaurant the owner plodded out, looking first at Shaw, then at the bodies in the dirt, one tangled in bloody curtains and sprinkled with broken glass. With a blank expression he turned his gaze up to the gaping hole where the window had been. Then he threw up his hands as if in surrender. He turned, walked back inside, and slammed the door.

"I don't know what to say to that fellow anymore," Shaw said, shaking his head.

The Kid, feeling Free Drink tug on his boot, looked out with his pals along the trail

254

leading into town. He looked back at Shaw and said, "Don't worry about what to say to him . . . look who's coming here."

Shaw raised his head enough to see the big Frenchman riding at the head of a column of men in a low swirl of trail dust. "Well, before I leave," he said, "I'm going to have to be sure they understand who did this and why." He raised his Colt, opened the chamber, dropped out his empty shells, and began replacing them with fresh rounds.

The Kid looked down silently at Free Drink, Sturgis, and Rudabaugh and gave them a knowing grin.

As the Frenchman and his men rode up on the dirt street, Shaw said, "Kid, now would be a good time for you and your pals to get off the street. I'm going to try telling them what just happened here and see where it takes me." He lifted his Winchester from its boot and laid it across his lap, his hand resting in position, his finger going inside the trigger guard.

"I believe I'll stick," said the Kid. Looking down at his pals, he said, "Anybody feels a sudden need to travel, he'd best get to doing it."

"Aw, hell," said Rudabaugh, "we ain't going nowhere without you, are we, boys?"

"Naw, not me," said Free Drink, adjusting

his gun belt.

"Me neither," said Sturgis. He spit and ran a hand over his mouth. "Not on account of this tub of guts."

"Do me a favor then," said the Kid without looking down at them. "Spread out some so one damn shot don't kill every one of us."

Behind them on the street, townsfolk had ventured forward to see what had happened between Shaw and Oakley; but upon seeing the Frenchman and his riders come into sight, the onlookers moved back warily and disappeared into doorways and alleys.

At the door of the livery barn, Foley had heard the shots. Now he stood looking on, rifle in hand as the Frenchman rode up to Shaw and stopped a respectable fifteen feet away, his men spreading out slightly behind him.

"You must be Mr. Shaw," LeBlanc said, looking first at the bodies of his two regulators, then up at Shaw's impassive expression.

"You must be the Frenchman," Shaw said, one wrist on his saddle horn holding his reins loosely, his other hand on his rifle.

"His name is Mr. LeBlanc!" Red Downing said in a bristly tone.

"This must have just happened," said Le-

Blanc. "The two shots we heard?"

"That's right," said Shaw. "They're lying where they landed. Look them over good; you'll see how it all played out."

"You don't tell Mr. LeBlanc what to do, Shaw," said Downing.

Without taking his eyes off of the Frenchman, Shaw said to Downing in a level tone, "That's twice you've spoken out of turn to me."

"Yeah, *and*?" Downing asked, not backing down an inch in front of his employer, especially with so many guns backing him up. Beside LeBlanc, Perls sat rigid in his saddle, staring with excitement, a monocle raised to his left eye.

"That's enough, Red," said LeBlanc, returning Shaw's stare. "You fired both shots?" he asked Shaw. "Neither of them had the chance to get a shot off?" He looked Shaw up and down.

"That's right, too," said Shaw.

LeBlanc nodded and looked up at the gaping window opening above the restaurant. "It's plain to see what these two had in mind. It looks like they picked the wrong man to double up on."

"Right again," said Shaw. He sat staring at the big Frenchman.

LeBlanc gestured a hand toward the

bodies of Hawkens and Reardon lying over their saddles in front of the doctor's office. "That looks like two more of my men. I recognize the horses." He gave a tight, smug grin.

"They followed us out of town," said Shaw. "Things got out of control. One died from a ricochet, the other from stupidity. Anyway, there they are."

"Yes, there they are," said LeBlanc, staring intently at Shaw. He gestured Red Downing toward the two bodies.

Downing rode over quickly, stepped down, and looked at the ricochet wound in Reardon's leg and the gaping exit wound in Hawkens's back. "Yep, it's Hawkens and Reardon, all right," he called out. "One's bled out; the other's shot clean through."

"Are you on the local rancher's side, riding against me, Shaw?" LeBlanc asked pointedly, concealing his embarrassment and rage at the deaths of four of his men today, in addition to the two he'd sent Oakley and these other three to investigate.

"I'm not on anybody's side," said Shaw.

LeBlanc cocked his big head to the side and gazed at him suspiciously. "A noted gunman like you, in a heated situation like we have here? Six men dead? It's hard to accept that you haven't taken sides."

"Accept it, LeBlanc," said Shaw. "If these men of yours had accepted it, they wouldn't be dead."

Having ridden up and heard Shaw's words, Red Downing said hotly, "Are you threatening Mr. LeBl—"

"Enough, Red!" said LeBlanc. The Frenchman could see something flicker darkly in Shaw's eyes, and recalled Shaw warning Downing twice about speaking out of turn to him.

The Kid also saw the look in Shaw's eyes, and he laid his hand on the butt of his Colt, removing any doubt of what was about to happen. "He told you we're not on anybody's side," the Kid cut in. "Shaw and us go our own way. Finish your piece."

"You are Bonney, William Bonney?" LeBlanc asked, turning his head slowly toward the Kid.

"That's my name, for now, anyways."

"Here is my piece," said LeBlanc. "How would you men like to hire on and work for me for a while?" He looked back and forth between Shaw and the Kid. "Just long enough to keep down any trouble? After all, you two have left me six men short."

"You rode all this way just to recruit a couple of guns?" Shaw asked, knowing better.

"I rode here looking for a man named Jim Blaine. He and two others ambushed and killed a couple of my Mexican drovers. I wish to hang him from a nearby tree."

"Not judge, no jury, no trial?" Shaw asked.

"Under these circumstances, I didn't think those things were required here in the land of the lawless," said LeBlanc.

"They're not; I'm just checking," Shaw said calmly.

"So, then, about the job offer?" said LeBlanc.

"I'm not looking for any work," the Kid said flatly.

"Neither am I," said Shaw.

"Perhaps we need to talk more about it," said LeBlanc.

"I'm all through talking. I'm leaving town." Shaw turned his horse and put it into a walk, knowing that all the Frenchman wanted was to pay him and the Kid not to get involved.

"I want your word that I won't be seeing you around Willow Creek again," LeBlanc called out in a firm tone.

"I only give my word to friends, LeBlanc," Shaw replied over his shoulder in parting. "You and I hardly know each other."

"Indeed, Mr. Shaw," LeBlanc said under his breath, watching Shaw's horse move away at a walk. "But we're getting better acquainted all the time."

CHAPTER 19

Seeing Shaw ride out of sight past the edge of town, the Kid backed his horse up a few feet and turned it toward the saloon. Free Drink, Sturgis, and Rudabaugh walked away half sideways, not turning their backs on the Frenchman and his regulators. "See how easy it is to get out of trouble when you're the fastest gun alive?" said Free Drink.

In the street, Downing sat atop his horse, seething, watching the Kid step down from his saddle and lead his pals inside the saloon. "With all due respect, Mr. LeBlanc," he said, "we shoulda killed them all while we had them rounded up together. You can't buy off men like Shaw or William Bonney."

"Ah, spoken like an uncultured Anglo-American, eh, Herr Perls?" said LeBlanc.

The German only nodded with a thin, knowing smile.

"Again, with all due respect, sir," said

Downing, ignoring the insult, "I'm afraid you don't know enough about this Fast Larry Shaw, or William Bonney and his pals. The Kid is treacherous and crazy. His so-called pals are stone-cold killers, to the man. Shaw is fast and dangerous — as these four stiffs go to prove." He gestured a hand toward the bodies on the street and in front of the doctor's office.

"Yes, of course I see," said LeBlanc impatiently. "I do not discount any of these frontier vermin." He settled and let out a breath. "But why take a chance on losing any more men here today, when I have the whole Katlin Gang itching to kill them for us?"

"We had them cold," Downing murmured.

"We still do," LeBlanc said confidently. He looked back and forth until he spotted the hotel. "Besides, we have other things to do here." He smiled at Herr Perls and nodded toward the hotel. "Let us get out of the sun and discuss matters at hand. I want this man Blaine found and hanged for what he did. We have the law on our side in that matter." He looked at Bertrim Sipes and Bobby Shoats and said, "Provided you two are telling the truth, and there are no witnesses to say otherwise."

263

"It's the truth," said Sipes.

"Absolutely," said Shoats.

"And you're certain he was wounded?" LeBlanc asked quietly, gazing toward the sign above the door of the doctor's office.

"I'd swear to it," said Sipes.

"Me too," said Shoats.

"That narrows our search considerably, gentlemen," said LeBlanc.

"Want me to go kick in the door?" Downing asked.

"Of course not," said LeBlanc. "Stop thinking like a brute Westerner." He nudged his horse toward the hitch rail in front of the hotel.

Above the bat-wing saloon doors, the Kid watched the regulators follow LeBlanc and step down from their saddles at the hitch rail. As the men filed inside the hotel behind the leader, he saw Dick Harpin walk toward the livery barn, leading his horse behind him. "The Frenchman is no fool," the Kid said, turning to face Free Drink, who stood three feet behind him, sipping on a mug of beer. "I bet it took him every bit of two seconds to figure where to find Blaine. We might just as well have pointed to the doctor's office for him."

"Why is it so all-fired important to him to get his hands on Blaine?" said Free Drink.

"He let you and Shaw get away with killing his gunmen."

"Like I said, he's no fool," said the Kid. "Had he ordered his men to try anything on me and Shaw, he knew he'd be the first to hit the dirt." The Kid gave a crooked grin. "But he still has to shove his weight around on somebody. Might as well be Blaine."

"So Blaine is what you call a Jonas goat," said Free Drink. "Somebody to take it all out on."

"A Jonas goat?" The Kid gave him a puzzled look. "I don't know what you're talking about," he said. "But the Frenchman knows he's not welcome here, and he knows there's a fight coming. He figures hanging Blaine for killing his drover is a sure way to put the fear of God into everybody for a while, at least long enough for him to fatten his cattle and move them on to market."

"I meant a *Judas* goat," said Free Drink.

"You meant a scapegoat, or whatever," said the Kid. "Anyways, all these waddies and sodbusters around here look up to Blaine." He added as if thinking out loud, "I reckon that's a good enough reason, too." He gazed out along the street. "It's up to us to keep them from doing it."

"Why is that our business all of a sudden?" Free Drink asked.

The Kid didn't answer. Instead he turned to Belan Foley, who stood at the bar, listening, looking out of place with two outlaws like the Kid and Free Drink Stemlet. "Did you find a buckboard at the livery barn?"

"Yep, I already told you I did," said Foley, not looking up from his mug of beer. Before the Kid could ask him, he said, "And I didn't do anything that might tip off Harpin about what we're going to do."

"Then we're all set come dark," said the Kid, giving Free Drink a look.

"As soon as Blaine is safe out of town, we ought to leave here ourselves," said Free Drink, "even if all three of us have to knock you in the head and drag you out of here."

"We'll leave before long," said the Kid. Looking out toward the hotel, he said, "Boys, it looks like a big powwow is going on. As soon as it's over this place will be crawling with regulators."

"But no trouble, right, Billy?" said Free Drink. "We keep everything going smooth, wait until after dark, then get Blaine out of here?"

"No trouble here," said the Kid. "But right there went the son of a bitch we'd better take care of." He nodded toward the livery barn, where Dick Harpin had gone moments ago. "If he sees Foley come get that buckboard tonight he'll squeal to Le-Blanc like a stuck pig." He turned to Free Drink and said matter-of-factly, "Maybe you ought to raise him up on your pig-sticker."

"Sure thing," said Free Drink. "Can I do it however I want to?"

"Within reason," the Kid said with a grin.

At the bar Foley fidgeted a bit in place and sipped his beer, the casual talk of killing a man making him uncomfortable. "You won't have to kill Dick Harpin," he said. "The buckboard is sitting out back of the barn. I can get it ready and ease it away without him knowing anything."

"Well, then, hear that, Free Drink?" said the Kid. "You won't have to stick him after all. Ain't that dandy?" But even as he said it, he gave Free Drink a look and nodded toward the livery barn. "Go make friends."

Free Drink smiled and batted his eye-lashes. He loosened his gun belt and hung it over a chair back.

When Shaw had left town, he'd ridden only a mile out before turning and circling back in a wide loop, avoiding being seen from the streets of Willow Creek. Taking a back alley that ran the length of the town, he made his way unnoticed to the back door of the doctor's office and slipped inside. The first to see him come into the room was Rita, who still sat by Blaine's bed with the baby sleeping on her lap. She looked at Shaw with a concerned expression. "Lawrence, what is going on out there? Are those men looking for Jimmy?"

"Yes, I'm afraid so," said Shaw. Hilda stepped into the room and let out a slight gasp at the sight of him. "I'm only here to see about getting Blaine out of town in one piece," he said. "I hope everybody will help me — help *Blaine,* that is."

Hilda's gaze turned icy, but she understood Blaine's situation. "I'm sure the doctor will want to —"

"Help Jimmy Blaine any way I can," said the doctor, stepping into the room and finishing her words for her. He looked at Shaw with the same icy stare. "I saw you ride out, but I knew you wouldn't leave Blaine at these men's mercy, in spite of what I think of you." He managed a look of contempt. "The Frenchman must know he's in here being treated. What is it you plan to do?"

"Tonight I plan on getting Blaine out of town, if you tell me he can ride," said Shaw.

"If he can't ride, I'll have to hide him somewhere in town until LeBlanc and his men leave. They mean to hang him."

"I can ride," Blaine said from his bed. "What about Ramon?"

"The only men interested in Ramon will be the ones who did the killing and don't want any living witnesses," said Shaw. "They won't try anything with LeBlanc around. But they will hang you, Blaine, just to make a point that he's the cock of the walk."

"Get me booted . . . give me a push." Blaine still sounded weak from having lost so much blood.

"That's good, Blaine," said Shaw. But he looked to the doctor for an answer.

"Yes, he can ride, if he must. They both can." The doctor looked at Ramon asleep on the other gurney. Then he let out a breath of exasperation. "There's a folding gurney in the shed out back. Take Blaine out there right now, before they come looking here for him."

"The baby and I must go with him when you leave tonight," said Rita.

"No," said Shaw. "It's far too risky. He can come back for you after things have cooled down some." Yet, even as he told her no, he pictured her perched on the buckboard seat with the baby on her lap.

"*Por favor,* Lawrence," she pleaded, seeing him consider it.

"Not now, Rita; we'll talk about it later," said Shaw, knowing this was no time to discuss it with her. He moved to the front room and parted the curtains an inch, checking the street before moving Blaine out of the office. Two regulators stood out front of the hotel. The street lay empty, as if in tense anticipation. But out of sight, Shaw watched Free Drink ease out the side door of the saloon and walk toward the livery barn. "Free Drink . . ." he whispered to himself. He saw the man was unarmed, but he knew full well that something was at hand.

At the door to the livery barn, the young outlaw stepped inside and looked around in the darkened barn for Harpin, calling out, "Yoo-hoo, Dick! Where are you?"

"Yoo-hoo?" Harpin stepped forward from a stall where he kept a bottle of whiskey. "You sound like a New Orleans whore warbling."

"Just trying to sound friendly," said Free Drink, shrugging, showing Harpin that his hands were both empty.

"I bet you are. You look drunk as a hoot owl," said Harpin. He palmed the cork back into the bottle. "What the hell do you want?

I told you before, I don't want you coming here."

"Hey, settle down," said Free Drink, walking closer. His voice sounded a little stronger. "Maybe I am drunk, but I don't have to take your insults."

"You do if Henry McCarty and your pals are not with you, *Wild Rose,*" said Harpin.

"He's not McCarty anymore," said Free Drink. "He's William Bonney . . . or *Billy the Kid.*"

"Yeah? Well, he's nothing in my book."

"I'll tell him you said so. He'll be *really* happy to hear it." Free Drink smiled demurely.

Harpin reconsidered his attitude and said, "Aw, hell, I didn't mean nothing. I've been riding with the regulators, now that *I'm* one. I'm a little saddle-weary."

"A regulator now! Well, congratulations," said Free Drink. "That's what I come here to talk to you about, sort of."

"Sort of?" said Harpin. "Either it is or it ain't. If you've got something to say, spit it out."

"Blaine is in the doctor's office," Free Drink said quickly, as if not wanting to think about the harm he might be doing Jimmy Blaine. "I thought you might want to take the news to LeBlanc." Free Drink

271

stopped less than a foot from Harpin, but the liveryman didn't back away.

"LeBlanc already knows, or at least suspects it," said Harpin, his voice a little friendlier. "Here, have one on me." He handed Free Drink the bottle and watched him take a step back, pull the cork, and raise the bottle to his lips.

"What the hell, I thought I'd give it a try," said Free Drink, after he'd taken a swig and passed the bottle back to Harpin. "You and me used to be pretty good friends back in Cheyenne, remember?"

"We never was as close of friends as you wanted to think we was," said Harpin. "Even if we was, things change. This is hard country. A man has to be careful who he sides with." He stepped back farther, putting another two feet between him and Free Drink. "Like I said, I'm a regulator now."

"I see," said Free Drink, satisfied, having seen how close he could get to Harpin. "Then maybe it would help you to know that Shaw is sneaking Blaine out of town after dark."

"Yeah? Go on." Harpin's interest was piqued.

"Blaine is wounded, sure enough. They'll be on what's called the old short trail that runs down alongside the creek before it comes down onto the flatlands. I heard Shaw tell the Kid. If the Kid knew I told you, he'd kill me stone-dead."

"He won't hear it from me," said Harpin, thinking over the information. "This might be worth something to LeBlanc. I'll pass it along."

"How about telling him I'm the one who told you?" Free Drink asked.

"Ah." Harpin smiled. "So you'd like a little something for your trouble?"

"Money ain't near as important as being friends," said Free Drink.

"Naw, forget all that *friends* stuff," said Harpin, brushing it aside. "If there's a couple dollars in it, I'll see you get half."

"You don't see me and you ever riding together for the Frenchman?" said Free Drink.

"I don't see me and you ever riding for anybody," said Harpin. "LeBlanc only hires the best." His chest broadened. He passed the bottle back to Free Drink. "Here, have another. I've got a few minutes."

CHAPTER 20

Dick Harpin left the livery barn in a manner that allowed him to make his way to the rear door of the hotel without being seen from the saloon. Once inside he took his information straight to LeBlanc. Upon hearing that Blaine was indeed convalescing in the doctor's office, the big Frenchman smiled at Perls.

"And this was told to you by one of William Bonney's own men?" he asked when Harpin was finished talking.

"It's reliable," said Harpin. "I pried it out of him with a bottle of whiskey," he lied, hoping LeBlanc might offer to reimburse him for the cost of the rye.

LeBlanc made no such offer. Instead he said to Perls, who sat beside him, "See?" He spread his large hands. "It is always better to rely first on intelligence sources rather than turn immediately to gunfire. This is how I operate the cattle syndicate, and this is what you and the other investors can always expect from me."

The old German nodded with admiration. "Vat will be our move now?"

"Thanks to Harpin here," said the Frenchman, turning his smile back to the livery tender, "we will all quietly ride out of town before dark as if headed back to the herd, but when Lawrence Shaw takes the wounded ambusher out tonight, I will have some of my top men waiting for them. With Blaine legally hanged, we will soon find the rest of the ranchers ready to cooperate."

"What do you want from me now?" Harpin said eagerly, feeling good about being so useful.

"Where is the man who told you this?" LeBlanc asked.

"He's passed out drunk in a stall full of hay where I left him," said Harpin. "I can kill him in his sleep or send him packing. It's your call." He smiled proudly.

"Right now," said the Frenchman, "go back to the livery barn, keep your eyes on him, and keep him with you. I don't want him going back to his friends and perhaps revealing what he has told you. Keep him drinking and keep him happy. If anything unusual occurs, come tell me. If not, sit still until you hear from me."

"You can count on it, Mr. LeBlanc," said Harpin.

Before he could turn to leave, the Frenchman said, "Oh, here, take this and buy another bottle for your friend and yourself." He fished a large gold coin from his vest pocket and gave it to Harpin. *"Bon boire, boire heureux,"* he said in French.

"Begging your pardon, sir?" asked Harpin with a puzzled look.

Perls cut in, saying, "He wishes you good and happy drinking. *Gutes trinken, glückliches trinken."*

"Oh, well, thank you, thank you both," said Harpin, curtsying a little as he backed away, turned, and headed for the door.

Perls chuckled and said to LeBlanc in German, "These Americans . . . they drink only to get drunk."

On Harpin's way through the lobby of the hotel, Bobby Shoats stepped in front of him, rudely stopping him. "Get out of my way, Shoats," Harpin said, his voice stronger than Shoats or any of the regulators had ever heard it.

"Well, now! What's got you acting so important all of a sudden?" Shoats asked, not backing away. Behind him stood Sipes and the others. "You've been spending a lot of time in the Frenchman's ear since we got to town."

"That's right, I have," said Harpin. "I'm on my way to do something important for him right now." He glared at Shoats. "Unless you want him to hear how you kept me from doing it, I think you'd best get out of my damned way."

"Whoa, Bobby! Let him pass!" Sipes laughed, a couple other men joining in. "Looks like our livery hostler has elbowed himself a better seat at the table."

"Yeah, maybe I have," said Harpin, "but with no help from any of you." He stepped forward, leaving Shoats no choice but to step aside or be walked over.

"Hey, come on, Harpin," said Shoats, making way but following alongside him. "Tell us what LeBlanc has in mind. Are we going to kick down the door to the doctor's office or what?"

Harpin gave a smug grin and said, "I'll tell you when he says it's *okay* to tell you."

Leaving again through the rear door, Harpin stopped long enough to purchase a bottle of rye whiskey from a small apothecary store, then hurried back to the livery barn with the bottle tucked up under his arm. When he slipped back into the darkened barn and to the stall where he'd left Free Drink, the young outlaw was sitting in a squat, his head in his hands. "Hey, Sal, how about a drink?" He held the bottle down to Free Drink. "I dug us up an eye-opener from the grain bin! What do you say?"

"Oh, Jesus," Free Drink whispered, "I'm afraid I've messed up something awful." He shook his disheveled head without looking up. "How long have we been asleep?"

"Not long," said Harpin. "I just woke up myself, went out back, and relieved myself. Here, take a drink; it'll make you feel better."

Free Drink looked up with sad, bloodshot eyes. "You . . . you didn't go anywhere? I mean, you didn't go tell anybody what I told you yet, did you?"

"No," Harpin lied. "I told you what I done. Here, give this a swig. It'll make you feel better."

Free Drink raised a hand toward the bottle, but hesitated before taking it and asked, "Are you sure you didn't —"

"Hell, I told you I didn't," said Harpin. He wagged the bottle until Free Drink took it, pulled the cork, and lifted a long drink to his lips.

"Ah, damn . . . that does feel better," Free Drink said, offering a weary smile. "I shouldn't have said nothing about Jimmy

Blaine being at the doctor's," he murmured. "I was just drunk and showing off. That wasn't really why I came here."

"Don't worry about it," said Harpin, taking a drink himself. "If you don't want me to tell the Frenchman, I won't. We'll forget you ever said anything." He didn't want Free Drink going back now and admitting to the Kid that he'd said anything he shouldn't have. That would ruin everything and make Harpin look like a fool to LeBlanc.

"Really?" said Free Drink. "That might be best, if it's all the same to you."

"Sure, forget it, Sal," said Harpin, squatting down close beside Free Drink and handing him the bottle again. "I'm sorry about calling you Wild Rose too. You and me ought to stick closer together than we have of late."

"I don't mind you calling me Wild Rose, just if it's between us, though," said Free Drink. He turned up a drink and gave a low whiskey hiss. "Obliged." He passed the bottle back to Harpin.

"Why was it you came here then? Just to see me?" Harpin asked. He raised the bottle high and took a long swig.

"Yeah, sort of," said Free Drink. He let the dagger slip down from his right shirtsleeve and gripped it tightly by its leather handle. With his left hand he reached up and took hold of the bottle to steady it.

Seeing Harpin's chest protrude as he swallowed the warm rye, the young outlaw swung the dagger in a wide, fast circle, plunged it into Harpin's heart, and held it firmly as the liveryman sank backward in the fresh straw, his feet kicking in feeble defense. Hovering low over the dying man, Free Drink wiggled the dagger back and forth, feeling warm blood gush up onto his hand. "So long, good pal," he whispered softly into Harpin's face.

When he stood up, he took one last drink from the bottle, corked it, and placed it by Harpin's side. Then he stooped down and tossed hay and straw over the body and walked out.

On his way past the saloon, he looked over the bat-wing doors and saw LeBlanc's regulators doing their drinking with little fanfare. The Kid, Sturgis, and Rudabaugh had left the saloon, each carrying a mug of beer. Free Drink spotted them at the corner of an alley a block away, where they set up their drinking camp, leaning against a dusty clapboard building rather than drink among LeBlanc's men. The Kid held two bottles of rye under his arm.

Free Drink walked past the saloon and joined them, taking a mug of beer that Rudabaugh offered. "Obliged," he said; then he sucked back a frothy mouthful and swallowed it in a single gulp.

"Well, how did it go?" the Kid asked, looking him up and down, seeing a dark stain along his right shirtsleeve.

"As well as it could," said Free Drink. He reached for one of the bottles under the Kid's arm.

Handing him the bottle, the Kid watched him yank the cork with his teeth, spit it away, and take a long, deep swig.

"Damn!" said the Kid. He took the bottle from Free Drink. "Don't give yourself the blind staggers. What went wrong?'

"Nothing," said Free Drink, catching his breath after the big drink of rye.

"It don't look like nothing," said the Kid. "Tell me what happened."

"Everything went the way it was supposed to," Free Drink said in a tight voice. "I just don't want to talk about it."

The Kid looped an arm over Free Drink's narrow shoulders and eyed him closely. "I've always been able to count on you, right?"

"That's right," said the young outlaw. He sipped his beer and stepped out from under the Kid's arm. "Take a look at this."

The four turned their eyes toward the hotel, where LeBlanc, Perls, Shoats, and Red Downing stepped out the front door and down to the hitch rail. Shoats trotted across the street and called out to the men above the bat-wing doors.

"Looks interesting," the Kid murmured, sipping his beer. He watched intently as the regulators walked briskly from the saloon and followed Shoats to the horses. "What do you suppose lit a fire under LeBlanc's ass all of a sudden, making him leave town this time of day?"

"Beats me," said Free Drink, staring intently alongside the Kid, Rudabaugh, and Sturgis, none of them making an attempt to hide their interest.

"All right, everybody put a few steps between us," the Kid said quietly, seeing the regulators mount up and follow LeBlanc across the street toward them. "Anything happens, I get LeBlanc and the German." He gave a friendly smile toward the Frenchman and tipping his beer mug as if in a toast.

"As you see, William Bonney, we are leaving this quiet little hamlet the way we found it, undisturbed," LeBlanc said to him from his saddle.

"Bye," the Kid said simply, with no further need of explanation. He held his beer mug close to his lips as if waiting for the regulators to leave before enjoying his drink.

But LeBlanc wasn't finished talking. He looked from face to face, then said to the Kid, "I have decided that even though Blaine might be hidden here somewhere, it is not my wish to upset the good citizenry by searching door-to-door for him."

"Adios," said the Kid, still waiting before sipping his beer.

LeBlanc's nostrils flared a bit, but he managed to keep his temper under control. "You can tell Lawrence Shaw that I will concede this visit to him. But rest assured I will find this Jimmy Blaine and hold him accountable for killing my Mexican drovers."

"Bon voyage," said the Kid, still with a smile, the suspended beer mug in hand.

"Mr. LeBlanc," said Red Downing, no longer able to tolerate the Kid's insolence, "take a minute. Let me step down and smack his rabbit teeth all over the ground for you, *please*?"

"Yeah, *please* let him, LeBlanc," said the Kid, giving Downing a cold, hard stare.

"As you were, Red!" LeBlanc commanded. He could see that the hot-tempered gunman was on the verge of drop-

283

ping from his saddle with or without permission. "There will be another day, William Bonney," said LeBlanc. "Perhaps on that day I will enjoy seeing him take you apart."

"Anytime will do," the Kid replied, still staring at Downing. "Right now I'm running out of ways to say good-bye." He kept the beer mug suspended until LeBlanc nodded curtly and nudged his horse away along the street, headed out of town. Once the last of the men filed by, the Kid raised the mug the rest of the way to his lips and took a long sip.

"Can we move to the saloon now, drink the way civilized men are supposed to?" Rudabaugh asked.

"Yep," said the Kid. He looked at the western sky and said, "It'll be dark before long. Time for Lawrence Shaw's buckboard to hit the trail."

CHAPTER 21

From his hiding spot just off the trail, Sipes watched the buckboard move into sight and bob easily along the pale, moonlit horizon. Lawrence Shaw's dark silhouette sat slightly hunched over the reins. "I'll be damned," said Sipes, seeing the silhouettes beside Shaw on the wagon seat. "He's brought along the woman and her child."

Next to Sipes, Bobby Shoats spit, then whispered, "He must've counted on this being awfully easy."

"It would have been, Bobby boy," said Sipes, "had it not been for one of the Kid's men spilling the news to Dick Harpin."

"Goes to show you what a few drinks of rye will get you at the right time and place," said Shoats.

Sitting restlessly atop their horses beside Shoats and Sipes sat two of the California gunmen, Peedon Otte and Carlos Antemeyer. "Are we going to kill Shaw and take this Blaine to LeBlanc to hang, or what?" Otte asked, his big dun pawing the ground restlessly beneath him, ready for the slightest tap of heels to send him racing up toward the trail.

"Hold your gawdamn horses!" Sipes whispered harshly. "This is Fast Larry Shaw! If we don't do this right, we'll get ourselves killed!"

"Do it *right*?" said Otte. "Me and Carlos haven't done it wrong. Have we, Carlos?"

"No," said Carlos, a tough-looking border gunman with the letter *T* (for *thief*) branded on his heavily whiskered left cheek, and a battered gold earring in one ear. "Nobody ever ambushed us and sent us hightailing either." He gave Sipes an accusing stare.

"Has somebody put your stinking California ass in charge?" Bobby Shoats asked. "Because if they did I never heard nothing about —"

"Easy, Bobby," said Sipes, cutting Shoats off, settling the hotheaded young gunman. "All right then," he added, turning to the other two, "you boys are stoked up for some action. . . . One of yas circle around in front with Bobby; the other follow me. Let's go get it done." He turned his horse quietly in the brush and gigged it up toward the trail. Otte turned his horse behind him, while

Bobby and Carlos eased their horses away through a tangle of brush and downed timber.

On the trail, Shaw heard the faintest whisper near his ear saying, "Somebody has started following us. I hear their horses."

"I know," whispered Shaw, "I hear them too." Behind him he detected the slight sound of hooves on hard dirt and stone. "I also heard somebody moving along the hillside below us." To the left of the buckboard a thin stream braided its way down the hillside.

"I have both hands on the baby," came the faint reply at his ear.

"Good." Shaw stared forward in the moonlight, realizing it was too late to start second-guessing himself. "Just sit tight," he said. "We'll see what happens once we reach the fork in the trail."

"Is everything all right?" came another whisper, this one rising up from the wagon bed.

"Yes, lie still back there," Shaw said over his shoulder, looking down at Blaine's washed but still bloodstained shirt. "Keep the blanket over you."

"Is everyth—"

"Yes, I said!" Shaw whispered, getting irritated. "Now be quiet, both of you." He gave the team of horses a quiet slap of the reins.

"I love you, Jimmy. I just want you to know that if anything goes wrong —"

"*Please* shut up!" said Shaw, trying to keep his voice lowered. *Jesus* . . . Ahead of the buckboard, Shaw could see the clearing in the moonlight where the trail forked down to the flatlands. So far, so good, he told himself, though knowing full well that the word had gotten out. Why else would anybody be using the old short trail this late at night?

Just as he expected, when he rolled the wagon slowly into the wide space at the fork, two figures on horseback stepped into the trail, one on either side, each with a rifle pointed at him.

Shaw raised a foot and set the brake handle forward, knowing right away that he would need the wagon steady.

"All right, Fast Larry!" said Bobby Shoats on the horse to his right. "Keep your hands up away from that gun butt. You know what we're here for. Hand him over!"

"Or what?" Shaw asked.

"You already know 'or what,' " said Shoats. He steadied his rifle in his hands. "So don't try stalling us."

"Just the two of you?" Shaw asked, wanting to hear something from the men behind him, get an idea of how many he was up against and from what direction.

"You're going to *wish* there was only two of us if you don't do like you're told, 'Fastest Gun Alive,' " said Bertrim Sipes, no longer trying to keep his horse quiet as he gigged the animal closer to the rear of the wagon. To Otte he said, "Get on that side; help me drag this bloody sonsabitch out of there."

Otte nudged his horse forward.

"Why only four?" Shaw asked. "I was expecting at least half a dozen, the way I've been knocking you blueflies down lately."

"Riling us won't help you none, Shaw," said Otte behind him. "We caught you cold, all because that girlie-looking pal of the Kid's jackpotted you for a few drinks and a pat on the head."

"Free Drink did that?" said Shaw. "He told you where I was headed with Blaine, the woman, and their baby?"

Over his shoulder, Shaw said, "Sorry, Blaine. Looks like I couldn't get you and your family out of there after all."

"Yeah, now you're going to hang, cowpoke," said Sipes. "You should have left us alone on the trail. All we wanted was the cattle. Now LeBlanc will make an example

289

of you, let you hang from a tree limb till you rot off the bone."

"What about the woman and the baby?" asked Shoats.

"Bring them along," said Sipes. "Let the Frenchman decide what to do with them."

"You heard him, ma'am," said Carlos. He eased his horse around to the side and reached out a hand. "Hand me the baby; then step down here on my lap."

As the blanket-wrapped bundle passed toward his hands, Carlos caught a glimpse of Otte and Sipes reaching into the wagon bed. "Come on, Blaine; ain't nothing going to change anything," said Sipes.

But instead of seeing Blaine reach up and accept his fate, Carlos saw a blaze of shotgun fire light up the wagon bed. Sipes's face disappeared in a spray of blood. At the same second he saw the Kid spring to his feet from the wagon bed and let out a loud battle cry.

In the split second it took for Carlos to react, he jerked his glance back toward the wagon seat in time to see the "baby" turn into a fire-breathing monster as it exploded, sending a blast of buckshot into his chest and face.

From his wagon seat, Shaw's gun came up as a bullet from Bobby Shoats's rifle sliced past his head and thumped into the wagon bed near the Kid's foot.

Shaw fired, seeing his bullet and another bullet hit the young gunman in the chest as the Kid's Thunderer exploded behind him.

"Oh, God! Don't shoot!" cried Otte, dropping his rifle and throwing his hands in the air. He looked at Free Drink's double-barreled shotgun pointed down at him from the wagon seat. "I . . . I . . ."

"You don't know what the hell to do now, do you?" the Kid said, also turning his gun toward the trembling ambusher.

"Don't kill me!" Otte pleaded. "I never should have come here!"

Shaw stood up and looked off in the direction of Sabo Canyon while he dropped the spent cartridge from his Colt and replaced it. "How come LeBlanc only sent four of you?" he asked. "Where are he and the others?"

"They . . . they went on back to the herd," Otte said in a shaky voice. "He said four to one was plenty!"

The Kid cut in, "What? Four is plenty, against the fastest gun alive? He must have been crazy." He grinned at Shaw and said, "You got anything else you want to ask this dead man before we close his box?"

"Aw, please!" Otte begged, unable to keep

tears from running down his cheeks. "You don't have to *kill* me, do you?"

"Well . . ." The Kid exaggerated giving the matter some thought. "Let's see, now, you came here to what? Wish Shaw here a safe trip?"

"I just want to live!" said Otte. "I know I was doing wrong coming here to do this. Hell, I ain't making no excuses! But damn, don't kill me! Let me go — I swear to God you'll never see me again!"

The Kid shrugged, looking at Shaw. "Hell, it was you they was going to kill. What say you?"

Shaw let out a breath. "Hell, turn him loose, Kid, far as I'm concerned. . . ."

"Hear that, Free Drink?" said the Kid before Shaw had stopped talking. "Turn him loose."

"I hear him," said Free Drink.

"Obliged, all of you," said Otte, his voice sounding sincere with gratitude. "If I ever —"

Free Drink's shotgun bucked in his small hands. The suddenness of it surprised even Shaw enough that he flinched as the orange-blue explosion blossomed in surrounding darkness.

The Kid said to Shaw with a solemn look. "Is that what you meant, turn him loose?

He did ride out all this way just to kill you."

Shaw felt a flash of anger, but he kept it in check. He said in an even tone, "Yeah, you're right, Kid. That's what I had in mind." Turning his gaze back out in the direction of Sabo Canyon, he said, "They ought to be well enough on their way by now."

Foley had kept a close watch on Blaine throughout the night while the two rode on, away from the old short trail where Foley had waited, the reins to a spare horse in hand, following Shaw's instructions. The two had heard gunfire echo from the old short trail; Blaine, even in his weakened state, had tried to get Foley to turn back with him. But Foley would have none of it.

"Lawrence told me to keep going no matter what," Foley insisted, "and that's what we're going to do."

By daylight, Blaine had begun to lag behind, bowed in the saddle and clutching an arm around his middle. "Damn it," he'd cursed when Foley slowed his horse to check on him. "How can a man like Shaw get shot and keep going like nothing happened? I get shot, and look at me . . . can't hardly sit a horse." He held his coat open, revealing a wide, wet circle of blood that seeped steadily through both his bandage and his shirt.

"I don't know," said Foley, already looking all around, wondering what to do about the wounded man. "It's just the breaks, I reckon."

Ahead to their far left lay the big herd beneath a constant blanket of dust. To their right lay their destination, the lookout from where Batson had spotted the regulators and the Mexicans driving the rustled cattle. But Foley could see that Blaine wasn't going to make it there on horseback. "Think you can make it to Farlin Clemons's place?"

"Yeah, I can make it there," said Blaine. "What happens there?"

"I recall he's got an old chuck wagon he bought from that English spread that went bust," said Foley. "We've got to get you into something that won't keep your insides pulled apart." He reached out and took the slack reins from Blaine's weak, trembling hand. Leading Blaine's horse, he veered to their right toward a deepening stretch of valley land filled with pine and rocky cliff edges.

"Let go of my reins," Blaine protested, yet his voice lacked conviction. "I can ride."

"Like hell you can," said Foley. "I'm getting you off that horse first chance. I ain't facing that wild-eyed William Bonney and Lawrence Shaw and explaining how I let you die on me."

"I'm not going to die on you," Blaine said with determination. "I'm a family man now . . . I got too much to live for."

"Keep reminding yourself of that," said Foley. He kicked up their horses' pace a little, carefully, and rode off the trail across the grasslands, realizing he'd be leaving a clear path for LeBlanc's men to follow should any of them be riding along the trail. But he knew there was nothing he could do about it if he wanted to keep Blaine alive.

Two hours later, at the end of a rough, rocky path, Foley sat looking down at the weathered face of Farlin Clemons, who stood alongside his Cherokee wife in his front yard amid stacks of tools and household items they had just started loading onto the chuck wagon. Once Foley had told him the situation, the old rancher shook his head, and he and his wife began unloading the wagon. "Every gawdamned time I've left for Texas, something like this happens!" Clemons said.

"You're going back to Texas instead of staying and fighting the Frenchman?" Foley asked as he helped Blaine down from his saddle.

"Running as fast as I can without falling," said Clemons. "I sold my cattle to Diekman last week." He gestured a rough hand toward his neighbor thirty miles north. "Far as I'm concerned the Frenchman or the buzzards can have what I leave behind."

Nodding at the wagon, Foley said, "We're obliged. I'll get this back to you soon as I get Blaine settled in up at the lookout."

"Hell, no hurry, I reckon." Clemons helped the black rancher lift Blaine up into the wagon bed. "I'll not make plans till I see you coming."

When Foley and Blaine rode away, their horses' reins hitched to the wagon's tailgate, Clemons walked over, sat down a dusty wooden step, and let his forearms collapse onto his knees. "Every *gawdamn* time," he said.

CHAPTER 22

At the rocky lookout point above Sabo Canyon, young Marvin Meeks stood up and waved his father's rifle back and forth slowly at the wagon on the trail below. In the converted buckboard, Belan Foley half stood from the wooden seat and waved his own rifle back and forth in reply, a cool evening breeze nipping at the collar and tails of his duck coat.

"Pa, it's Mr. Foley," Marvin called back over his shoulder. "You best come look."

Albert Meeks stood up from the fire with a battered pair of binoculars in hand. Still chewing a bite of roasted sage hen, he walked over to his son at the edge of the cliff. Marvin stood watching as his father raised the binoculars, looked down through them for a moment, then spoke thoughtfully, almost to himself.

"That's Jimmy Blaine in the back," he said. "Looks injured." He squinted into the lenses and looked at the two horses trailing behind the wagon. "Wonder what all this means?"

"I signaled them on up," said Marvin. "I reckon we'll soon see."

An hour later, after the buckboard had disappeared onto the trail leading up to the lookout point, Belan Foley drew the rickety wagon to a halt on a stretch of rocky level ground and stood again. "Ummm-ummm, I am glad this trip is over," he said, looking back over his shoulder as if making sure he hadn't been followed.

In the buckboard Blaine sat up weakly and looked all around.

"What happened?" the rancher asked as Foley stepped down from the seat. Together they helped Blaine from the wagon bed.

"The Frenchman and his regulators are all-fired set on lynching Blaine if they find him," said Foley. They took Blaine over near the small fire and seated him down against a rock. "They're accusing Jimmy here and Batson and Springer of ambushing some of their drovers." Foley opened Blaine's coat and shirt and checked the bloody bandage. The bleeding appeared to have stopped since Blaine had gone from saddle to wagon bed. Foley looked relieved.

"Hogwash!" said Meeks. "This man has never ambushed anybody in his life."

"Hogwash is right," said Foley. "There's a wounded Mexican in town who even says it was the Frenchman's men who started the fight." Buttoning Blaine's coat, Foley went on, saying, "Anyways, I saw the whole thing from right here. The Mexican told the truth: It was the regulators started it."

"How . . . does it look?" Blaine asked.

"It's stopped bleeding," said Foley, with a pat on Blaine's slumped shoulder. "Lean back and get yourself some shut-eye. You're out of Willow Creek. That's the main thing."

"Yeah, that's the main thing," said Meeks. "The *next* thing is: What are we going to do about the Frenchman and his thugs wanting to hang one of our own?"

"The whole situation could be sorted and settled if we had a way of putting it before the territorial judge," said Foley.

Meeks said with skepticism, "The only judge around here for a while is going to be the Frenchman himself." He rubbed his whiskered chin in grim contemplation. "Where does Lawrence Shaw stand in all this?"

"He says he's not taking sides," said Foley. "But he and William Bonney brought Blaine out of town and met me at the begin-

299

ning of the old short trail. There's no telling what happened after that. I heard gunfire later in the night, but Shaw told us to keep moving no matter what, so I did. Shaw and William Bonney already killed some regulators. I expect the rest of LeBlanc's men are busting to see them both in the dirt."

"I expect it's time we gather everybody together the way we had planned," said Meeks, motioning his son, Marvin, toward him from where the young man stood looking out across the rolling grasslands and stretches of pine woodland below. When the boy ran up and stood before him, Meeks said, "It's time, son. Get a horse twixt your knees and round everybody up."

"Bring them here, Pa?" Marvin asked, a glint of excitement in his eyes.

"Yes, bring them all here," said Meeks. "We'll need to mull this over between us some before we ride into Willow Creek."

Foley and Meeks watched over tin cups of hot coffee as the boy gathered and saddled a wild-looking brindle barb stallion. The brush-scarred little plains stallion snorted and bucked and crow-hopped until Marvin won control long enough to put it into a reckless pace down the narrow trail. "He's ridden like that ever since his second birthday," said Meeks with a thin smile of admiration. "You ought to see him when he's in a hurry."

By the time the dust above the trail had completely settled Foley had draped a blanket around Blaine's shoulders, and Meeks had taken up his son's position on lookout. But twenty minutes later, at about the time young Marvin should have reached the main trail into Sabo Canyon, a volley of gunshots resounded up from the lower hillside.

"They've gulched him!" Meeks shouted, running a few steps toward the trail instinctively, then stopping as if in realization. "I've got to get down to him!"

"Wait, Meeks! Don't go down there!" Foley shouted. He knew that if what they'd heard was the regulators having come upon Marvin along the trail, there would be nothing Albert Meeks could do for his son but pray the young man had been able to race through them.

But Meeks wouldn't hear of waiting. "That's my boy!" he shouted, running to his horse and jumping atop it bareback. "Keep watch!" he shouted over his shoulder as he batted his heels against the big dun.

"Damn it!" said Foley, finding himself standing alone at the small campfire, Blaine sleeping so soundly the gunfire from below

301

hadn't awakened him.

T. J. Katlin stepped his horse out from behind the rock where he and Lane had hidden in wait at the sound of the little barb's hoofprints coming down the hill trail. He looked back and forth at the rest of his men, who appeared from various hiding spots along the trail. "None of you hit him?" he asked, both amazed and infuriated. "None of you big, bold outlaw sonsabitches managed to hit one gawdamn man on horseback?"

"More than likely some of us did hit him," said Uncle Linton, hurrying his horse over to T. J., "but he was moving faster than anything I've seen in a long time. He might ride a mile or more before falling. Like some kind of wounded elk."

"A wounded elk?" T. J. said with sarcasm. "Who the hell do you think you're talking to, Uncle? You all missed him! Every damn one of you!" He didn't mention that both he and his brother Lane had also fired and missed. He turned in his saddle and said to the two Russians, "Go get him. Bring him back. Catch up to us along the trail. We're going to ride up and grab Jimmy Blaine."

The Russians turned their horses and punched their spurs to the animals' sides, sending them bolting off after the fleeing barb and its rider. T. J. and Lane swung their horses around and gigged them up the steep trail, Bratcher McBain and Uncle Linton following them.

Putting his horse alongside T. J. and Lane, Uncle Linton cautioned them, saying, "Nephews, we don't have any notion how many ranchers might be waiting up there."

"I don't give a damn how many there are!" said T. J., still angry over everybody allowing Marvin Meeks to ride through them. "We know Blaine is up there. We've followed his trail all night and all morning. Once we get a rope around his neck, we'll start making Fast Larry Shaw dance to *our* tune."

"What about the Frenchman?" asked Uncle Linton. "What's he going to think about us not taking the cattle back to the herd like he told us?"

"To hell with him," said T. J. "We'll drag Blaine to Willow Creek for him, tell him we spotted Blaine getting away from town, and had to decide which was more important: capturing Blaine for him or chasing steers." T. J. gave a sly grin. "Giving Blaine to him will make that Frenchman happier than a beetle in a bucket of shit."

"Besides, Uncle Linton, you worry too damn much," said Lane. "Chances are there's nobody up there but Blaine and the nigger."

"Yeah," said T. J. He nodded in the direction Marvin had taken on the barb. "That one was probably the lookout, gone for help."

"Blaine's in bad shape, according to what the rancher told us back where they got the wagon," said Lane. "All we've got to do is —"

Lane's words were cut short as a rifle shot whistled past his head, and Albert Meeks came riding down on them with a rebel yell. "Get him, gawdamn it!" shouted T. J., already drawing his Colt and firing toward the quickly charging rifleman.

Before Meeks had gotten within fifty yards of the Katlins, gunshots nicked and grazed him and his horse and sent them both tumbling and sliding off the trail. They went down through breaking brush and lower tree limbs and over the edge of a four-foot drop, out of sight.

"Well, by God, that's more like it" said T. J., looking around in surprise at Uncle Linton and McBain. "It's about damn time we chewed somebody up and spit them out! I was starting to wonder if I was riding with a bunch of old maids!"

They pulled their horses to the side of the

trail and looked down the long, sliding impression that man and horse had made down the hillside. "Want me and Uncle Linton to go down and check?" asked McBain.

"Volunteer yourself, not me, McBain!" Uncle Linton growled at him.

"No, forget him," said T. J. as he looked down, seeing neither man or animal. "He's either dead or damn near. Let's get on up before the nigger and Blaine manage to slip away from us." He turned his horse and rode up the thin, steep trail.

Atop the hill at the lookout point, Foley had wasted no time getting Blaine up and behind a large rock at the edge of the cliff. He put a rifle in Blaine's hands and laid it over the rock for him. "I can still . . . pull a trigger," said Blaine.

"We're going to be finc . . . just fine," said Foley, not really believing it himself.

When T. J. eased into sight, having stepped down from his saddle and led his horse the last few yards, he stood behind a thick pine, looked all around the camp, then called out, "All right, black man! Don't put up a fight and we won't kill you."

Surprised to see that it was T. J. Katlin instead of the Frenchman's regulators, Foley called out a defiant reply: "Come a step closer and it won't be me getting killed!"

"Yeah, yeah." T. J. smiled to himself, realizing he'd been correct — that there were only Foley and Blaine up here. "I know Blaine's about had it, and I know you're by yourself. So don't fool around with me. Come out, give me Blaine, and get the hell out of here, *alive.*" He paused to let it sink in. "Do you understand that I'm going to let you live? I wouldn't have to, you know."

"That's white of you," said Foley, "but I ain't coming out, and you ain't getting Blaine! I told Shaw I'd take care of him . . . and I will!"

"Shaw, huh?" said T. J. "That troublemaking son of a bitch is what brought us here in the first place. I'm taking Blaine to Willow Creek and using him to get Shaw out into the street and kill him."

"You're taking him to LeBlanc," said Foley, "so he can hang him!"

T. J. grinned. "Well, that too," he admitted. "But either way, the trail ends for you right here if you don't give him up."

Foley looked over at Blaine, who in spite of their predicament lay with the side of his face against the rock, half-conscious. Shaking his head, he murmured, "Shaw, I done my best. I never gave him up without a fight."

From behind the tree, T. J. saw Foley rise

306

up atop the rock, brace himself, and let out a loud cry as he levered and fired round after round from his Winchester. The first shot hit the pine tree, but each shot after that moved farther away from T. J. until he saw his opportunity and stepped out from the cover of the tree with his Colt raised and cocked.

Son of a bitch! T. J. said to himself. One shot exploded from his pistol. It hit Foley high in his shoulder and sent him spinning off the rock, his rifle flying from his hands, his coattails windmilling. Turning to the others who had taken cover off the trail, he said, "Now, fellows, there's what I mean when I tell you to shoot somebody!"

"Good shooting, brother," said Lane as he stepped forward leading his horse, followed by Uncle Linton and McBain.

The four walked to the large rock and stepped atop it, their guns pointed and cocked. All that remained of Foley was his sweat-streaked hat lying at the edge of the cliff. Blaine lay leaning against the rock, trying to raise his rifle for a shot.

"Here, now, we'll have none of that!" said T. J. He stepped over and kicked the rifle from his hands. "Don't make us kill you, cowpoke. We got to turn you over to the Frenchman, get you healed up and ready for your hanging."

"My . . . my baby . . ." Blaine said in a weak and trailing voice.

"Oh, yeah, we heard you became the father to that whore's baby," T. J. said, grinning. He reached down to drag Blaine to his feet. "Congratulations, I reckon."

CHAPTER 23

Marvin Meeks heard the gunfire behind him. He looked back but never slowed down. After having made it unscathed through the ambush the Katlins laid for him along the trail, he wasn't about to go back until he'd carried out the task his father entrusted to him. For seven miles the Russian brothers had dogged him hard, at one point coming within fifty yards of him on their larger, leggier horses. But while their big mounts began to tire and slow down, the little barb just seemed to put more heart into the race and moved even faster, as if sensing the urgency of his rider's situation.

"To hell wit dis," said Vladimir as he and Jerniko finally reined their horses to a walk and watched the dust from the brindle barb boil up and spread wide across the trail. He shook the big revolver in his hand and said in their native tongue, "We did not get even a shot at him!"

"No," said Jerniko, "and I will not kill my horse chasing him any farther." He patted his horse's withers and turned it back in the direction of the trail up toward the lookout point. "If the Katlins want this man so bad, they can chase him. My behind is sore from sitting this foolish American saddle."

"Tell them we killed him; they will never know the difference," said Vladimir. "What do we care?" The two looked at each other and laughed heartily.

When they arrived at the lookout point and saw wagon tracks leading back down, they decided the Katlins had found Blaine and headed back to Willow Creek. They rode on and followed the tracks for three hours until they caught up with the Katlins and the slow-moving wagon on the main trail across the grasslands.

"Did you catch him?" T. J. asked as soon as the Russians arrived.

"Of course we caught him," Vladimir lied, straight-faced.

"Then where is he?" Lane asked.

"He is dead," said Jerniko with a slight shrug, as if it went without saying. "You did want us to kill him, did you not?"

"Yeah, that's exactly what we wanted," said T. J. with a dark chuckle.

But Lane didn't trust them. "Where's his

body?" he asked sharply.

"He is lying dead in the tall grass alongside the trail into Sabo Canyon, where we left him to feed the buzzards," Vladimir said firmly and clearly, as if Lane might be having a hard time understanding him.

"We didn't think you would have us drag a stinking, bloody corpse all the way back here," Jerniko added, giving Lane a disdainful look.

Lane had more questions, but before he could ask them, Uncle Linton stood in his stirrups and pointed back along the trail toward the big herd. "Nephews, it's the Frenchman coming," he said, sounding excited, "moving at a good clip!"

"Relax, Uncle," said T. J. "We got Blaine for him, didn't we?" He gestured a hand all around the grasslands at the strewn-out cattle they had abandoned. "Hell, here's the cattle if he wants to round them up." Looking at his brother, he chuckled and added, "What the hell more could he ask of men like us?"

The Russians joined Uncle Linton and McBain, glad the questions had stopped. "So, now you have Blaine," Vladimir commented, looking down into the wagon bed and seeing Blaine rolled into a ball with a blanket wrapped around him.

"Yeah, and I don't like it much," McBain commented quietly.

"Oh?" Jerniko asked.

Leaning to keep himself from being heard by the Katlins and Uncle Linton as the three stared at the advancing horsemen, McBain said, "All this trouble, just to get to Fast Larry Shaw? Hell, if they want him dead so bad, we ought to be bold enough to ride in, call him out, and kill him."

The Russians only nodded and sat patiently while the Frenchman and his regulators drew closer and finally stopped in a half circle around the wagon.

"Oh, my goodness!" said LeBlanc, unable to conceal his surprise when he and Red Downing looked into the wagon.

Downing said, "Yep, this has to be Blaine. He fits Harpin's description."

"Oh, it's Blaine, all right," said T. J. "We caught him and the nigger rancher hiding out. The nigger told us it was Blaine before we killed him."

"And there were no witnesses when you killed Foley?" LeBlanc inquired.

"Naw, just a few rock lizards, boss. They never tell anything." T. J. grinned. He enjoyed seeing LeBlanc so impressed by their work, and the look of envy eating away at Red Downing's eyes.

"It's not *boss,*" Downing corrected him soundly. "It's Mr. LeBlanc."

Ignoring Downing, T. J. said to the Frenchman, "You tell us which you prefer, boss. We only aim to please." He gestured a hand toward the wagon bed as he spoke.

"Pay no attention to Red," said LeBlance. "I do not mind being called *boss* . . . not by men who produce such amazing results for me." He gave Downing a dark stare, as if he were responsible for the four men not returning with Blaine from the old short trail. "Lately I send men to do a job and I never see them again. This is good work!"

"Begging your pardon, boss," said T. J., "but you ain't seen nothing yet. We're going to take this wretch into Willow Creek, use him to flush Shaw out in the street and kill him like the dog that he is — William Bonney too, if he tries sticking his beakin." He tipped his hat brim and added with mock humility, "That is, with your permission, of course."

LeBlanc seemed to consider the matter for a moment, then said, "I must admit, I have been looking forward to hanging him, having never actually seen a hanging except in travel pictures." He turned a questioning glance to the German, who had sat rigidly in his saddle, watching and listening. "What

313

about you, Herr Perls? Have you seen a hanging in person?"

"Oh, yas, many times," said the German, "with the bands and the food, and all the fanfare."

"I see," said LeBlanc. "Then you wouldn't mind awfully if we didn't get to see Blaine hang?"

The German looked mildly disappointed, yet before he could answer, T. J. cut in. "Don't worry, boss. You can always hang him after we flush out Shaw. We just turn around, leave town with him, and bring him back to you."

"Not if something goes wrong and Blaine ends up dead in the street alongside yas," said Downing, cutting into the conversation.

"That's not going to happen," said T. J. "You're confusing our way of doing things with your own."

"Why you . . ." Red Downing took a step toward him; T. J. never backed off an inch.

"Oh, stop it, Red!" said LeBlanc. He could see that it was no more than a posture on Downing's part anyway. To T. J., he nodded and said, "I will go along with this." He looked up across the afternoon sky. "We will ride through the night and be at Willow Creek by morning. You take Blaine into

314

Willow Creek and execute your plan with Shaw. We will wait outside of town. But" — he raised a thick finger for emphasis — "Red will ride in with you. If he sees it is not going as it should, he will come get us and I will have to take over. Do you agree with this?"

"Sure," said T. J., "but nothing's going to go wrong." He stared at Downing and said with confidence, "Now that you've got the right men on the job."

"These damn range wars . . ." Lawrence Shaw murmured. He stood for a moment at the hotel window, hat in hand, saddlebags over his shoulder, and looked down onto the street. Finally he said to Rita, who sat behind him breast-feeding the baby, "Jimmy Blaine will stay among the ranchers around Sabo Canyon until he's fit to be up and around."

"Did you tell Jimmy that I love him?" Rita asked. "The way I asked you to do?"

"Yes, I'm pretty sure I did," Shaw lied.

"I should have gone with him," Rita said in a prickly tone of voice, the same tone she'd used with Shaw since he and the Kid and Free Drink had returned to Willow Creek after turning Blaine over to Belan Foley.

"It wasn't a good idea," Shaw said. "Maybe in a few days, you and the baby —"

"You know what I think?" said Rita, cutting him off. "I think that secretly you want me and the baby, but you will not admit it to yourself. That is why you did not take me along to be with Jimmy. You want me, but you cannot tell yourself so, because your heart has been broken so badly by the death of your wife. You are afraid to take a chance and love again. You are a big, bold pistolero, when it comes to matters of the gun. But you are a coward when it comes to facing life, because life is the only thing that beats you — you and your fast draw. You have no defense for what *life* does. You can only try to hide and imagine what terrible thing life has planned next for you. You must try to avoid anything or anyone who gets too close —"

"Jesus! Are you through?" Shaw said, abruptly stopping her as he turned from the window. "I only came here to say good-bye, Rita." His voice softened a bit. "I was trying to tell you that you and the baby will be all right here until things settle down some and you can join Blaine."

"Then say good-bye and go, Lawrence," Rita said crisply. Yet as she turned her dark eyes away from him, he saw a tear glistening on her cheek. "I love Jimmy, and I want nothing more to do with you or any other man except him."

Hanging his head, Shaw nodded and said quietly, "Well, good-bye then." Stepping past her toward the door, he raised his hat halfway to his head and stopped and said indirectly to the baby at Rita's breast, "Good-bye, little darling. You're going to be happy here. . . ."

"You have never looked at her, Lawrence," Rita said. She turned toward him, pulling the baby's face from her breast with a gentle sucking sound.

"Don't, Rita," said Shaw, ducking his face away, but not before seeing the baby's face. Bright brown eyes drifted up and appeared to be looking into his. A sheen of mother's milk bubbled at the corner of tiny lips.

"I am naming her after you," said Rita. "I want you to know that you will always have a namesake."

"*My* name for a girl?" Shaw asked without facing either her or the baby.

"Well, yours and Billy's," said Rita. "As soon as I decide how it sounds best."

"Oh, I see," said Shaw, putting his hat on and reaching for the doorknob.

"Lawrence," she said as she heard the

door open, "I'm sorry. I do not mean to say things to hurt you. I am going to miss you."

"I understand," Shaw said softly. "I'm going to miss you too."

"I will never forget all you have done for me and my baby," she said, her tone turning softer, more sincere. "Take care of yourself?"

"Yes, I will," he said, as if giving his word.

In the hallway, he pulled the door shut behind himself, took a deep breath, and whispered, "Damn . . ." Then he adjusted the saddlebags over his left shoulder and walked to the stairs and down to the street.

Across the street inside the Fair Deal saloon, the Kid tossed his cards into the middle of the table, where he'd been sitting alone, dealing himself poker hands over and over. "I have not had a lick of sleep since we killed those sons of bitches out on the old short trail," he said, standing and stretching and adjusting his gun in its holster.

"You're getting to where you do that more and more often," commented Free Drink. He stood at the bat-wing doors, looking out toward the hotel in the early morning light.

"Yeah, I know," said the Kid. Picking up his shot glass of rye, he tossed it back and emptied it in a single swallow. "They say it's a sign of an unhealthy mind, doing something like that after a shooting."

"*They* who?" Rudabaugh asked, leaning back against the bar, dry-shaving his cheeks with a long boot knife.

The Kid grinned. "*They* who said it," he replied. He walked over beside Free Drink and looped an arm over the small outlaw's shoulder.

Free Drink idly let his eyes drift from the hotel to the livery barn, where Dick Harpin's body lay thinly covered with hay, having been sniffed out and prowled over by rodents, cats, and reptiles. "I sleep good every night, and my mind is too troubled to talk about."

"My good pal," said the Kid, jostling him against his side, "you are much too young to have such a troubled mind."

Free Drink gave a what's-done-is-done shrug and took his eyes off the livery barn and back to the hotel. "Shee-*it,* Billy, I'm too young not to!" he said.

"Here he comes!" The Kid dropped his arm from around Free Drink's shoulder. The two watched Shaw walk out the door of the hotel and head toward the doctor's office.

"I can't believe he's got the nerve to show

his face there!" said Free Drink.

"Nope, he's not," said the Kid, watching Shaw stop on the boardwalk just short of the doctor's office as if having changed his mind. "He's thought better of it." The Kid gave a crooked grin. "He's coming here to visit us instead."

But as Shaw turned and walked away from the doctor's office, the Kid and Free Drink saw Hilda step out onto the boardwalk and hurry toward him. Shaw turned again at the sound of Hilda calling his name.

"He's the busiest man I've ever seen." The Kid chuckled.

On the boardwalk, Shaw watched Hilda stop self-consciously. She gave a guarded glance all around, making sure no one could tell she had almost met him with an embrace. Her fingers nervously pushed back a fallen strand of hair. "You're leaving?" she asked, but it was not really a question that required an answer. "I wanted to tell you that I have thought about what you said in the restaurant, and I know you said it to get us out of there . . . to keep Adrian from getting hurt."

Shaw sighed in relief. "I was afraid I'd have to leave here with you thinking I meant those things I said." He looked into her eyes, the two of them standing close, yet

320

unable to offer each other a parting embrace. "You're right. I had to get you and your husband out of there."

"I . . . I can't say I wish you had not come back to Willow Creek," Hilda said. "I can't say I regret what we did. But I will say that I am responsible for everything. I welcomed you, perhaps even threw myself at you." She paused, then said, "I'm sorry this turned out the way it did."

"So am I, Hilda," said Shaw, "but I'm glad I'm not leaving here with you hating me."

"I couldn't hate you, Lawrence." She smiled, and resisted the urge to hold him.

Across the street the Kid said under his breath, "Kiss him, lady, damn! He's leaving, never coming back." But seeing her take a small step back, the Kid said, "No dice, huh?"

On the boardwalk Hilda continued to Shaw, "I have never known anybody like you. You have a reputation for being a bad man; yet I see the things you do." She shook her head slowly. "You are not a bad person."

"Obliged, Hilda," Shaw said. He looked past her shoulder toward the office door. "I expect we'd better go now."

"Yes, I know," said Hilda. As she stepped farther away, she said, "But I also wanted to tell you that Ramon is doing fine. He'll be

321

leaving anytime . . . says he's headed back to Mexico."

"Good to hear." Shaw nodded, touching his hat brim as he turned and walked on.

Still watching above the bat-wing doors, the Kid murmured to Free Drink, "Uh-oh, look at this."

As soon as Hilda walked back inside the doctor's office, Dr. Hauler stepped halfway onto the boardwalk and stared angrily at Shaw. "Better hope this sawbones ain't a backshooter," said Rudabaugh, having heard enough to be drawn from the bar to the doors beside the Kid. "Else Shaw's a dead man!"

"Naw," said the Kid. "This doctor ain't going to do nothing. He considers himself too civilized to —" His words stopped as he saw Dr. Hauler raise a battered Army Colt and cock it. "Shaw, look out!" he shouted, springing through the bat-wing doors, his Thunderer coming up from his holster.

Shaw crouched and spun on his heels, his gun already out, cocked, and ready. But at the second he caught sight of the doctor aiming at him, he heard the Kid's shot explode and saw Hauler stagger backward as the bullet hit his head and slammed him back inside the office.

"Oh, no!" said Shaw. He glanced over and

saw the Kid standing with his Colt smoking in his hand, a strange, cruel smile of satisfaction on the Kid's lips.

CHAPTER 24

In the waiting parlor of the doctor's office, the Kid stood leaning against the wall, twirling his Colt on his finger, his Winchester rifle propped against his side. On the boardwalk townsfolk had gathered and stood crowding the door. Rudabaugh, Sturgis, and Free Drink stood just inside the door, separating the townsfolk from the Kid. Watching the Kid's gun twirling, Shaw felt like telling him to sit down and put the gun away. But he dismissed the urge, reminding himself that, after all, the Kid might have saved his life.

"You have to admit," Free Drink said in a low, guarded tone, "that was a damn fine shot." He looked to Shaw as if for a comment of approval. "I mean . . . there's not one man in a thousand could fire that quick, that far away, and hit a man right smack in the —"

Free Drink stopped talking as the door to

the treatment room opened enough for Hilda to slip through and stand wiping her hands on a bloodstained towel. She avoided looking at the Kid, and spoke directly to Shaw as he stood up, hat in hand, saddlebags on the floor beside him. "He's resting right now," she said. "Ramon is with him. I've cleaned the wound and will put stitches across his forehead shortly, as soon as I can determine whether or not he has a fracture to his cranium."

"Thank God he's all right," said Shaw. "Hilda, I want you to know how sorry I am this happened."

Hilda's demeanor had changed again. She spoke politely, but curtly, as if saying only what needed to be said. "He tried to shoot you, Lawrence. I expect any man would do the same."

"It wasn't Shaw who shot him," the Kid cut in. "It was me." He had enough respect to have dropped his gun into its holster when Hilda had stepped into the room.

"Yes, I know," she replied coolly, without looking at the Kid.

"Begging your pardon, ma'am," said Rudabaugh, "but a man goes around pointing a gun at folks' back, he ought to expect to catch a bullet sooner or later."

"I daresay my husband did not make it a

practice to go around pointing guns at people," said Hilda in the doctor's defense.

"I bet he won't from now on either," Rudabaugh said with a thin smile.

"If there's nothing I can do . . . that is, nothing we can do," said Shaw, "maybe it would be best if we all leave?"

"Thank you, Lawrence," said Hilda. "That would be considerate of you. Perhaps you should leave through the rear door. I will step out front and speak to the townsfolk. I'll let them know that this was no one's fault but my husband's."

"Obliged," said Shaw. He motioned for the Kid and the others to follow him to the rear door. But the Kid turned stubborn. "Huh-uh, I came in through the front door; I'm leaving through the front door. You heard her — this wasn't our fault."

"Yeah, Kid," said Shaw, "but just for the sake of good manners, let's do this." He gestured toward the rear of the office.

"Damn, you're too obliging, Shaw," said the Kid. "No wonder you run into so much trouble." He grudgingly pushed himself from against the wall. "Come on, pals; let's be accommodating."

On their way to the rear door, Free Drink said, "Are you still wanting to leave town, Shaw?"

"Oh, yes," said Shaw, "now more than ever. You might all think about leaving too. I believe we've all worn out our welcome here."

"I was only trying to graze him some, Shaw," the Kid cut in out of the blue. "If I meant to kill him, he'd be dead right now."

Shaw knew better. Reaching for the rear doorknob, he said in a lowered voice now that they could not be heard by Hilda Hauler, "Well, like Free Drink said, it was a good shot."

"Yeah?" The Kid grinned crookedly, running the sleeve of his coat under his nose.

"Damn right it was," said Sturgis. "And had you killed him deader than a dead monkey, you'd have been in the right, no two ways about it."

"With all due respect, Shaw," Rudabaugh said as the four of them filed out the rear door into the alleyway behind Shaw, "Billy did you a good turn. Not saying you wouldn't have handled it, but you have to admit he —"

"Most likely saved my life," said Shaw, finishing his words for him.

"Ah, hell, Rude, hush up," the Kid said, turning shy.

"No, Kid, he's right," said Shaw. He turned facing the Kid. "I wish this had never happened, but I'm obliged to you for what you did."

"All right." The Kid raised his eyes and grinned. "Then you can buy me a drink or two before you get in the wind, show your appreciation."

Shaw let himself relax and said, "Sure, why not? A couple of drinks before I leave." They walked away toward the rear door of the saloon, sticking to the long alleyway to avoid the townsfolk.

In front of the doctor's office, Hilda explained to the concerned townsfolk that their doctor was going to be all right. She avoided giving a detailed explanation as to why the shooting had occurred, but simply called it a terrible misunderstanding and let the townsfolk make of it what they would.

"No one can be blamed for what has happened here," she said in closing. "That is my husband's wish. He thanks all of you for your concern." She slipped back inside the office, closed the door, and leaned on it for a moment to clear her thoughts. Then she went to the treatment room and went to work.

She gave her husband a strong dose of laudanum. While she waited for the numbing effects of the medication to take hold, she ran a length of heavy surgical thread, needle and all, through a ball of wax and laid it on a tray beside the gurney where Dr. Hauler lay in a half-conscious stupor. Ramon, who had stood back watching, stepped forward now to assist. He laid his hands on the doctor's forearms.

"Will . . . this hurt?" the doctor asked incoherently as Hilda swabbed camphor oil along both edges of the open gash at the doctor's hairline.

"You tell me," she said, concentrating on the wound, picking up the needle, and taking a deep breath. "Here we go."

Ramon winced at the sight of the needle piercing the bruised purple flesh. But he managed to hold down firmly on Dr. Hauler's forearms lest the doctor try to resist.

Almost a full hour later, Hilda knotted the last stitch, snipped the thread with a pair of scissors, and stepped back and said, "All finished." Ramon sighed and stepped away.

"Santa Madre," he murmured, a nauseous feeling stirring low in his stomach.

"Save all the praying, Mexican," said T. J. Katlin, stepping suddenly into the room from the rear of the building. "You'll be needing it later if you don't do as you're told."

Hilda gasped. "Who are you? What do you

want?" As she asked, she saw the rest of the gang shove their way into the room, Blaine hanging limply between Uncle Linton and McBain. Red Downing was the last to enter. He stood aside, watching, seeing how T. J. handled things.

"We're moving in here for a spell," T. J. said to the stunned doctor's wife, "while our ol' pard here recuperates."

"Oh, my, Jimmy!" Hilda rushed over to Blaine as McBain and Uncle Linton dropped him roughly onto the empty gurney beside the doctor.

Looking down at Dr. Hauler, who still lay in a stupor, the line of black thread stitched across his hairline, T. J. grimaced and said, "*Damn,* woman! What are you doing, scalping this poor sonsabitch?"

Hilda quickly jerked Blaine's shirt and coat open. "His head was grazed by a bullet. I sewed and dressed it," she said in an icy tone to T. J. as she looked at the purple flesh around Blaine's wound.

"Well, ain't you the busy lady today," T. J. scoffed. "Who shot him?"

"The baby . . . ?" Blaine managed to say in a whisper, unable to finish his words.

"Shhh, be still," Hilda said to Blaine. To Ramon, who stood watching anxiously, she said, "Heat some water for me, *por favor*!"

Then, replying to T. J., she said, "William Bonney shot him, but it was an accident."

"An *accident*!" said T. J. with a wide grin. "I'll have to remember that the next time I shoot a sonsabitch. It's going to be an accident!"

Responding to Hilda's request, Ramon turned and hurried, limping toward the other room for a pitcher of water. But as he got to the doorway, McBain, standing by it, threw an arm up to the doorjamb, blocking him. "Where do you think you're going, Ramon?" he growled.

Ramon looked at Hilda, who in turn looked at T. J. "I need water!" she said, refusing to be intimidated.

"Sure, let him get some water," said T. J. "He's going to be leaving in a minute anyway." He looked at Ramon and said, "Get the water. Then I want you to go find Fast Larry Shaw. You're going to tell him the Katlin Gang came by to say "howdy.""

Inside the saloon, Shaw had finished his second drink and set his empty glass on the bar top for a refill. The Kid had asked only half jokingly if Shaw truly thought that trouble seemed to follow him around. Shaw didn't have to think about it before replying, "Yes, Kid, I think it does. I don't think there's anything weird to it. It's just something my reputation causes."

"You mean the way sick and injured people are drawn to the doctor?" Free Drink asked with his shot glass halfway to his lips.

"Yep, something like that, I suppose," said Shaw. He watched the Kid lean over enough to pick up the bottle of rye and fill his shot glass for him. The bartender stood at the far end of the bar, drying wet beer mugs and stacking them on a shelf. "I believe a man creates his fate as he goes along. A doctor draws the kind of folks his profession attracts — the ill, the injured. I do the same, except I draw the killers and the crazies." He tipped his glass slightly toward the Kid and said, "Present company excluded, of course."

"There seems to be a lot of blood and bandaging wherever you are," said the Kid. "Maybe you should have been a doctor yourself." The Kid tipped his glass in return.

"Like I said, Kid, that's the life I created." Shaw gave a sad look at his shot glass before taking a drink.

"I don't believe that," said the Kid, also tipping his shot glass. "I think life just happens. Who cares why or how? What we are or who we are's got nothing to do with it."

He threw back his drink as if in conclusion.

"You're still young, Kid," said Shaw. "Maybe you'll think different down the trail." He tossed back his drink and set the glass on the bar.

"I hate it when people do that," said the Kid.

"What's that?" Shaw asked, picking his saddlebags up from the floor and his hat from the bar top.

"Talk down to me the way you just did," said the Kid.

"I didn't mean to," said Shaw.

"If I thought you meant to, we'd be locking horns," said the Kid, offering a thin, crooked smile. "But saying that I might think different down the trail is just another way of saying I've got a lot to learn . . . meaning that right now I don't know *nothing*." He remained smiling, but Shaw saw a tightness to it.

"No offense intended, Kid," he said.

The Kid shrugged. "Maybe I do have a lot to learn. But I'll learn it as I go. If it turns out you're right, I'll look you up and tell you."

"I hope you'll do that, Kid." Shaw pushed his empty glass away with his fingertips. "And now, fellows," he said to the Kid and his pals, "it's time I get out of Willow Creek while the dust is settled."

The Kid, trying to keep Shaw around and drinking with him, said, "Ah, come on. Let me buy you one more round, just to keep the —"

"*Señors!*" said Ramon, with a frightened look on his face, "there is trouble at the *oficina del doctor*!" He'd rushed through the swinging doors with such urgency that the Kid and his pals spun toward him, their hands gripping their gun butts, ready to draw.

But Shaw only looked at him in the mirror above the bar before turning and asking, "What kind of trouble at the doctor's office?"

"The Katlin Gang is there!" said Ramon. "They have Jimmy Blaine. He is in bad shape! T. J. Katlin said to tell you they will kill him if you do not step out into the street and drop your guns." Ramon looked at the Kid and his pals, then back to Shaw, and said, "They mean to kill you, *Señor* Shaw."

"You're right, Ramon: They do mean to kill me," Shaw said. "What about the doctor and his wife? Are they all right?"

"*Sí,*" said Ramon, "for now. But these men . . ." He hesitated, giving the Kid and his pals an appraising glance, then said, lowering his voice, "They are desperadoes. I

334

saw them when they came to ride for Le-
Blanc. Who knows what they will do to any
of us if they do not get their way? They
threatened to kill not only Jimmy Blaine,
but also the doctor and his wife if I do not
return with your answer."

"How many are there?" Shaw asked. He
lowered his saddlebags from his shoulder to
the floor beside him, raised his big Colt
instinctively, and checked it.

"Hay siete!" Ramon said, looking worried
for Shaw's safety.

"Seven, eh?" said Shaw. He tossed a look
at the Kid and said, "So much for the dust
being settled."

The Kid and his pals had straightened up
at the bar, watching and listening closely.
"You're not going to do what they're telling
you to, are you?" the Kid asked Shaw.

"They've got Blaine, the doctor, and his
wife," said Shaw. "I expect I don't have
much choice." He looked at Ramon. "Tell
them I'm coming out."

"Tell the sons of bitches we're *all* coming
out," said the Kid. He snatched up his
Winchester from against the bar and
stepped forward.

"Wait, Kid, this ain't the way to play it,"
said Shaw, raising a hand toward him and

335

his pals, stopping them. To Ramon he said, "Tell them I'm coming out alone."

Chapter 25

"How do you like the way it's going so far?" T. J. asked Red Downing. He half turned from the front window, looking out at the nearly empty street.

"I haven't seen anything worth mentioning yet," Downing said with a shrug, looking unimpressed. "If I was the one wanted to have it out with Shaw, I'd be walking the street toward him right now."

"Oh, we'll have it out," said T. J. "The thing is, when he killed our brother, he took it upon himself to face every one of us. That's the way us Katlins always stick together."

"I see," Downing said, "and him being unarmed is some sort of safety precaution, just your way of making sure he doesn't blow your damn head off?"

T. J. gave a dark chuckle and said, "Keep it up, Red Downing. See if I don't blow your damn head off without hesitation."

Downing took a step forward, showing no fear.

"Just so you don't mistake where I stand in all this, Katlin. I can ride out at any time and let LeBlanc know that things ain't going the way he wants them to. We'll ride in and circle this town. You and your men won't be looked upon favorably if that happens. In fact, you won't be looked upon at all, if you get what I'm saying."

"I get what you're saying," said T. J., seething.

Stepping up beside T. J., Uncle Linton said, "Don't take any shit off this regulator stiff, nephew. If he jackpots us, the only thing circling will be buzzards over his dead ass."

Downing didn't flinch.

"Easy, Uncle," said T. J. "I'm betting the Frenchman and this jake-leg have it all worked out: If he doesn't show up by a certain time, LeBlanc will ride in anyways. Right, Downing?"

Downing grinned with a mock look of amazement. "Well, well, you ain't as stupid as you look, T. J." With a hand resting on his Colt, he said, "You boys talked so much about killing Shaw, you'd better hope to God you can get it done; else it'll be my pleasure to bring in LeBlanc and see to it

338

all of your peckers get nailed to a hide board."

Listening from his gurney as he began to regain consciousness, Dr. Hauler blinked to make sure he wasn't having a nightmare. He looked over at Blaine, who lay shirtless, pale, and limp, a fresh bandage on his wounded side. "My God," Hauler whispered. He reached out a hand and gripped Hilda's forearm, letting her know that he understood their situation.

Hilda brushed his hand down, lest one of the Katlin Gang see it. "Stay asleep," she whispered.

Turning his attention back out the window, T. J. said to Lane and the others, "Here he comes!"

"Let's go kill him and cut his head off," said McBain, levering a round into his rifle chamber. "The quicker we stick his head on a pole, the quicker we get over to Mexico and whoop it up some."

"Don't get too excited, McBain," said Lane, standing beside his brother at the window. "You're staying here and keeping an eye on Blaine and these folks, make sure they don't get away on us."

"What?" McBain looked stunned by the blow. "They ain't going nowhere! I'll tie them down to a chair! Don't do me this way, T. J., Lane, please! I'm one of us! Don't make me a damn prisoner guard." He pointed at Downing. "Let this son of a bitch guard them! He ain't doing nothing!"

"You're guarding them; now shut the hell up about it," said T. J.

"Besides, guarding them is an important job," said Lane. He watched Shaw step out onto the boardwalk of the Fair Deal and down onto the street. "Shaw's knowing we've got a gun to Blaine's head is the only thing that'll make him knuckle down and do what we tell him. Anything goes wrong here, we're in trouble."

"Yeah," said Downing, "then you'd have to fight him like a man. Couldn't stand that, could yas?" He turned and walked away to the back door. "I better find a good place to watch from."

Before T. J. could respond, Lane said, "Look at this. He's just standing there; he ain't coming any closer."

Standing over fifty yards away, Shaw unbuckled his gun belt and held it out at arm's length. "All right, Katlins," he called out. "You said 'unarmed' — here's my gun." He pitched the gun belt a few feet away. From behind his back he pulled up a smaller Navy Colt from beneath his shirttail and pitched it over by his gun belt. "There, I'm

340

unarmed. Send out Blaine and the doctor and his wife."

T. J. and Lane stepped out onto the boardwalk in front of the doctor's office and spread apart, letting Uncle Linton and the Russians step out behind them. "Shut up, Fast Larry," T. J. shouted. "You're not the one calling this play; I am!" He pounded a hand on his chest. "They come out when I say they come out."

In unison the Katlin Gang stepped down and walked forward, spreading farther apart in the dirt street. Seeing what was at hand, the few people along the street ducked out of sight; the scarce horse and wagon traffic hurried out of the way.

"Oh, no!" said the restaurant owner, who had been making repairs on the front of his eatery. Leaving his tools on the boardwalk, he hurried inside, slammed the new door shut, and bolted it.

Shaw stood unarmed, allowing himself to realize once again that if he really, truly wanted out of this hellish life he created, there would be no better place to let it happen. He looked at the sunlight in the clear sky, the sway of a warm breeze across the tops of distant pines. Then he leveled his gaze back down to earth, at the Katlins as they walked toward him, six abreast in a wide half circle.

Maybe this was the way it had been meant to be all along, he told himself. Unarmed, outnumbered, in a dirt street — how else could the fastest gun alive step off and call it quits? He was still calling all the shots, even in his own death. How many men got that in life? he reminded himself. Not many. "All right, Katlin, let's get it over with," he called out to T. J., the half circle drawing tighter around him. "Come any closer and I'll think you want to dance, not fight."

"This is not a fight, Fast Larry Shaw," said T. J. "This is a straight-up execution — vengeance for your killing our brother Brady."

"Then get to it," said Shaw. "I see him in hell, I'll tell him you sent me."

T. J. stopped twenty feet away. A trace of a tight smile came to his lips. He raised his Colt as if he had all the time in the world and cocked it. Around him, rifles and pistols cocked. Lane and the others stood aimed and ready. "I'll say one thing: You was one cool sonsabitch, even at the end," said T. J. "I'll tell that to anybody wants to know."

Shaw did not look at his gun belt, his big Colt, or his small backup Navy Colt lying in the dirt; but he knew where they were and about how far away. One quick lunge, and he knew he could wrap a hand around the butt of the Colt and go to work from right to left. He'd made this sort of lunge in the past, more than a few times.

First T. J., he told himself, his mind racing in spite of his cool demeanor — a shot to his middle would either kill him or take him out of the fight. Next, the rifleman on his right, the one standing closest — one shot, *bang!* Then he'd roll before they could get their aim back on him. Next, *bang!* — the man to his left —

Stop it, damn it! he mentally shouted at himself. *It's over; let it go!*

Shaking his head a bit to clear it, Shaw said, "I don't need you telling folks how cool I was. All I need is for you to get this done and let Blaine and the Haulers go, the way you said you would."

T. J.'s smile widened. "Did I say that? Hell, I must've just been funning with you."

"Well, hell . . ." Shaw murmured to himself under his breath; but he wasn't surprised.

"Naw, you see, Blaine's hide belongs to the Frenchman," T. J. continued. "I promised I'd bring him out to be hanged after we killed you." He shrugged a shoulder. "Maybe I should have mentioned that sooner."

"Maybe you should have, you dog turd!" came the Kid's voice from atop the clapboard restaurant building. He stood up from behind the low front facade, a double-barreled shotgun in his hands, both hammers cocked. "Guess who I'm going to kill, T. J."

T. J. swallowed a knot in his throat. "Kid!" he said in surprise. "We've got no fight with you. Hell, we do business together. You and the Wild Rose, and Rudabaugh, right? We always deal with yas!"

"Wrong," said the Kid. "I can't deal with a dead man."

"Me neither," said Free Drink. He stepped from the alley beside the restaurant, also carrying a shotgun, this one a sawed-off eight-gauge single-shot with a barrel flared on its end like an army bugle. "Nobody calls me Wild Rose anymore and lives to tell about it."

"Aw, come on, the both of yas!" said T. J. "This ain't nothing to do with you boys. Billy, what the hell do you care about a hardscrabble rancher like Blaine?"

"He's the father of my child," the Kid said. "Shaw's too."

"I heard all that nonsense," said T. J. "But you know why we're killing Shaw — he shot our brother."

Time to make that lunge . . . Shaw pictured his guns lying in the dirt. *I tried, Rosa,* he told himself, seeing her face, seeing the soft, warm smile that had welcomed him only a moment earlier. Now he watched her smile and her face fade from his sight.

From an alley across the street from the restaurant, Hyde Rudabaugh stepped out with a big Colt in each hand. "Had your pa had any mind, he'd have shot Brady the day he was born," he called out.

Behind Shaw, he heard Sturgis call out, "Lane! You once screwed me on a horse deal. It's time to settle up!"

"Everybody hold fast!" said T. J. "Shaw, do you want the blood of the doctor and his wife on your hands as well as Blaine's?" He took a step backward and slowly raised his free hand above his head. "One wave of my hand, and you'll hear three shots. Bratcher McBain will have himself a private slaughter in that doctor's office; yes, sir, he will!" His grin came back in spite of the guns pointed at him and his men. "Want to hear them shots, Shaw? I'll *damn* sure enough give them to you!" He appeared on the verge of giving McBain a signal.

"Make that signal and you'll be dead before Blaine or the Haulers!" said the Kid.

"Hold it, Kid!" said Shaw.

"Now you're using your head, Shaw." T. J. grinned.

But from the doctor's office came a scream as the door flew open and Bratcher McBain half ran, half staggered wildly toward them down the middle of the dirt street.

"Jesus!" said Lane Katlin, watching along with the others as McBain struggled with the handles of a pair of scissors stuck deep into the center of his chest. Blood spewed freely. Screaming, the old outlaw spun in the street, one hand leaving the scissors and reaching behind him, grappling and clawing at the long handle of a surgical instrument planted deep in his back, between his ribs. More blood spewed.

Lower down the center of McBain's spine, another instrument handle jiggled back and forth with each tortured step he took. "Pull them *ooooout*!" he bellowed at the Katlins.

On the boardwalk, Hilda Hauler ran out covered with McBain's blood. "We're all right, we're all right, we're all right!" she shouted, jumping up and down as if offering proof of her well-being.

Get ready; here comes that lunge. . . . Shaw thought to himself, watching McBain stagger down to his knees; the outlaw seemed to melt into the dirt, falling onto the scissors and driving them deeper, the sharp

346

points slicing into his heart.

Standing at the rear of the doctor's office watching the scene unfold in the street, Red Downing cursed under his breath, tried the rear door, and found it had been locked from inside. Looking back to the street, he saw Shaw make the lunge for his big Colt. *Time to go,* he told himself. Whoever stabbed McBain and locked that door would have armed themselves by now.

"Those stupid sonsabitches!" he said aloud to himself, seeing the Katlins encircled by the Kid and his pals. Wasting no time, he sprang to his horse, jumped up into the saddle, and nailed his spurs to the animal. LeBlanc would have to hear about this right away. The Katlins had ruined everything, as far as he was concerned. He wasn't about to make a play at taking Blaine back to LeBlanc, not after seeing what happened to McBain. This was all the Katlins' fault, not his.

On the street, Shaw caught the handle of his big Colt as he dived past and rolled onto his belly. He put his first shot just where he'd planned, dead center of T. J.'s chest. Two bullets whistled past him; but he'd rolled onto one knee and made his second shot at the rifleman to his right.

The shot hit the big Russian high in his

chest. Vladimir's rifle flew from his hands just as a shot exploded wildly from its barrel. But Vladimir only spun on his heels until a blast of buckshot from the Kid's shotgun rained down on him, seeming to pound him into the ground.

"Look out, Shaw!" Free Drink shouted, not realizing that Shaw's plan had already been to make his next shot at the man to his left — Uncle Linton.

"You gawdamn girlie sonsabitch! I've got you!" Uncle Linton raged, hearing Free Drink warn Shaw. But, swinging his rifle toward Free Drink, the old outlaw caught the full blast of the eight-gauge in his chest and face before Shaw got his shot off.

Shaw saw Lane Katlin go down when Sturgis and Rudabaugh both fired on him at once. But then he saw Lane roll to his feet and run wounded down the middle of the street toward the doctor's office, blood streaming from his left shoulder. "Don't shoot, gawdamn it! Don't shoot!" Lane called back over his shoulder, reaching back and firing his Colt wildly in Shaw's direction.

"Yeah, right," said Shaw, taking quick aim and dropping the outlaw with single shot to the back of his head before he reached the boardwalk.

Standing on the boardwalk, Hilda Hauler screamed as she saw a thick spray of blood and brain matter explode from Lane Katlin's forehead.

"Shaw, beside you!" shouted the Kid from the roof. Shaw ducked instinctively and spun as a bullet from Jerniko's rifle sliced through his coatsleeve. "Get that damn Russian!" shouted the Kid. He climbed hurriedly down a ladder he'd leaned against the building as Jerniko leaped up onto the boardwalk in front of the restaurant and kicked down the brand-new door to get inside. But upon hearing the Kid single him out, the Russian turned into the open doorway and fired his rifle from his hip, letting out a long, angry war cry.

As one, Shaw, the Kid, and his pals turned and fired. Their shots, both buckshot and bullets, enlarged the door opening, picked Jerniko up in a blast filled with bone, blood, and wooden door frame, and flung his mutilated carcass the length of the restaurant. He knocked the wood stove onto its side and landed atop it, sizzling. Black suet rose from the downed chimney pipe and began to settle heavily. A dark cloud boiled out through the front door.

"There goes one of the regulators!" said Free Drink, pointing at Downing as he rode away at a hard clip.

"Stop him!" the Kid shouted, still in a frenzy of excitement.

"No, wait," Shaw said. "He's not going far. LeBlanc won't stop until he gets Blaine. Let him ride in. I'm going to kill him."

The Kid looked at him, still wide-eyed, wearing a tight, crooked smile. Gesturing toward the dead lying in the street, he asked, "Does this mean you're about to take sides?"

"No," said Shaw. He dropped the spent cartridges from his big Colt. "It just means I'm concerned about our child's father."

The Kid laughed, still tense with excitement. Then he broke open the shotgun in his hands as if in afterthought and began reloading it. "I knew it, by gawd, I knew it!"

"You knew what, Kid?" Shaw asked.

"That you had a card up your sleeve," the Kid replied, stepping back and forth excitedly among the dead on the ground as he reloaded. "Free Drink!" he shouted. "Didn't I tell you Shaw wasn't about to give up and let these warthogs kill him without a fight? Huh? Didn't I?"

"You sure enough did, Billy," said Free Drink. Smoke still curled from the wide bugle-ended eight-gauge. "He sure enough did, Shaw," he added for Shaw's sake, as if

Shaw had asked him to confirm the Kid's words.

"You had that diving-for-your-gun trick already worked out, didn't you?" the Kid asked, snapping the shotgun shut and leaning it against a post in front of the shot-up restaurant. "I knew you did," he answered before Shaw got the chance. "Hell, it would have been suicide otherwise, not having a plan of some kind in mind, wouldn't it?"

"Yeah, Kid, it would have been suicide," said Shaw, reloading his Colt. Looking all around at the dead on the street, and at the gunsmoke hanging in the air, he murmured, "The ol' toss-your-gun-away-and-dive-for-it-at-the-last-minute trick. It gets them every time."

"I knew you was up to something." The Kid grinned and winked. "That's why I figured you wouldn't mind too much if me and my pals sort of slipped in here and there and gave you a hand."

Shaw took a deep breath and let it all settle in his mind for a moment. "Naw, Kid, I didn't mind. In fact, I'm glad you did."

CHAPTER 26

Red Downing hadn't gone more than a mile out of town when he met LeBlanc and his men riding hard toward him. When he saw the furious and frightened look on the Frenchman's face, Downing's first impulse was to rein his horse around and flee; but upon seeing a broad cloud of dust coming up behind the Frenchman from the direction of Sabo Canyon, Red circled up to Le-Blanc and said, "The Katlins made a mess of things! I got here as quick as I could."

Instead of reining to a halt, the Frenchman only slowed a bit, gave a worried look toward the cloud of dust, and said, "Where is Blaine?"

"In town at the doctor's," said Downing. "The Katlins let him slip through their fingers. I'm afraid Shaw has killed that whole bungling lot of them!"

"Oh, and what did you do to keep it from happening?" he asked pointedly.

"There wasn't much I could have done," Downing said in his own defense. "You told me to watch, and I watched. You told me to come tell you if things started going wrong." He shook his head. "Well, they started going wrong, sure enough. When I left, Shaw had started making a play against the Katlins, with the Kid and his pals backing him up."

"Damn it! I thought as much," said Le-Blanc. "We heard the shooting and knew it was too much gunfire to be just the Katlins killing Shaw. But no sooner had we started toward town than one of our drovers rode in from the herd and said there's a band of ranchers from Sabo Canyon riding down on us." He nodded toward the cloud of dust advancing quickly on them.

"How many men do we have left?" Downing asked, already running odds through his mind.

"I have these few Mexican drovers with me. The rest are tending the herd," said Le-Blanc. He looked back among the men, seeing a mixed group of Mexican drovers and a few hired gunmen.

"Damn," said Downing. "These drovers won't make it in a fight! You can't expect it of them. Half of them don't even carry guns!"

"It's too late to worry about that," said LeBlanc, staring straight ahead with determination.

"Maybe we'd best cut away from here, get back to the herd and turn them back to Texas," said Downing. "Good grazing ain't the only thing in life."

"I have investors to answer to," said LeBlanc.

"To hell with your investors! You can't answer to them if you're dead," Downing fumed.

"Is that your best advice, Downing — cut and run all the way back to Texas?" asked a young gunman named Frank Cardwell, who sidled up to LeBlanc with three other young men around his own age. Cardwell and the other three had been riding, eating, and bedding down in the drovers' camp until LeBlanc's sudden shortage of gunmen prompted him to bring the tough-looking young men up in rank.

"Listen to me, you young whelp," said Downing. "We need to get away from here before we get caught short between the ranchers and Shaw and the Kid. You can learn gunfighting some other time. This is no place for beginners!"

LeBlanc cut in, "The ranchers from Sabo have *already* gotten between us and our

354

herd! We have no choice but to go on into Willow Creek and hope we can fend them off! Having Blaine in my grip would have kept this from happening!"

"It's too late to think of that now," said Downing. "But it's not too late to clear out of here."

"We're riding in," LeBlanc said with finality.

Beside LeBlanc, Herr Perls said, "Perhaps it would be wise to retreat."

LeBlanc only gave him a harsh stare.

Downing looked around quickly. Among the faces of a few Mexican drovers and the young gunmen following LeBlanc, he saw two old gunmen named Elm Thompson and Curtis Lindly. The two sat with resolved expressions on their weathered faces. "Thompson, Lindly!" Downing called out to them. "Tell him what kind of bloodbath this is going to turn into if we get caught between two forces here."

Lindly tilted his head up long enough to say, "We're already caught between the ranchers and Willow Creek. Fight is all we can do now, 'less we want to run like scared chickens."

"Is that what you'd have us do, Downing?" asked young Frank Cardwell.

Without answering, Downing cursed

under his breath and jerked his horse in beside LeBlanc. "You're about to get us all killed," he said; then he rode on in silence.

Shaw, the Kid and his pals, and few of the merchants from along the storefronts had dragged two freight wagons into the street, turned them onto their sides, and piled empty wooden shipping crates against them, building a barricade.

Seeing the boiling rise of dust coming toward their town, other citizens of Willow Creek had armed themselves and taken up positions in windows and doorways. Shaw and the Kid stood behind the barricade and watched Dr. Hauler walk toward them from his office, his forehead bandaged, another bandage on his ear from his earlier wound.

"I wish he'd just stay away," Shaw said sidelong to the Kid. "No good can ever come from him and me crossing paths. Can't he see that?"

"He must think that your screwing his wife makes you two friends in some way." The Kid snickered, a hand covering his mouth.

"That's not funny, Kid," said Shaw.

"I know," the Kid said. He turned and walked just far enough away to be able to eavesdrop.

Shaw looked at Dr. Hauler as he walked up and stopped a few feet away. "Shaw," the doctor said bluntly, "I'm asking you in my capacity as peacekeeper here, Is there any way to stop all the senseless killing and keep this fight from happening?"

"Not that I can see, Doctor," said Shaw. "The Frenchman wanted Blaine before. . . . He'll still want him now. If Blaine was in any shape to ride, I'd take him and clear out of here. But he's not. You said so yourself."

"You're right, of course." The doctor nodded, unable to argue against Shaw's logic. "I felt I must ask."

"I understand, Doctor," Shaw said respectfully.

Hauler paused for a moment, then asked curiously, "How is your wound, Shaw? Are you in any pain?"

"None worth mentioning, Doctor," Shaw replied. "Why do you ask?"

"It's just that you seem to have recovered remarkably fast, while the rest of us appear to mend so slowly," he commented, as if healing quickly were an accusation of some sort.

"Maybe I'm just more used to bullet wounds than some folks, Doctor," said Shaw, unsure of what the doctor was implying. "Maybe you just do good work."

Dr. Hauler only stared at him for a moment. "I hate all of this violence and ugliness that seems to have followed you to Willow Creek, Shaw," he said, as if he needed to tell him so now, lest he never get another chance. "I especially hate the way circumstance has led both my wife and myself to participate in it."

"Doctor," said Shaw, hanging his head a bit, "I can't tell you how sorry —"

Cutting Shaw off quickly, the doctor said, staring at him intently, "I'm referring to my wife and I having to kill that man." He gestured his head toward the body of Bratcher McBain being dragged off the street by two townsmen.

"Yes, I know," said Shaw, quickly sidestepping any other issues that might still lie between them. "But, Doctor, you can't really say that was my fault."

"Oh, yes, Shaw, I do," said the doctor. "I don't know how, but somehow everything that has happened here has happened because of you." He gestured toward the Colt on Shaw's hip. "You and your big gun, your big presence, your big reputation." He expanded his chest and continued, saying, "I long for the day when men like you have gone the way of the dinosaur. Guns and

358

violence have no place in the world I want to live in."

"I know you don't believe me, Doctor," said Shaw. "But I long for that same kind of world." As he spoke he pictured himself and Rosa hand in hand, no gun at his hip. "But here is where I live today, and if killing keeps good folks like Jimmy Blaine alive, and folks like you and your wife and these others, then like it or not, killing *is* what I do best."

"You're right, Shaw. I *don't* believe you," said Dr. Hauler. "I believe this is what you thrive on. . . . In fact, if I believed in heaven and hell, I would have to say I think you are the devil, Shaw! The devil sent to torture Willow Creek. But since I do not believe in such things, I will only say that you are a vile, loathsome, repulsive —"

"All right, that's enough out of you, sawbones!" said the Kid, stepping over and giving the doctor a shove. "Get your ass out of here before I gun-butt you!"

"Easy, Billy," said Shaw, seeing a harsh, dark look come over the Kid's face. "He's got a right to say what he thinks. I'm good for it."

"You're *good* for it?" The Kid gave him a disbelieving look. "Like hell you are!" He turned to the doctor and said, "You want to talk about the ugliness? You want to talk about all the bad that's come about since Shaw showed up here?" The Kid took a step forward in spite of Shaw's having raised a hand to keep him back.

"Please, Mr. Bonney!" said Hauler, relenting in the face of the Kid's anger. "This isn't about you. This is between Shaw and me —"

"Let's talk about the bad that *didn't* happen because Shaw and his *big gun,* and his *big-gun* reputation, have been here to stop it."

"Kid, you don't need to do this," said Shaw, keeping a low, even tone.

But the Kid ignored him, although he did stop advancing on the frightened doctor as he said, "Jimmy Blaine would have been dragged out of your office and hanged in the street had Shaw not come up with a plan, and hard enough nuts in his bag to carry it out! As for the Frenchman coming, bringing trouble to Willow Creek, he'd have been here long before now if he and his men hadn't all been worried about whose side Shaw's big gun was on."

"All right, Kid," Shaw said quietly, "that's enough."

But the Kid wasn't through. "Now that the Frenchman is coming, he's coming with half the men he started out with. Why? Because Shaw has killed them . . . blown their heads off! Shot their guts out! You think he's brought violence and ugliness? Picture what would have happened by now if he'd ridden on by."

"That may very well be so," said the doctor, frightened but still prepared to argue his point. "But the fact remains —"

Before he could finish, a townsman called out from the direction of the livery barn, "Dr. Hauler. You'd better come take a look-see. We've found Dick Harpin in the livery barn. He's dead."

"Dead, you say?" the doctor called out, dismissing the kid and his heated exchange and hurrying off toward the livery barn. "I know I haven't seen him around. . . ."

"Nobody has seen him; now we know why," the townsman called out. "We followed a terrible stink into one of the stalls, and there he was — rats have eaten his ears, lips, and eyeballs."

"Oh, my goodness," said the doctor. "I thought perhaps he rode off with the Frenchman!"

Free Drink drifted in beside the Kid, as if for protection. The Kid threw his arm around the small outlaw's shoulders and chuckled. "Harpin didn't ride off with the

Frenchman," he said, "but they're both damn sure headed in the same direction."

Looking at the Kid, Shaw said, "Obliged for what you said, Billy."

"What do you think?" The Kid grinned. "Did I spread it on a little thick?"

"A little, maybe, but obliged all the same," said Shaw. He leaned back against an upturned wagon to take a quick rest; but no sooner had he relaxed than he heard Sturgis's voice call out from the roof of the shot-up restaurant.

"Here they come!" Sturgis shouted, standing atop the front facade, looking out at the oncoming charge of man and horse in a wide cloud of dust.

"No rest for the wicked," the Kid said. He and Shaw ran with rifles in hand to the center of the barricade.

At the head of the riders, LeBlanc veered away enough to look back and see that the ranchers had gained considerable ground on them. In front of him he saw rifles atop the rooflines and in doorways. In the street he saw the barricade, with rifles pointing from behind it.

"We've got to stop, LeBlanc!" shouted Red Downing, riding right beside him. From the windows, doorways, and the barricade in the street, rifle fire exploded heavily. Behind them the guns of the ranchers from Sabo Canyon opened fire.

Realizing he'd ridden into a box with no way out, LeBlanc gave a quick glance at Herr Perls as if seeking his advice. But Perls stared at him and shouted above the melee, "You fool! You have gotten us killed!" No sooner had the words left Perls's mouth than LeBlanc saw a bullet slice all the way through his head just above his ears and fling him backward from his saddle in a bloody mist.

Catching fire from front and rear, the Frenchman panicked and posted high in his stirrups. Swinging a big revolver above his head, he bellowed back at the top of his lungs to his drovers and gunmen in desperation, "Charge!"

But as his and Red Downing's horses pounded up the street into Willow Creek, all of his drovers and half of his gunmen had fallen back, broken up, and raced away in every direction.

Behind the barricade, Shaw, the Kid and his pals, and a handful of townsmen had to cease firing and duck down as bullets from the ranchers cut through LeBlanc's men and thumped loudly into the freight wagons. "Damn it!" said the Kid. "Looks like the ranchers are out to kill us instead of Le-

Blanc!" He jerked a ragged red bandanna from his neck, tied it quickly to the barrel of his Winchester, and raised the rifle and waved it back and forth.

Peeping out through a crack in the plank floor of a freight wagon, Shaw could see that the firing from the ranchers had stopped. In the street less than twenty yards away, LeBlanc's remaining regulators had leaped from their horses and scurried to take whatever cover they could find. LeBlanc lay on his side in the dirt, propped up on one elbow, holding his free hand up in surrender.

"Stop, please!" he pleaded loudly, almost wailing.

"Too late to stop!" the Kid shouted, holding his rifle up but drawing his Colt from his holster and taking aim through a slim opening in the barricade.

"Kid, don't!" shouted Shaw.

But the Colt Thunderer's hammer fell, and the Frenchman flipped backward in the dirt. "Oops, sorry," the Kid said to Shaw. Realizing that the firing had stopped from all directions, armed townsmen ventured forward. Shaw and the kid climbed atop the wagon barricade and jumped down into the street, side by side, their Colts in hand. "Keep us covered, pals!" the Kid called over his shoulder to Free Drink, Sturgis, and Rudabaugh.

In the street only three of the younger regulators were still alive. They raised their hands, letting their weapons fall to the ground. Cardwell sat with LeBlanc's blood splattered on his face. "Don't shoot, gawdamn it! My gun jammed!" he said, as if offering an excuse for his poor performance.

The Kid chuckled and asked a young man sitting next to him in the dirt, "Is that true? His gun jammed?"

"I think so, Billy," said the thin young regulator. He sat looking at the Kid, blood and dirt smeared down his cheek. Instead of throwing his gun away, he'd laid it in the dirt, less than arm's length away.

"Do I know you?" the Kid asked, looking closer.

"We ran across each other down at Fort Sumner last year, and Las Cruces, and Greasy Springs. Remember?"

"Watch his gun, Kid," said Shaw, nodding at the pistol near the young man's hand.

"I got him, Shaw." Recognition came to the Kid's face. "I know this ol' boy. He wouldn't try throwing down on me." The Kid grinned. "Garrett, what are you doing riding with regulators? You was eating other men's beef last I saw you." He reached down and pulled the lean, dark-haired young man to his feet.

Dusting himself off and giving a glance toward the pistol in the dirt, the young regulator said, "Regulating is as close as I've gotten to doing law work."

"Still badge-hungry, eh?" The Kid chuckled. As he spoke the Kid bent down, picked up the young man's gun, and shoved it down into his waistband. The young gunman shrugged; it was all right with him. "What about these two?" The Kid waved his Colt toward the other two regulators seated in the dirt. "They any good for anything?"

"Yeah," said Garrett, "they're pals. Both of them good men. We just drew a bad hand riding with LeBlanc."

"Yeah?" The Kid looked the other two regulators over appraisingly. "What're you going to do now?" Behind him, Free Drink, Sturgis, and Rudabaugh moved forward from behind the barricade and closed in around them, their guns slumping in their hands.

Shaw walked on, his Colt still cocked and ready, seeing the Sabo Canyon ranchers ride into town, four abreast and he couldn't tell how many deep. He reached out with a toe and kicked a rifle away from Red Downing's dead hand. He stood looking at the ground until the ranchers half circled him, and he heard a familiar voice say, "Shaw? I thought you was leaving after I took Blaine out of town. Thought you wasn't taking sides?"

"I'm not," said Shaw. He looked up at Belan Foley and young Marvin Meeks, who sat a few feet closer than the rest of the ranchers. "Things just worked out this way. I'm obliged you showed up when you did." He saw the bloodstain on the shoulder of Foley's ragged shirt, the countless scratches and knots on his face.

"I wouldn't have made it," said Foley, "if it hadn't been for Marvin here and these ranchers coming back and finding his pa and me left for dead."

Shaw looked at Marvin. "Good job, young man."

Marvin touched a gloved finger to his battered hat brim, then backed his horse and rode at a walk to where LeBlanc lay dead in the dirt. Foley and the ranchers rode with him.

"We ought to cleave off his ears or something," one of the ranchers commented, loud enough for Shaw to hear.

Shaking his head, Shaw flipped the cylinder of his Colt open and punched his spent rounds out into the dirt. Gazing along the street, he saw Blaine step onto the board-walk in front of the doctor's office with the assistance of Rita Vargas and Hilda Hauler.

"We are going to name her Lawrencia after you, for what you've done," Rita called out, jostling the tiny bundle on her free side.

"That's beautiful," Shaw replied halfheart-edly, as he took four fresh rounds from his holster belt.

"What about me?" the Kid shouted, hav-ing overheard them.

"What about you?" Rita asked indiffer-ently.

"I'm the father too, remember?" the Kid called out.

Shaw heard Rita and the Kid argue back and forth as he looked all around the dirt street at the dead. In spite of their bloody, violent end, he considered their peaceful, mindless repose for a moment, then — *Stop it . . .* he told himself, feeling his mood darken as he caught himself envying the dead.

What a hell of a day, he told himself, look-ing up across a clear and perfect sky. But a bad day in Willow Creek had to be better than no day at all. "What did you say, Kid — no rest for the wicked?" he murmured to himself. Reload complete, he clicked the cylinder shut and holstered the big Colt.

Touching a finger to his hat brim in Jimmy Blaine's direction, he said to himself, "Take care of our baby," and turned and walked toward the livery barn, where his horse stood saddled, ready, and waiting.

The employees of Thorndike Press hope you have enjoyed this Large Print book. All our Thorndike, Wheeler, and Kennebec Large Print titles are designed for easy reading, and all our books are made to last. Other Thorndike Press Large Print books are available at your library, through selected bookstores, or directly from us.

For information about titles, please call:
(800) 223-1244

or visit our Web site at:
http://gale.cengage.com/thorndike

To share your comments, please write:
Publisher
Thorndike Press
10 Water St., Suite 310
Waterville, ME 04901

CPSIA information can be obtained
at www.ICGtesting.com
Printed in the USA
FFOW04n0702011113
2226FF